"Eli, I've be … **for ten year** … **demanding profess** …

Aubrey leaned back and stretched her long, shapely legs in front of her.

He could so easily entangle his feet with hers.

"Rewarding, too, of course," she added. "But hard."

"That it is."

He reached out and slowly removed the paper from her hands. His sole purpose in doing so was to feel her soft, warm skin against his. He had to touch her even as he knew he needed to quit stealing these moments. He needed to find a place where they could peacefully coexist, one that didn't include touching her and wanting to kiss her.

She watched him, her green eyes all soft and bright and full of questions...and he knew he wasn't imagining the desire swimming in their mossy green depths. Twelve years may have passed, but that was a look a man could never forget.

Carol Ross lives in the Pacific Northwest with her husband and two dogs. She is a graduate of Washington State University. When not writing, or thinking about writing, she enjoys reading, running, hiking, skiing, traveling and making plans for the next adventure to subject her sometimes reluctant but always fun-loving family to. Carol can be contacted at carolrossauthor.com and via Facebook at Facebook.com/carolrossauthor, Twitter, @_carolross, and Instagram, @carolross__.

HEARTWARMING

Christmas in the Cove

———

USA TODAY Bestselling Author

Carol Ross

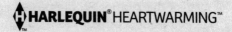
HARLEQUIN® HEARTWARMING™

Recycling programs
for this product may
not exist in your area.

ISBN-13: 978-1-335-08175-9

Christmas in the Cove

First published in 2016. This edition published in 2019.

Copyright © 2016 by Carol Ross

This edition published by arrangement with Harlequin Books S.A.

For questions and comments about the quality of this book, please contact us at CustomerService@Harlequin.com.

Printed in U.S.A.

I happily dedicate this book to
Alec Cadan Benson.

For many reasons—not the least of which is because he has the coolest name in the world (you're welcome).

And to Ethan Benson, who is always up for a brainstorming session. Thank you!

CHAPTER ONE

AUBREY TAPPED A rhythm with her foot as the song "Respect" played inside her head. The words sounded as clear and pure as if Aretha herself was strapped in the helicopter's seat beside her.

The copilot, Lieutenant Jensen, interrupted her mid-verse. "Three minutes."

Signaling that she heard, she resumed her internal checklist. Not the equipment list every Coast Guard Rescue Swimmer is always prepared with—mask, fins, knife, radio, beacon and assorted supplies. She'd already done that one about fifty times. No, Aubrey was executing her "mental prep." Breathing deeply, she imagined blood flowing to the furthest reaches of her body from her heart to her liver and all the way to the tips of her toes, while she silently sang Aretha Franklin's classic tune over and over again. Was this weird? Maybe. She had no idea. But she knew other rescue swimmers who had their rituals, too. So, in that regard, she assumed it was normal. She didn't really care one way or the other. It was her normal.

"Almost there." Jensen spoke into her ear again.

She had noted the change in airspeed as they'd approached the coordinates. They were now moving slowly, searching. She embraced the surge of adrenaline that kicked in as she prepared for the task at hand. *There* could be literally anywhere, she mused as she looked out at the vast grayness beyond the rain-splattered windshield of the Jayhawk helicopter.

The emergency call had reported that the *Respite*, a forty-foot fishing boat with a crew of three, was in immediate distress. The captain of the vessel had relayed that the engine was dead, they were taking on water in the high seas and the bilge pumps could not keep up. The latest communication had confirmed they were abandoning ship. Time was of the essence. She shot an impatient glance at Oliver.

The flight mechanic and hoist operator, Petty Officer Terrence "Osprey" Oliver, opened the helicopter door. Looking out, she assessed the situation as well as the conditions permitted. She could make out the floundering vessel and the spreading debris field, but couldn't see anything in the water that looked remotely like a human. As they circled the scene, her eyes scanned, the fog thinned... and there! Splashes of orange. Survivors in life jackets waving their arms. She looked at Oliver. She could tell he'd seen them, too, which was no surprise as Osprey had earned his nickname for a reason. She'd seen him spot survivors at distances that would make a real bird jealous.

She was anxious to get into the water now.

He signaled for her to get ready.

She quickly unbuckled from her flight seat and began to add the rest of her water deployment ensemble. Already outfitted in her dry suit, she removed the onboard communications, or ICS, and adjusted her swim helmet. For the duration of the rescue she would rely mostly on hand signals to communicate with her crew.

She waited some more. It was only a minute, but still, slower than usual and she felt a surge of anxiety as the seconds ticked by. This delay was not typical. What was going on?

Oliver signaled for her to slip her ICS back on.

Lieutenant Jensen spoke. "We're experiencing mechanical difficulties. Returning to base."

"Wait, no!"

"We don't have any choice, Wynn."

"Yes, we do. Let me drop."

"Negative. We're not leaving you without an exit."

"The forty-seven is at least thirty minutes out." Aubrey was referring to the forty-seven-foot motorboat that would have to be deployed from Station Cape Disappointment and the time it would take for it to arrive on scene. She didn't have to add that the survivors might not last that long.

"Another helo will have to— Hold on."

A delay could mean the difference between life or death. The least she could do is get them into a life raft and provide some comfort during the wait.

She knew the pilot, Lieutenant Commander Vincent, was going to give her an order. She needed to make a last-ditch argument in an effort to save three lives. She could get to the survivors, at least, do what she could to give them comfort and keep them alive until help arrived. She would risk the censure. So Others May Live was the Coast Guard's Rescue Swimmers' motto, and that's what she did. That's what she would do. Always.

"Sir, I can—"

"Stop talking, Wynn. We've got another chopper en route. It's on a recon mission and is only minutes out. If you're willing, you've got the go-ahead to deploy. They will execute the recovery."

"Yes, of course I'm willing."

"Lieutenant Commander Holmes is piloting the aircraft. Petty Officer Johnston is the flight mechanic," Oliver added. "The two new guys are also on board. You're all set. Go save some lives."

She hadn't met the new guys yet, but she had a ton of respect for Lt. Cdr. Holmes. And Jay Johnston was a friend, someone she flew with regularly and trusted. He was also an excellent hoist operator and Aubrey was glad to hear he was part of the crew.

She secured her equipment bag, put the mask and snorkel on her forehead, and pulled on her fins. Still wearing the requisite gunner's belt, she moved forward and seated herself in the doorway of the chopper, gripping the handholds situated on either side. From this vantage point she could now see that the boat was lying very low and listing heavily to starboard. Swamped. She could hear nothing but the scream of the helicopter combined with the roar of the wind and the ocean. The sound fueled her determination. Ready, she signaled. Oliver gave her a firm tap on the chest to indicate she could proceed.

The helo moved right and dipped as Lieutenant Vincent lowered it into position. She released the gunner's belt, positioned the mask on her face and, after one last equipment check, gave him a thumbs-up. Three more taps to her shoulder indicated she was good to go on his end.

She could never deploy without thoughts of her childhood "Coastie friends" Eli and Alex flashing through her mind. Their dads had served together and were the best of friends. That connection had brought their kids together, too, but a mutual love of adventure, the beach and water in any form had sealed the bond into their own solid, unwavering friendship.

The three of them would practice rescue jumping for hours on end: slight bend in the knees, fins pointing up, one hand on the mask and the other across the chest. Just like she did now. Steeling herself, she took a deep breath, timed her free fall to catch the top of a big swell, and dropped into the ocean.

She surfaced, her mind now fully in rescue mode. Raising her arm high into the air, she positioned her palm up and out in the "I am all right" signal, and swam to the first survivor.

LIEUTENANT COMMANDER, COAST GUARD pilot and rescue swimmer, Eli Pelletier wasn't technically doing either of those jobs today. Rather, he was enjoying his ride as a passenger touring the Pacific Northwest's coastline. His friend and fellow pilot, Lieutenant Commander Gale Kohen, was in the helicopter seat beside him, also taking in the view.

He and Gale had only arrived in Pacific Cove the day before and reported for duty at Air Station Astoria in Warrenton, Oregon, early that morning. They'd been transferred to District 13, also known as Sector Columbia River, under the auspices of performing an evaluation of the base's search-and-rescue operations. Commander Pence had recommended a flyover in order to familiarize themselves with the area and conditions the SAR teams regularly worked in. Eli thought the reason for the ride sounded a little thin, but no one was going to second guess the commander. The real reason for their sudden transfer here didn't have anything to do with

SAR procedures, although they were both highly trained in the field.

They were bombing up the coast, chatting with the crew about past rescues, when the call came in that another helicopter at a rescue scene was experiencing mechanical problems. They'd been asked to take over, which was no problem. Regulations ensured that each helicopter was interchangeable as far as equipment went and he could see that this crew knew their bird.

"Pelletier, Kohen, you guys ready to go?"

"Affirmative," they both agreed. The question was rhetorical. Like every Coastie, both were always willing to put their knowledge and skills to use whenever and wherever needed. That fast and Eli went from passenger to RS at the ready.

Eli knew the pilot, Lieutenant Commander Holmes. They'd flown together right after Eli had graduated flight school at Air Station Elizabeth City, North Carolina, where they'd both been assigned at the time. He'd only met the other crewmen, Petty Officers Johnston and Reeves, that morning. He was impressed with how quickly they now shifted from practice mission to life-and-death emergency. This was undoubtedly due to the fact that there had been no shift—they'd been ready. *Semper paratus*. Always Ready, as the Coast Guard motto stated.

D13 included one of the most dangerous stretches of ocean in the world—the Columbia River bar, where the formidable Columbia River emptied into the Pacific Ocean. Having spent the happiest years of his childhood here, Eli knew it well. His dad had been a Coast Guard officer before him and he knew training here in the Columbia River Sector was top-notch. Flexibility was the hallmark of a Coastie and just being stationed here had given these men plenty of experience.

Lt. Cdr. Holmes maneuvered the helo closer so they could get a better view, hovering next to the scene to avoid exposing the swimmer and survivor to the powerful blast of the helicopter's rotor wash. Eli could see the swimmer and three survivors in the water below, two were in close proximity to each other, with the third a short distance away. Should be a simple, straightforward rescue, he thought.

Flight mechanic and hoist operator, Petty Officer Johnston, was evaluating the scene. "Swimmer is with two survivors. Swimmer is signaling for basket. Thirteen minutes since survivors have been in the water."

With instructions from Johnston, Holmes

flew the helicopter into position. Upon seeing the signal from the RS already in the water, Johnston dispatched the basket. A few short minutes later he added those sweet words every member of a rescue crew longs for. "Survivor One in basket. Survivor on the way up. Survivor halfway up…"

In less than three minutes they were hauling the first drenched fisherman on board the chopper. Gale, who was also an EMT, went to work evaluating and warming the cold, shivering man.

Soon, Johnston safely pulled up another survivor and said, "Swimmer is okay. Swimmer is away, headed for the third survivor."

With direction from his crew, Holmes moved the helicopter into place again and the third survivor was soon on board. The young man appeared to be hysterical, shivering, crying and jabbering excitedly.

Gale attempted to calm him. He had a way with people and Eli wasn't surprised when the kid immediately settled down. He reported, "Survivor is telling me there's someone else in the water—"

Johnston broke in. "Swimmer has radioed and confirmed. She's headed toward the wreckage. Can anyone see another person in the water?"

She? Eli felt a jolt of fear shoot through him. Eli knew that D13 had exactly one female RS at this point in time. There were only a few women currently certified in the entire Coast Guard. That meant Aubrey was down there doing the rescuing. Anxiety knotted his gut, creating a personal problem for him, he realized. Because, apparently, even after all these years, Aubrey in danger meant that the knight in him wanted to take over. That's what she used to call it when he would try to help her or to do things for her. "Stop being such a knight, Pelletier. I can do it myself." And usually she could, but that wasn't the point.

They were all scanning the ocean below, looking for the fourth person.

"Swimmer is near the bow of vessel," Johnston reported.

His tension lessened slightly. Aubrey was an excellent swimmer, like a fish in the water. Or a mermaid. That's what he used to call her. And, for a while there, she had been his mermaid. That had been the best time of his life.

"Swimmer circling the bow, approaching the stern. Survivor Four spotted. Survivor in the water. Survivor appears entangled in debris. Twenty-five minutes."

Time crawled by as Johnston relayed Aubrey's efforts to free the final survivor.

Finally, Johnston said, "Survivor is seriously stuck in that net." He muttered something unintelligible as a huge wave engulfed the boat.

They all watched as Aubrey briefly disappeared from sight. Eli held his breath, expelling it when she finally surfaced several feet away.

"Did that piece of debris hit her?" Johnston wondered aloud. "Did you guys see that?"

Eli kept his eyes glued on her form, waiting for her to give the distress signal. What if it had hit her and she was disoriented and couldn't signal? Eli felt the knot constrict as the danger of the situation sank in.

THE FIRST TWO rescues went smoothly. As smoothly as they could in high winds and rough seas, anyway. Aubrey approached the survivors one at a time, letting them know who she was and that she was there to help. She assisted each one into the basket and then the crew on board the helo successfully aided them into the aircraft. The third is where the situation evolved.

The young man was highly stressed with hypothermia rapidly encroaching. After approaching him, she quickly signaled for the basket as he informed her through bouts of violent shivering that there was "one more."

"Person?" she asked. "One more person? On board?"

"Yes, yes," he cried.

"Where?" she shouted.

He shook his head. "I don't know. I don't know. But Danny was with us, too. In the cabin and I… I couldn't find… Please…" She couldn't make out the rest of what he was saying as his sobs mingled with the roar of the ocean.

"Calm down and tell me."

"By the boat. Look near the boat."

"Got it."

"You'll go look?"

The basket lowered and she worked quickly to get him inside.

"Yes, but sir, you have to calm down and stay inside the basket, so we can get you on board. You'll be fine. You're almost there."

"But—" He reached for her again and Aubrey batted his hands away.

"Keep your hands inside the basket at all times. If someone else is in the water, we'll find him. I promise."

He nodded, crying pitifully now. She signaled to the helo to bring him up.

She didn't add that she was worried about the state that person might be in at this point. With high winds and water temperatures hovering around fifty degrees, hypothermia was almost a given at thirty minutes. It had been at least twenty since the captain had reported they were abandoning ship. Exhaustion, panic and waning consciousness tended to facilitate drowning beyond this time frame.

As the basket ascended, she retrieved her emergency radio and informed Johnston of the situation. After the basket was safely inside the helo, she kicked hard with her fins, propelling herself toward the half-submerged vessel. She circled the bow and slowed, not seeing anything that looked remotely human. A large wave crashed over the vessel and that's when she saw a flash of something... What was that? She watched, waited for it to show again.

There it was. It wasn't orange. But it was white—a common color for life preservers. She swam closer. As she neared the spot she realized it was, indeed, a person. Not a man, though, as she'd been expecting. A girl. Maybe a teenager? What was she doing out here? And without a life jacket?

She heard a weak shout as she neared the girl who had her arms gripped tightly around the small, circular life preserver. Aubrey realized why no one had immediately spotted her from above. She was completely entangled in a mass of netting, so much so that from the air she was sure they couldn't make out the form of a person. She would likely appear to be a blob of debris.

What a mess, Aubrey thought, removing the knife from her equipment bag. She swam closer, taking care not to become entangled herself. A bolt of concern went through her as she noted the bluish color of the girl's lips. But she was shivering and holding on, which meant the final stages of hypothermia weren't setting in yet. She must have managed to stay out of the water until the boat began to submerge. She speculated that as the girl abandoned ship and the vessel tipped, the loose pile of netting had slipped overboard along with her, essentially trapping her right there with the wreckage.

Aubrey called loudly when she reached the girl, "I'm a Coast Guard Rescue Swimmer and I'm here to help you."

The girl's response was incomprehensible.

"What's your name?"

It was difficult to hear her over the ocean's angry roar. She repeated what she thought she'd heard. "Danielle?" Something occurred to her and she asked, "Danny?"

"Yes." The answer came out along with a choked sob and Aubrey sent up a silent thank-you. She'd worry about what the girl was doing out here without a life jacket later. Much later. After they'd survived this ordeal. Both the wind and rain had let up somewhat, but the fog was regrouping and settling in again like gobs of grayish-tinted cotton candy.

"I'm Aubrey. It's kind of cold for a swim today, huh? What do you say we get out of here?"

All of this was said as she evaluated the situation. There was too much net for her to lift it off. With her swim knife, she began cutting away the netting. She tamped down her despair as she realized the extent of her entanglement. If she didn't get her out soon, the sinking boat would pull her under.

"I… I…can't swim."

"Don't worry, Danny. You won't need to. I'm here now and luckily I swim pretty well. Are you injured?"

"My leg," she said. "I hurt my leg when I slipped off the boat, but I can't feel it now…"

"We'll get it fixed up as soon as we get in the helicopter."

She glanced at the helicopter, her airborne

sentry serving to keep her calm. Just a couple more minutes, she thought as she continued clearing the net, thankful that sharpening her knife was a part of her personal equipment check ritual.

She kept talking to the girl as she worked. "Hold on, Danny. I'm almost finished. We'll be out of here soon."

As if in argument, a giant wave rolled over the boat, swamping everything in its path. It brought with it a piece of debris, smacking Aubrey hard in the shoulder and grazing her head. The force knocked her backward as the wave pulled her under. Even submerged and disoriented, she knew not to inhale. Lungs burning, she waited patiently for the force to let up as she knew it would. Grateful for the often-tortuous but invaluable training instilled in her during "A" school, she finally broke the surface, inhaling a breath. Looking around, she realized she'd ended up a few yards away from Danny.

Swimming back, she was afraid she'd find her survivor entangled even worse. Instead she was relieved to see that the wave had done them a favor, taking the remaining vestiges of the nylon netting with it. Danny was free. She reached out and pulled the girl into her arms, kicking hard with her fins, propelling them away from the wreckage. It would be easy to become tangled in something else in the floating and rapidly spreading mass of boat debris.

That's when she realized the helo had deployed another swimmer. She saw the form slicing cleanly through the water and imagined the situation must have looked far worse from the air. Her fellow swimmer stopped when he approached them.

"Aubrey?" a deep voice called out to her. "Are you okay?"

Her heart nearly stopped. Even with a mask and swim hood, she knew exactly who was now treading water before her. Removal of his mask and snorkel confirmed it. Finding herself face to face with Lieutenant Commander Eli Pelletier, former friend and one-time love of her life, a current of shock went through her. Not that she had time to think past the reaction, though, because she had a life to save.

Far enough away from the wreckage to avoid potentially flying debris from the rotor wash, she signaled for the basket. The helicopter moved over them.

"We're good," she shouted back.

Seconds later and the basket was lowering toward them. She watched as he repositioned his mask and, in his irritatingly Eli way, he moved as if to take over.

"I told you we're fine. I've got this."

He backed off while Aubrey kept talking, encouraging the terrified girl as she assisted her into the basket. "You're doing great, Danny. You're going to be all right." She signaled to raise the basket. Danny's terror-filled eyes remained locked on hers as she rose up out of the water. "Almost home." A sense of satisfaction settled upon her as the basket headed toward the helo.

"What are you doing here?" she called after she signaled for the hoist hook to be lowered for their retrieval.

"Helping you out?" he returned hopefully.

She narrowed her eyes menacingly. He wasn't helping, he was saving. Or that's what he'd thought he was going to do. The first time she'd seen him in twelve years and he was trying to *save* her? How annoying.

She didn't need help or anything else from him. She certainly didn't need saving.

As the cable came down she reached for the hoist hook and deftly secured it to his V-ring. She lifted an arm, holding a thumbs-up, signaling he was ready to be hoisted.

CHAPTER TWO

"ARE YOU SURE you want to be here?" Aubrey's sister Nina asked her again. Both she and their younger sister, Camile, kept looking at her like she might tip over at any second.

"Yes, absolutely. I'm off duty, so I'll take a nap later and be as good as new." Aubrey studied one of the several lists she had attached to her clipboard. "We've got sixteen people signed up for this work party. I need to be here."

The three sisters were standing in the basement of the First Methodist Church surrounded by boxes, bags and baskets full of snacks, toys and children's books. The items were ready to be stuffed into Christmas stockings for handing out at A Visit With Santa. It would be the second event in the DeBolt Realty Crazy About a Coast Christmas competition.

Aubrey, along with the mayor, was co-chair of Pacific Cove's Christmas Committee, which put them in charge of the town's participation in the contest.

Eligible beach towns up and down the Pacific Northwest coast had signed up for the competition. Back in July, each interested town had applied for entrance by submitting a proposal for four tourist-and/or community-friendly holiday events to be held the first three weeks of December. The categories included food, entertainment and fun for the family.

"You've been awake for who knows how many hours, part of that time on a rescue in freezing cold water where you saved four people," Camile said, crinkling her face skeptically. She tucked a blond, chin-length curl behind one ear and plopped a hand on one petite hip.

Aubrey often marveled at how her little sister had ended up so…well, little. In comparison to her and Nina, anyway, who were both just a few inches shy of six feet. And while Nina was thin and willowy like their mother, Aubrey was curvier but athletic like their dad. Camile was barely over five feet, with "bones like a bird," their grandma liked to say.

"I *helped* save four people, along with my flight crew. Two flight crews actually," Aubrey corrected. Being a rescue swimmer might be one of the toughest jobs in the Coast Guard, but there was no way she could do it without her crew. Yesterday's rescue had gone smoothly. Aside from Eli being deployed to assist her, she was feeling good about it.

Upon returning to base, she'd tried not to glare at Eli as she'd discussed the rescue with her team. She'd learned that after being rolled by the wave and hit by debris, coupled with the amount of time both she and the survivor had been in the water, the crew's concern had escalated. The decision had been made to send down another swimmer, in this case Eli. She understood, yet it troubled her just the same.

Because it was Eli. She couldn't help but wonder how hard he had pushed for it.

Even though as kids they'd both been wild and adventurous, and often competitive with one another, he'd always had an overly cautious streak where she was concerned. Trying to protect her, help her, save her. She couldn't stop wondering exactly what had happened on that helo.

She'd been tempted to ask Jay, but didn't want to give away the fact that she and Eli had any kind of romantic past. It wasn't relevant and she didn't need to be ribbed about it. Or have anyone thinking she was receiving special treatment. Anxiety bubbled within her at the thought. She needed to put it out of her mind for now and focus on the task at hand.

"*You're* going to take a nap? Right," Nina drawled wryly. Nina had been living with her for almost a year now and knew that she didn't do naps. Aubrey powered through fatigue, shaking it off like a beesting or a twisted ankle.

She couldn't help but be touched by her sisters' concern, but enough already. She lifted her arms and held them aloft. "You guys, please stop worrying. I promise it was no big deal. Just another day at the office. Did you count these books?"

Nina answered, "Yes, I've counted them several times. You love using that office line, don't you?"

Aubrey shrugged a shoulder and grinned. "I do." She couldn't help it. She loved that her "office" was the ocean. She loved her job, too. She was proud of what she and her fellow Coasties accomplished on a daily basis.

"Okay, but I could have handled this work party, you know?"

"Of course I know that," Aubrey said. And she could have. But Aubrey needed everything to be perfect. "What kind of an example would that be setting for the rest of the team if I bailed in this crucial time?"

Camile snorted. "The team? The Christmas committee is a team? Do you even know how much you sound like Dad right now?" Camile had only returned home from college a few days ago for winter break, so this was the first Christmas committee meeting she'd been able to attend.

She deepened her voice and added an uncanny impersonation of their father. "'To expect commitment and one-hundred-percent effort from your team members, a good leader needs to be an example.'"

In tandem, she and Nina burst into laughter.

Aubrey couldn't help but grin herself. "Thank you," she said, even though they all knew it wasn't really a compliment. The sisters disagreed on the effectiveness of their now-retired Coast Guard father's parenting techniques as they'd been growing up. Aubrey had hung on his every word while doing her level best to emulate him. Nina had not. Camile had fallen somewhere in the middle.

Aubrey looked down at her clipboard. "How are we doing with the goodies?"

Nina flipped a page in her own notebook. "Two hundred and twenty-six Baggies—

three pieces of saltwater taffy per bag for a total of six hundred and seventy-eight pieces. Two hundred and thirteen pouches of roasted almonds and three hundred string cheese sticks."

"Perfect."

"Ah, yes, almonds and cheese, those most traditional of holiday treats," Camile drawled sarcastically. "Couldn't we have scored some fudge or a frosted sugar cookie or something? You know that June, the owner of Bakery-by-the-Sea, is a friend of mine, right? She makes the prettiest cookies."

"I know, and that's a sweet offer. But we have plenty of candy with the taffy. Why not take the opportunity to show kids that healthy foods can be treats, too? Sandpiper Nut Roasters donated the almonds. Cove Aged Cheeses donated the cheese. And Salmon Crackers *made* the crackers' whole-grain deliciousness. It's good stuff. And tucked into these little stockings that Mom's quilt club made? Not only are the kids going to love them, they're going to be a hit with the contest judges—a super-high scorer."

Each event would be attended by a member from DeBolt Realty's judging panel. Input from attendees would be encouraged and factored into the final scoring, as well.

Events included everything from Christmas concerts and plays to fancy dinners and wine-and-cheese tastings—anything that would "generate a feeling of community and holiday enthusiasm." Scores were based on creativity, attendance, execution and Christmas spirit.

"Whole-grain crackers?" Camile shot a horrified look at Nina. "Next thing you know, she's going to be passing out those little boxes of raisins on Halloween. She'll be *that* house…"

Nina reached out and placed a hand on Camile's shoulder. With exaggerated solemnity she said, "Camile, honey, I hate to tell you this, but she's already *that* house. I begged her, but… She passed out protein bars this year."

"They were chocolate chip!" Aubrey protested. "Plenty of sugar in there to constitute a treat, but the protein and fiber mixed with the sugar helps to prevent that blood sugar crash that no parent wants their child to be subjected to."

"Protein bars?" Camile pressed her fingers against her temples. "And her house didn't get egged?"

"I'm sure it was only because everyone in the neighborhood knows she's Coast Guard.

Most of them also know she's Captain Brian Wynn's daughter." She added a slow, sad head shake. "But I'm afraid that will only shield her for so long before—"

Aubrey rolled her eyes. "You are both hilarious. I will admit they weren't that popular with the trick-or-treaters. Next year I'm thinking about fruit cups. Now, can we get back on track? Our volunteers should be showing up any minute now. I want to have everything ready so we can start stuffing these stockings. I need to win this thing."

When Aubrey had heard about the competition, she'd pounced on the opportunity, teaming up with Mayor Jack Hobbes as co-chair. The mayor was on a quest to attract wealthy tourists as well as new property-tax-paying residents to Pacific Cove. Aubrey wanted Pacific Cove to win the community improvement money. The town council had agreed to a deal where the bulk of the prize money would go to a project that was dear to her heart, the refurbishment of Pacific Cove's swimming pool. Their combined efforts would bring exposure to the town and its businesses and, if things went smoothly, would also save the pool in the process.

"So, who's going to be your Santa?" Camile asked as she scooped up a box of taffy and set it off to one side. In addition to her position as co-chair, Aubrey had taken the lead on this fun-for-the-family event, "A Visit with Santa."

"Pete Stahl has committed to doing it. Isn't that perfect? He even looks like Santa."

"He's a great choice. And I do like the books," Camile said, opening a cardboard box to reveal a collection of holiday titles for kids. "And the coupons for bowling at Fast Lanes and free admission to Saturday Swim at the pool. I can see what you're trying to accomplish here. Not only is a visit with Santa family friendly, so are these activities."

"Not to mention, she's drawing attention to the plight of her pool," Nina added.

"You guys can stop trying to appease me. I'm confident."

"Isn't she always?" Nina added, exchanging a smile with Camile.

Camile laughed. "I can see how jumping from helicopters and dangling from cables over sea cliffs might prepare a person for volunteer work here in Pacific Cove."

Aubrey laughed even as a current of discomfort flooded through her at the reminder of what she was trying hard not to think about; Eli was back. She hadn't even known that he was returning to Pacific Cove. Of course, she'd known two new transfers were arriving on some kind of special assignment, but she'd never heard their names, hadn't bothered to find out because she'd learn them when she needed to and—

Camile's voice interrupted her thoughts, "I've noticed there are several titles. Are we letting the kids choose what books they want? Or do they just get what they get?"

Good questions. And an even better distraction from the inevitable encounter with Eli.

As ELI AND GALE jogged through the streets of Pacific Cove, or "The Cove" as locals often referred to it, Eli marveled at how little things had changed in the twelve years he'd been away. Mission Street was still the main thoroughfare through town, both sides lined with quaint shops selling sand toys, shells, snow globes, plastic pirate swords and other assorted beach trinkets. Colorful flags were waving outside Kassie's Kites and the saltwater taffy pull was busy working in the window of the Wishing Well Candy and Fudge Shoppe.

He noticed that Salmon Crackers still smelled like the heavenly fresh-baked buns they served their sandwiches on. On the next block, he was thrilled to see Rascal's Bookstore still in existence. There was a new coffee shop and the smell emanating from Beach Beans Coffee Roasters made his mouth water.

The first day of December and already Christmas lights and garland were strung on every single light pole in town. Shop windows were painted. Many displayed festive holiday scenes and/or gift ideas.

The end of Mission Street featured a large cul-de-sac with a gazebo overlooking the beach. It was a popular meeting spot and a place where community events often centered. They jogged up to the structure and stood off to one side for a quick breather. A large sign advertised that Santa would be visiting there this coming weekend.

They stood side by side for a moment, gazing out at the stunning view of the horizon. Eli closed his eyes for a few seconds and focused on the roar of the ocean—the unique sound that was Pacific Cove. In spite of everything he was facing here, he was glad to be back. So far in his career he'd lived near the beach in Connecticut, New Jersey, North Carolina and San Diego, California. He was positive that if someone blindfolded him and plopped him down on the shore at any of those locales, he'd able to identify each one.

But the Northwest coast was different to him and Pacific Cove was special. He and his father had moved every few years until Eli was twelve. That's when they'd landed in Pacific Cove. His father had been lucky enough to score back-to-back assignments here and Eli considered it the closest thing to a hometown he'd ever had.

Connected to this place were a billion memories, most of them including or featuring Aubrey. They had spent so much time on this very stretch of beach. He'd kissed her right here once, at the bottom of the stairs, sheltered from passersby under the edge of the boardwalk.

He felt himself shifting from one foot to the other as a fresh bout of anxiety coursed through him. Clearly, she was upset by the fact that he'd gone into the water after her. She'd barely glanced his way as the team had discussed the events back at the base.

Lt. Cdr. Holmes had explained to Aubrey their fear that she'd been knocked silly by the piece of debris. They'd immediately deployed Eli in case she needed assistance. By the time he'd been lowered into the water, the rest of the crew could see she had the situation handled. The consensus had been that she'd executed her duties perfectly.

But the fact was he'd pushed for it. He hadn't been able to handle the idea of Aubrey being in danger. He'd wondered if Gale had picked up on it. He'd been waiting for his friend to quiz him about it, could feel his questioning gaze on him now. Gale knew that he, Aubrey and Alex were friends, that they had grown up here together. But Eli hadn't mentioned that, for a time, he and Aubrey had been more.

"Are you up for a few more miles?" he asked. A sudden urge came over him to run by his old house. "We still have another hour before we meet Danielle Cruz and her parents." Their first official task of the day was to interview the survivors from yesterday's rescue.

"Sure," Gale agreed.

They took off running again, heading east toward the other end of Mission Street. Here it crossed the two-lane Coast Highway, bisecting the town—and its socioeconomics right along with it. The community's wealthier residents lived in the upscale beachfront and ocean-view mansions. The more modest "middle class" homes began a few blocks from the beach and stretched up toward the highway. The less fortunate and view-deprived lived "across the highway."

It was funny because he and Alex and Aubrey hailed respectively from each of these locales. The St. Johns lived in the grandest of all the grand beachfront homes. The Wynn family enjoyed a comfortable existence in a well-kept bungalow right in the middle of town. And the Pelletiers had made their home "across the highway."

They turned into the now nearly empty parking lot of the Starfish Charmer where Eli explained, "This establishment used to be the place in town to drink hard and not go home alone."

Gale chuckled in understanding. They were crossing the lot when a familiar figure emerged from the tavern. Eli watched as the man stopped, shoved his phone into a pocket and raked his hands through his hair. Same gesture of frustration he'd employed since they'd first become friends in the sixth grade.

"Hey, that's my buddy, Alex."

Alex saw them, gave a hearty wave and headed in their direction. They stopped and Eli introduced the two men. He silently hoped these two guys, his best friends, would hit it off.

"Are you okay, buddy? You looked a little wound up when you came out of there."

"Oh, yeah, um…town council business."

Alex looked around like he'd just realized where they were. "What are you doing hanging around in this part of town, anyway?"

Eli lifted his arms in a wide shrug. "What are you talking about? These are my old stomping grounds. I'm showing Gale around."

Alex chuckled. "True enough."

"I think the real question is what are you doing here, St. John? Pardon my political incorrectness, but this is slumming for you. I, on the other hand, used to enjoy a basket of clam strips here almost every Saturday night with my dad."

He glanced toward the somewhat run-down establishment, annoyance again creasing his brow. "Polly Simmons has started yet another petition to shut this place down."

"On what grounds?"

"She claims it's unsanitary." Twisting his face into a grimace, he pointed across the highway and asked, "You guys headed to your old neighborhood?"

"We are. Is it?"

Alex clapped him on the shoulder. "I'll go with you for moral support because it's going to break your heart, buddy. And, no, it's not. I wouldn't eat off the floor, but it's nowhere near condemnable. Polly is irritated because Jaycie won't sell the place. Jaycie keeps getting these obscene offers from developers, but she won't even consider them. This further infuriates Polly because she is on the mayor's bandwagon where this subject is concerned. Polly and the mayor and their cronies want to turn Pacific Cove into one of those upscale tourist traps full of—" he paused to add air quotes "—'high-end boutiques and gourmet eateries.'"

He rubbed the back of his neck and then gestured at the Starfish Charmer. "What is wrong with this place the way it is? Once you lose that small-town feel? Bam, it's gone forever. Am I right?"

He turned and motioned them forward. "Cool your heels, by the way. We're walking. I couldn't run across the street if a tiger was chasing me. Honest truth, I would literally lie down and take my chances with a tiger—that's how out of shape I am."

They all laughed and started walking.

"So, Gale, what do you think of our little town so far?"

"It's great. I'm a small-town boy myself. It reminds me a lot of our little coastal towns back east in Connecticut."

"But without the history or the New England–style charm?"

Gale grinned. "Well, a couple hundred

years can make a big difference history-wise. Although, Astoria is pretty cool and you've got your own history with the fur trade and Lewis and Clark's big adventures along the Columbia River. Plus, the old forts and the Native American culture. And all these spectacular lighthouses I've been reading about. Excited to check those out."

"That's true," Alex said, a tinge of pride in his voice. After a thoughtful pause he asked, "How long do you think you guys will be here?"

Eli answered. "Uh, we're not sure yet. As long as it takes us to make a thorough evaluation."

"Of search-and-rescue training procedures?"

"Yep."

"Air rescue or all operations?"

"We're doing air, water and vertical surface. Someone else will be assigned to the boats, probably sometime this spring, from what I understand." This wasn't true, but luckily the powers that be had planned for this question and formulated the official answer they were to give if asked. Even though it was part of the job, it made him uncomfortable to have to lie to his old friend.

Alex nodded thoughtfully.

This would be the perfect opportunity to confide in Alex. He and Gale had been cautioned to proceed as if they didn't trust anyone. The admiral knew Eli had roots here, yet he'd trusted him not to let those connections cloud his judgment. Eli and Gale had agreed that they'd discuss and be in accordance before they sought advice or help from anyone else, Coast Guard or civilian. There was also the fact that he could conceivably be putting his friend in danger by getting him involved. For the time being he would hold off.

As they walked and talked, Eli wondered how many hundreds of times he and Alex had covered this same path together. It was crazy how it suddenly seemed like they'd done so only yesterday.

The cozy gray-and-white saltbox he and his father had shared was gone now. They paused on the newly-poured sidewalk in front of a cardinal-red mailbox marking the address where it had once been. Memories tumbled through his brain like a slide show; his dad making him breakfast every single morning when he wasn't on duty, playing on the rope swing he and his dad had hung from the limb of a huge spruce tree, his cat Willow greeting him when he got home from school...

"Man, we had some good times here," Alex

said. "Remember all the card games we used to play? Dang, Aubrey was good at that one where you have to get rid of all the cards in your pile. She has freakishly fast hands. Remember how we would cheat? We'd get frustrated and throw her cards so she'd have to scramble around for them while we would frantically try to catch up." His deep belly laugh was contagious. "She'd get so mad, but she'd giggle at the same time. It's been great having her back in town—and Nina, too. I love those Wynn girls."

Eli chuckled in remembrance. He hadn't had fun like that in a very long time.

"Speaking of rescues... That was kind of a scary one yesterday, huh?"

Of course Alex would know about it. He knew everything that happened in town. Plus, Aubrey and Alex were still close, just like he and Alex were. Unlike him, Alex was still friendly with the entire Wynn family.

"You heard, huh? Aubrey was great. They are lucky to have her." Eli wasn't about to give away how scared he'd been. He didn't even want to admit that to himself.

"Yeah, I talked to Nina last night. I called Aubrey first thing this morning because I knew she had a Christmas meeting. She's a little obsessed with this competition. The woman goes nonstop as it is. If she's not on base or working out, she's swimming or giving lessons at the pool or helping somebody with something—or worrying about someone. Nina is on the receiving end of that these days. You know about how Nina's been living with her since her divorce?"

He knew, but only because Alex had told him months ago over the phone.

"She's been through hell, and Aubrey's been there for her every step of the way. Don't get me wrong, she's amazing, and I'm not begrudging her any of it…" His head fell to one side as if pondering. "Most of it, anyway. I just wish she'd take a little time for herself once in a while."

Eli wasn't surprised by any of this. She'd always exhibited that kind of compassion. He'd been drawn to it as well as her courage and unshakable drive. At times he'd been almost jealous of the phenomenal amount of energy she possessed. Even when they were teenagers, she'd been tough to keep up with. When she'd told him she wanted to be a rescue swimmer, he'd never once doubted her ability to achieve that goal.

"What's a Christmas contest?" Gale asked.

"Oh, there's this competition, sponsored by DeBolt Realty. Their goal is to find the beach town with the most Christmas spirit. They specialize in oceanfront property and they're trying to expand their footprint here in the Pacific Northwest. Aubrey is co-chair of Pacific Cove's effort, along with the mayor, Jack Hobbes. She *really* wants to win. I'm not super thrilled about the venture because, if she wins, the town gets included in a national advertising campaign. Don't let them fool you. Not all publicity is good publicity. But I'm being supportive for Aubrey's sake because also included is prize money, which she wants to use to spruce up the community's pool. That part I'm on board with. We spent an awful lot of time in that pool when we were kids, especially Aubrey."

Alex pointed at what used to be Eli's yard. "Remember how we would get those whiffle ball games going in your yard? Your dad would always play when we needed to make the teams even. He was so cool. He made being a single dad look easy. How's he doing?"

Tim Pelletier had been a great dad, caring for Eli in the best way he knew how and steadfastly making their house a home. Eli's mom had taken off when Eli was only three months old, so his dad had been left to fulfill as much of the mom role as he could.

In spite of his dad's bouts of depression, his childhood had been great, right up through his teenage years.

But everything had changed soon after his high school graduation when his father had been transferred. Closing in on two three-year assignments, it had been time for him to move on. But not in this way. The new assignment, which he'd had no choice but to take, had essentially been a demotion for his father, marking the end of his career advancement. Depression had kicked in and he'd retired soon after.

The situation had been bad for Eli, too. He'd been left with no choice but to break up with Aubrey while a burning anger and hatred had born for the man who had caused it all—Brian Wynn. Aubrey's father. Because how could Eli be with the girl whose father had ended his own dad's career? How could he be with her and not tell her all of the things that weren't his to tell, like why he'd really broken up with her and what her parents' role had been in it all?

Eli realized Alex was waiting for an answer. "He's good. Really good, actually. He's thinking about flying up for Christmas." After his retirement, his father had moved to Florida, bought a boat and become a sport fishing guide. After several rough years of adjustment, his dad finally seemed content. The last couple of years in particular he'd been especially busy and seemed to be flourishing.

"We should go fishing with him again. Man, that was a blast." Three years ago, he and Alex had taken a trip to Florida to visit him.

"Alex caught a marlin that weighed in at—what was it?—four hundred and twelve pounds."

"Four hundred and twelve point two pounds," Alex answered, launching into his fish story.

Eli took the opportunity to study his old neighborhood. Alex was right. Unlike the west side, or "beach side" as they'd called the upscale part of town, this side of town *had* changed. Dramatically. A few years ago a developer had bought a huge chunk of land here, torn down the old houses and put up one of those cutesy subdivisions where the houses looked different and yet matched at the same time. It reminded Eli of a set of snap-together toys.

"Isn't this a crying shame?" Alex asked a few minutes later. "It looks like a bunch of gingerbread houses have been smacked down in the middle of Candy Land. I did my level best to block approval of this project. But the developer…he's got his shizzle together. I tell you what…"

Alex rambled on while Gale asked questions.

Amazingly, the giant spruce tree that had stood in their front yard was still there, sans swing, but Eli could see the scars where a succession of ropes had spent years relentlessly rubbing into the thick limb. He stared at it as Alex ranted on about the injustice of unfettered construction in their town.

He wondered how long he and Gale would be in Pacific Cove.

The real question was how long could he work so closely with Aubrey and yet keep the distance he knew he needed to maintain? And what about Brian Wynn? Alex had told him that since his retirement, Brian and his wife, Susannah, had been spending a few months of the year down south in Arizona. He'd also mentioned that they would be home for the holidays.

Avoiding him was completely unrealistic. Could he be around the man and not reveal the hatred he harbored for him? Did he even want to? Maybe a confrontation was the answer to this long-held animus. Eli knew his train of thought was nothing but a vicious, ugly circle with no end. Because the problem with this scenario was that Susannah was still Brian's wife—and Aubrey was still their daughter.

CHAPTER THREE

AFTER THE CHRISTMAS meeting Aubrey headed across town to visit Danielle Cruz. She'd learned that the girl had suffered a bad sprain to her knee along with a variety of scrapes, bumps and bruises. She was lucky. Aubrey had seen people suffer much worse after becoming entangled in boat rigging or debris.

Danny's mom answered the door and she spent a quiet, emotional moment thanking Aubrey. She then led her up the stairs to Danny's room and left Aubrey there with a grateful, encouraging smile. The door was open and the pretty teenager was sitting up, eyes closed, reclining against the headboard. Straight black hair was tucked behind her ears and a magazine lay open on her lap. Bare feet with purple-painted nails were sticking out from the end of a green-and-blue comforter. One foot was busy tapping a rhythm. The other was sporting a black brace around the knee.

"Hey," she said, wrapping her knuckles on the doorjamb.

The girl's eyes snapped open as her head turned, fingers reaching for the turquoise ear buds nestled inside her ears. Recognition dawned across her features. "Oh…" One hand flew up to cover her mouth and she promptly burst into tears.

Aubrey hurried toward her bedside. "Danny, what's the matter? Are you all right?"

The girl reached for her hand and squeezed it tight. "I'm so happy to see you." She snuffled out the words. "I was so cold and out of it, I didn't have a chance to thank you. Thank you for saving me. And for saving Brendan and his dad and his uncle, too." She dabbed at her face with the white sheet.

"Of course." Aubrey smiled gently and lowered herself onto the chair next to the bed. "You're welcome. It's my job and you did great."

"Yeah? Well, I can't imagine having your job. You are so cool, you know that? Like, totally badass. I thought I was going to die. That net, it was going to pull me under. I couldn't believe it when you came swimming over to me and I hoped I might actually be saved. And when I realized you were a woman? I was, like, shocked. I thought you might be an angel, even though you were wearing all that Coast Guard stuff."

Aubrey let out a soft laugh. "Believe me, I was just as happy to see you as you were to see me. And just as surprised, by the way. I didn't realize I was looking for a girl, either. You know, you weren't part of the original distress call?"

Her head bobbed as fresh tears sprang to her eyes. With her free hand, Aubrey reached for the tissue box on the bedside table. She placed the box between them.

Danny plucked out a couple of tissues and used one, dabbing her eyes and blowing her nose. "I'm so sorry. I'm really emotional for some reason."

"That's perfectly normal after what you've been through."

She sniffled. "Yeah. I've been crying a lot. I go from really, really happy to, like, the saddest of sad in one heartbeat. It's been rough. I mean, I'm super grateful to be alive and everything, but…everyone is mad at me and Brendan. Especially at Brendan."

"Why would they be mad?" Aubrey placed a hand on her own chest. "I'm not mad at you."

Danny nibbled on her lower lip. "I wasn't supposed to be on the boat. Brendan stowed me away." She added a raspy chuckle. "That's what he called it. He called me his stowaway. I thought it was cute…"

"Where were you headed?" She couldn't help but wonder how the young couple thought they would get away with the scheme when they reached their final destination.

"Brendan's dad and his uncle? They drop off these parts sometimes down the coast. It was just supposed to be one of those trips. There and back. Drop off the stuff and then turn around and come back. Brendan said it would be easy. He was going to pretend like he was getting seasick and then come into the cabin where I was hiding. I know it probably sounds really bad…" She trailed off with an apologetic shrug.

It had been a stupid thing to do, but they were kids. She was struck by the memory of the time she had been Eli's "stowaway."

During his teenage years he had worked for Quinley's Berry Farm. Sometimes he'd deliver berries as far away as Portland. One time he'd suggested Aubrey hide under a blanket in the cab of the pickup so she could ride along. It had been a perfect day filled with sunshine and laughter. On the way home they'd stopped for frozen custard and watched the most incredible sunset from a bluff overlooking the Astoria Bridge. For a few seconds she let the happiness of that memory sink in, refusing to spoil it with thoughts of the un-happily-ever-after that followed.

Danny dabbed at her eyes with a fresh tissue. "My parents have been pretty good, though. I think they're just happy I'm alive."

"Of course they are."

Her head started an agitated shake. "But Brett, that's Brendan's dad, has, like, blown a gasket over the whole thing. Usually he's a really nice guy, but this…?" She gave Aubrey a pleading look. "He's… Brendan is worried."

"Worried, how?" The loss of a boat was a pretty big deal and definitely a reason to be upset. Hopefully it was insured.

"I'm not sure. He just keeps saying that his dad is in a serious rage. He can't let it go. Keeps asking Brendan questions and going over and over what went wrong."

Near-death experiences hit people in dif-ferent ways. She wondered if she should fol-low up on this for Danny and Brendan's sake. Talk to his dad or recommend some counsel-ing? She would brief her superior officer Se-nior Chief Nivens and get his opinion. What she didn't need to do was upset Danny any further.

"You know what? I know it's difficult to

believe right now, but chances are this will all blow over. Just do me a favor. Next time you decide to stow away or participate in any activity at all anywhere near the water, wear a life jacket, okay? Promise me."

She let out a giggle. "That's funny. That's exactly what that other Coast Guard guy said this morning."

Coast Guard guy? "Who?"

"Lieutenant Commander Pelletier." She enunciated the title proudly. "That's right, isn't it? He told me to call him Eli, but he looks more like a lieutenant to me. A really good-looking one. And the other guy was totally hot, too. He looks like a movie star or a model or something…"

Eli. And the "hot movie star" had to be Gale. Why would Eli and Gale come here to talk to Danny? The girl had already been officially debriefed. Danny's unknown presence onboard had thrown a wrench in the midst, but wrenches like that were thrown into rescues all the time. Yet a niggle of concern began to form in her mind. If they were questioning Danny again, did that mean she herself was being investigated for some kind of misconduct?

Aubrey replayed the entire series of events over and over again in her mind. She reassured herself once again that she hadn't done anything wrong. Had she? Maybe she should have radioed that she was fine and didn't need assistance. But time was always a factor… These were the kinds of details she could stew about for days. She wanted to quiz Danny about what they'd asked her, but felt it would be wrong somehow.

Besides, she told herself, not only was she a big girl, she was good at her job. She would wait it out, with confidence, until she knew for sure what this was all about.

Instead she focused on Danny and what she could do for her.

"I HAVE AN IDEA," Gale said from the passenger seat of the pickup as Eli drove back toward the base.

"What's that?" Eli asked.

"It occurred to me earlier while we were talking to Alex. It made me think about what I'd do if we were trying to solve this case in Falls Terrace. I know you haven't lived here, or even been here, in a long time, but you still have a lot of connections in the community."

"Yeah." Eli was already realizing how true that was. Twelve years didn't seem that long now that he was back.

"All this Christmas stuff going on? *This*

could help us solve this thing—getting out there and meeting people and socializing. A town this size, with this close-knit feel? People talk. There's not much that is really and truly secret. Folks might not even know they are sitting on important information because they only have one piece of the puzzle. But if we gather some of these pieces, make some connections, we might get somewhere."

He had a point. Eli guided the pickup into a space in the air station's lot.

"Which reminds me." Gale pulled his phone out of his pocket. "I got a text from Yeats." Yeats was their contact at the DEA, keeping them informed about news on the case from California. He slid a finger across the display as he explained, "The crates have been sent to the lab for examination."

For the last year a potent strain of heroin had been flooding the West Coast. Early indications had the DEA believing the drugs were being shipped up from the south. As a result, they'd focused most of their resources there even as the drugs continued to flow. He and Gale had been stationed in San Diego when a tip had come in to the DEA that Coast Guard personnel may be involved. Because of a connection Eli had in the DEA, he and Gale had been consulted about the case.

The DEA had seized a shipment of drugs from a boat off the coast of San Diego. Upon reviewing the evidence, it had been the wooden crates, not the drugs, that had got Eli thinking. They had been constructed from various woods, including maple and larch. Eli knew that larch was a wood that could only have come from much farther north where maple was also very abundant. He had speculated that the drugs were being smuggled into the Pacific Northwest, where they were being broken down into smaller units then shipped out again to lower level dealers in these locally constructed, and hopefully traceable, crates.

It was just speculation on his part, but soon after that, Eli had been at a Coast Guard luncheon where he'd mentioned the theory to Admiral Schaefer. The admiral had seized upon the notion and, a few short weeks later, Eli and Gale had been added to the task force and transferred to Astoria.

The admiral's blessing and enthusiasm had been welcome, the assignment essentially like a promotion for him and Gale. For Eli, the importance of solving the case had increased exponentially. Not only did he want to solve the case for his own career, he didn't want to let the admiral down. Failure, in any form, was Eli's worst nightmare. Nothing, and no one, was going to stand in his career path the way it had his father's.

"You have a history here, right? Plus, your friendship with Alex and Aubrey. Can you get us involved in some of this community stuff?"

"Yeah, probably," he said with much more confidence than he felt. He had no idea how things stood between him and Aubrey.

Gale reached into the backseat and grabbed his notebook. He pulled a sheet of paper from inside and began to read in an overly enthusiastic tone. "'It's okay to be crabby this Christmas! At Pacific Cove's crab races and crab feed you can be a crab and eat one, too' et cetera and blah, blah, blah."

"Crab races?"

"Yes. I just happened to pick up the Crazy About a Coast Christmas schedule of events. The first item listed is the crab races and crab feed this Friday night. At a place called The Shoals Hotel. Attending doesn't sound like that much of a hardship. There's an all-you-can-eat crab feed and buffet. But, if we could volunteer? Mingle with the folks? That would be even better."

Eli grinned. "This actually isn't a bad plan. I'll see what I can do."

CHAPTER FOUR

"Okay, guys, that's it for today. Great job, my little minnows! Don't forget to practice your crunches and push-ups at home. Remember what we say?" A chorus of little voices joined hers. "Strong on land means strong in the sea."

"Awesome! That's right. You guys are smart as well as super swimmers."

The fitness standards for a rescue swimmer were some of the most stringent in all of military service. Regulations required that they pass a monthly fitness test in order to remain on duty. The training on base, while intense, wasn't enough. So, on her off days, she worked out. A day rarely went by when she didn't get into the water and she liked to do it here at "her" pool, Pacific Cove's community pool. And two or three times a week when she wasn't on duty, she taught swimming lessons.

Six little bodies scrambled out of the pool. This group had made a ton of progress in the last few weeks. This fueled her resolve, even as it killed her that the pool she'd literally grown up in, and that she loved with all of her heart, was crumbling around her. She refused to accept what others were calling inevitable.

"Is anyone sticking around to practice today?" Aubrey had a policy that the kids could stay after class for fifteen minutes and practice what they'd learned in their lesson that day. They could practice anything, really, as long as they were in the water.

Two hands shot up into the air. One belonged to George, a shy little guy with huge brown eyes and a sweet smile featuring one front tooth. The other hand belonged to Eleanor, a tiny girl with blond pigtails and a bright purple swimsuit. Eleanor was one of her all-time favorite students, a foster child who'd been bounced around from relative to foster home her entire short life. For now, she'd found a home with stable parents who were motivated to bring her to swim lessons.

She qualified for free lessons through a program Aubrey had started for youth who couldn't afford them otherwise. And Aubrey could see what swimming did for Eleanor because it was the same miraculous, confidence-building phenomenon she'd experienced as a child.

"Excellent, George and Eleanor. I'll see the rest of you yahoos on Thursday?" With waves and goodbyes, the remaining crew headed toward the locker rooms.

"Do you guys want to jump off the diving board?"

"I do! I do!" This from Eleanor.

Ever cautious, George said, "I think I'll practice treading water some more first."

"Sounds good, buddy. You can never be too good at treading water." Aubrey knew this was his way of gathering courage. She wouldn't push him.

He climbed back into the pool while Eleanor hustled over to the diving board.

"Whenever you're ready, El," Aubrey called to the little girl.

She took a few steps, bounced on the board, sailed through the air and splashed into the water with all the force her forty-two pounds of weight could manage. She surfaced and began to swim toward the edge exactly as she'd been taught.

"Perfect!" And it was. The girl reminded her so much of herself at that age. She'd always been the first one in the water and the last one out. The first one to jump off the diving board. The first to swim across the deep end. The first to hold her breath while swimming the entire length of the pool under water...

A giggle sounded. "Can I do it again?"

"Absolutely. Good job, Georgie. You're doing great."

"Fearless," a familiar voice said near her left shoulder, startling her.

"Eli, hi."

He came around and sat beside her on the bench. "Reminds me of a girl I used to know. She would literally jump off of anything, no matter how high, as long as there was water to land in below."

Aubrey gave him a casual smile even as her heart kicked hard against her rib cage. She focused on the pool where George was now practicing his freestyle stroke from one corner of the pool to the other.

"Really?" she said, her tone dubious.

"Really. She's all grown up now, but I don't think she's changed all that much. In fact, now she jumps out of helicopters and allows herself to be lowered by cable onto sinking boats or to the sides of cliffs to help people who are stranded."

"Wow. It sounds to me like she totally rocks."

"Oh, she does, but…" His mouth formed into this adorable half frown as he glanced around as if to confirm no one would over-hear. "Between you and me? I think she might be a little crazy."

She couldn't stop the smile playing on her lips even as recalling the memories tight-ened her chest with emotion. They used to call each other crazy after some of the stunts they'd pull together: jumping off cliffs and bridges, swimming across icy-cold rivers, ex-ploring treacherous cliffs and caves.

His head dipped until his mouth was only a few inches from her ear. "But then, I've al-ways been a little partial to crazy."

Aubrey felt her cheeks grow warm as a blast of heat flooded her bloodstream. Ap-parently twelve years had done nothing to weaken her body's response to Eli Pelletier. She was going to have to draw on her much more dependable brain when dealing with him. Luckily, her brain was stronger than her heart, and knew better than to fall under his spell. Her brain she could trust.

"What are you doing here?" she asked, glancing at him again. He didn't appear to be here to swim, attired as he was in soft, worn jeans and a faded blue-and-gray Gonzaga Bulldogs T-shirt. His black hair was damp and he'd draped a soggy rain jacket over the bench beside him. She turned her attention toward Eleanor who was now bobbing in and out of the water like the dolphin Aubrey had nicknamed her after.

"I came here to talk to you."

She frowned. "How did you know I'd be here?"

"Alex told me. I ran into him this morning and he mentioned that he'd talked to you. I had already stopped by your place and tried your phone. He told me you can always be found here on Tuesdays and Thursdays when you aren't on duty."

"That's true."

"You always loved teaching lessons."

"I have. I do. Ever since Jason Redmond almost drowned in the ocean. I've done other stuff, but teaching the world to swim is still my goal."

"I remember," Eli said. "That was your...? Let me think... Second summer as a life-guard on the beach, right?"

"Yep. I was fifteen." The first time she'd ever done CPR on a real-life person. Changed her life.

The episode still sometimes woke her up at night. As she'd executed compressions on Ja-son's cold, blue, bony chest, time had seemed to shift into slow motion. It had felt like hours before the ten-year-old finally gasped and coughed out the ocean that was literally choking the life out of him.

"And that's when you started teaching the free lessons, right?"

"Stretch out your arms, Georgie," she called to the little boy. "Reach really far… That's it. Good job!

"Yes. Thanks to Betty. You remember Betty Frye, right?"

She felt like she was giving back to the pool that had helped to make her who she was. Unfortunately, she was only one person and the need was great. And because her beloved pool was falling into ruin, attendance was way down.

"Of course. Betty was great." Betty used to run the pool and coach the swim team. The competitive swim league where she'd flourished throughout her youth had disbanded years ago.

"She was. She loved this place as much as I do. She helped me restart the program."

Eli was looking around as if just now noticing his surroundings. "It's looking a little sad these days, huh?"

She nodded. "Betty passed away two years after I left for the Coast Guard. The program fizzled out after her death and the pool has been on a slow decline ever since. If it wasn't for the St. Johns, it would probably be closed already."

He frowned. "What do you mean?"

Aubrey explained how Alex and the St. John family had made a series of donations to keep the pool open, but without the revenue it needed, it was only a matter of time before it closed for good.

"No one wants to swim here anymore. People are taking their kids to lessons in Astoria or Lancaster. Without the revenue…" She trailed off with a sigh.

"This is a tragedy. I had no idea. So many great memories here."

The comment turned her insides to mush because she knew how those memories were intertwined with hers. She, Alex and Eli had been nearly inseparable for years and they'd spent countless hours here at the pool.

Keeping her eyes on her still-swimming charges, she smiled and said, "I don't remember ever not knowing how to swim. I spent so much time in the water when I was a kid, I thought it was normal. I didn't realize until I was way older that not everyone lives part-time in the water."

"I know what you mean. When I moved

here, I was happy to join you. I don't know
if I would have passed 'A' school on my first
attempt if Dad and I hadn't moved here—if
I hadn't met you. I give you so much credit
for pushing me in that way. In a lot of ways
actually."

Aubrey felt a warmth spread through her
at the comment. He'd pushed her, too. She'd
had the same thoughts about him when she'd
entered the brutally difficult rescue swimmer
school. As the only woman in her class, she'd
often told herself to imagine the guy next to
her was Eli. If she could swim as far as Eli,
then she could swim as far as him, too. There
were days that thought had been what literally kept her afloat.

"Yeah, I kind of feel that way about you,
too. So many races in this pool."

"What's your time these days in the 500
meter buddy tow?"

She told him.

"Wow. I still think there's a chance you
might, in fact, be part mermaid," he teased,
referring to the nickname he'd given her when
they were kids. "Alex and I used to just mar-
vel at how long you could stay under."

Before she could respond he twisted around
on the bench again. "There has to be something that can be done…" She felt heartened

by his reaction. Less silly about her own plans.

"I, uh, actually have a plan."

He leaned forward, resting his elbows on his thighs. "Let's hear it."

"I know it probably sounds insane... You've heard about this Christmas contest going on in town?"

"I have. It would be tough to miss."

"That's good." She grinned. "That means I'm doing my job as co-chairperson. You may or may not have also heard that I'm a little over the top about the whole thing?"

"'Obsessed' I believe is the term I heard."

She gave her head a shake. "I'm sure that came from Alex. He thinks I'm nuts, even though he's helping, albeit grudgingly. But the reason for my enthusiasm is because I plan to win."

"You?" he repeated sarcastically. "You plan to win?"

They shared a laugh and she went on to explain her strategy. Then added, "The money isn't enough to restore the pool to its former glory, but it's enough to get started. I have ideas on how to raise the rest. A refurbished pool and some proper management, and I know this place could pay for itself again. I would love to get the swim team up and running and expand the swim lesson program."

They spent a few minutes discussing the details until it was time for Eleanor and George to pack it up. She tossed each child a towel, delivered some encouraging words and watched them head for their respective locker rooms.

She could feel Eli's eyes on her the entire time. She couldn't help but wonder what he was thinking.

"You never said why you were looking for me."

His expression turned sheepish. "I wanted to apologize. I, uh, kind of pushed to be deployed yesterday. I saw you down there in the water and when that piece of debris hit you, it took me back… And I couldn't—I can't—stand the thought of something happening to you. Apparently that hasn't changed."

She swallowed, but it was difficult what with the gigantic lump lodged in her throat. She tried to think of something to say. There was so much she wanted to say, she didn't even know where to start. And yet another part of her didn't want to say anything at all. It seemed better not to revisit their history.

"We both know friendship means more than anything in the world to me. I have always done, and will always do, anything for my friends." *Except for* our *friendship. Except for* me, she wanted to add but didn't, knowing how pathetic that would sound.

She blew out a breath and looked around, wanting to focus on something besides his beautiful face. It felt painful to meet his eyes. After all these years, it surprised her how much it still hurt. Because they had been friends. Best friends. And she'd relied on that—on him. Too much, she'd realized after their breakup. She'd confided in him, depended on him and, yes, she'd been young but she'd loved him with all of her heart. For seven months they'd been more than friends and she'd given him everything she had— body, mind and soul. And more. She'd promised him her future, and he'd done the same.

Except he'd changed his mind. In what seemed like the blink of an eye *he'd changed his mind*. He'd broken up with her, saying only that a long-distance relationship would be too difficult. The Coast Guard Academy was intense and he'd need all of his energy to focus on that. She'd understood—as much as her shattered heart had allowed her to. After all, she kept telling herself, they were both intent on their Coast Guard careers, and she still had two years of high school left. Eli did need to focus. So did she. Even though she'd hoped they could do so together.

Three days later he was gone. His dad's transfer came through and Eli moved with him.

Within a month he was attending the Coast Guard Academy and starting a new life. Without her. And as much as that hurt, she couldn't hate him. She'd never hated him. Mostly she'd been shocked. She couldn't blame him for moving on, but she couldn't help but wish he hadn't abandoned their friendship in the process.

The reliably practical part of her kicked in again, banishing this unhelpful sappiness. He was here now and she needed to get used to that. She would get used to it. She kind of wanted to get used to it. If she could ignore the physical attraction, weed out the warm fuzzies from her heart, which shouldn't be that tough because they served no constructive purpose, then maybe they could even get some semblance of that friendship back.

But first she needed to make something clear.

"I appreciate the apology. On some level, I even appreciate the gesture. But you cannot do it again, you know that, right? You're lucky no one caught on. Actually, I'm the lucky one. I have to work with these guys, Eli. It's tough enough to be a woman in this profession. I've earned their respect, but for any of them to think that you don't trust my abilities? Or, even worse, that you are somehow giving me special treatment? That would be devastating to my reputation."

ELI HADN'T INTENDED for this to happen—this revisiting of old feelings and sharing of some kind of moment. He should have anticipated the depth of feelings he'd still have for her. And why wouldn't he, when, in typical Aubrey fashion, she was making this reunion, and his near screwup, so easy on him?

She'd done this when he'd broken up with her, too. She'd been all composed and sweet, even though he'd been able to see how much he was hurting her. No screaming or shouting or crying. Just those light green eyes brimming with unshed tears and a quaver in her voice as she'd told him she understood. She'd turned and calmly walked away, her thick blond braid swaying at her waist. It killed him even now to think about it.

In a perfect world, they would have remained friends. But he'd known, even at the time, that he couldn't do it. He couldn't just be friends with her. Could he be just friends with her now? Seeing as how that was the only option, he needed to figure out a way. And quickly.

Rekindling a romantic relationship was not possible. If anything, the obstacles were even bigger than they'd been twelve years ago. Back then, when he'd had to let her go, his father's career and reputation had been on the line—as well as Aubrey's happiness. If he'd told her all of the truth, she would have been devastated. It would have torn her family apart and shattered her happiness right along with it all.

Now that he was back, the stakes were even higher. *His* career was the one on the line, and he wasn't going to let anything—or anyone—stand in his way. Not like his father had. He was going to fulfill his dreams. Not to mention that the same complications still existed surrounding Aubrey and her family. As evidenced by his actions regarding the rescue, the instinct to protect her was still as strong as ever.

She was right about her own reputation. It wouldn't be good for her if her crew thought someone in his position doubted her. Or that he was trying to protect her by giving her special treatment.

"You're right. It won't happen again."

"It better not," she said firmly. "Or I will have to kick your butt."

"I would be okay with that," he shot back. "In fact, if you want to try, I'm available any night after work. Could we have dinner first?"

Her lips twitched and then she laughed.

Eli felt his heart take flight, even as he told himself to ignore the sensation. But she was just so...irresistible. She always had been. Even when they were kids and had been nothing more than friends, he'd loved being around her. She was smart, funny, athletic, driven and focused, yet she could also be a little shy. She was also adventurous to the point of being wild. Fun. Hard-core fun. They'd always had so much fun together.

And the way she was watching him now was nothing short of dangerous because, in spite of their history, and their breakup, attraction still simmered between them. Good sense told him he should get up and walk out right now.

But he couldn't seem to stop staring at her, couldn't quite believe he was finally sitting here next to her. And he had a chance to make things better between them. Back in the day she'd possessed a steely courage and, at some point over the years, a quiet, solid confidence had seeped in to replace the shyness she'd battled as a kid. He liked that, too.

"Aubrey, I know I should have come to you a long time ago to...explain somehow." That was a dumb thing to say. It was unrealistic because he couldn't really explain without giving everything away. "I should have at least tried to make things right between us. I never intended them not to be. I just... It was difficult for me to—"

"You don't have to explain anything to me," she answered flatly. "I get it, Eli. I got it a long time ago. We were young. Your career was important."

He swallowed, knowing he should just let it go at that. It stung, reminding him of how deeply he'd hurt her—how much it had hurt him, too. But if he started explaining, where would he stop? No one here in Pacific Cove seemed to know about the circumstances of his dad's transfer all those years ago. Except Aubrey's dad.

Yep, Brian Wynn knew all about it. Still, after all these years, Eli wanted to take the man down. The only thing holding him back was the promise he'd made to his own father, and his desire to protect Susannah Wynn. Lately he'd been thinking about that, though, wondering if he could manage one without the other. Could he be satisfied by getting revenge against Brian Wynn even if the man wasn't aware of who had extracted it?

"Look, Eli, if you're worried about me, about something personal regarding our history affecting my job performance or making things difficult for you, I can assure you that won't happen. My job always comes first. And I think we've established that it's important for you to treat me like anyone else. I will give you the same courtesy."

"I know that, Aubrey. Your record is impeccable. Your colleagues love you. Everyone on base respects you. I'm proud of you. You should be really proud of yourself."

He hoped he wasn't imagining the hint of blush on her cheeks.

She shifted on the bench to look at him. "Alex says you're here to check up on us?"

Now she was referring to what he was "officially" doing here. The paperwork said that he and Gale were in District 13 to perform an evaluation of the base's airborne search-and-rescue missions.

"To ensure that proper procedures are being followed."

She stared back at him, a thoughtful expression on her face. Without her signaling distress or radioing for assistance, it was debatable as to whether he really should have gone into the water after her. No one was questioning what he'd done—yet, anyway. Still, not exactly a stellar example of what he'd just claimed he was here to do. If he was trying to maintain his distance where she was concerned, his actions had pretty much blown that, too. He needed to get his head together where she was concerned, and he needed to get his act together where his job was concerned.

This case had to come first.

His gaze traveled back to the diving board. "How many 'rescue jumps' do you think we practiced off that diving board?"

He ignored how her gravelly chuckle sent a jolt of heat through his bloodstream.

"Um, approximately one million and fourteen? Remember how we used to tie towels onto a swim noodle to use as our 'survivor.'" She added air quotes.

They laughed again, reminiscing about the elaborate "rescue missions" they would invent.

"I can't stand the thought of this place closing." He swiveled so he was facing her again. "You think you can win this contest, huh?"

"Of course," she answered confidently.

"How can I help?"

She smiled. "That's really sweet, but you just got to town and all. I'm sure there are a million other things you'd rather do with your off time."

"None of them this important," he said, ignoring the eye-roll from his conscience. He suddenly wished his motives were as pure and selfless as hers. "I'm serious. I want to help."

"Well, the crab races are first on the agenda. If you're serious, I'll give you Gabby's number and you can ask her. I'm sure she could use the extra hands."

Just then her newest student limped out of the locker room wearing a bright blue swimsuit and a knee brace around one leg. She lifted a hand and waved.

Eli's gaze followed hers, along with a dose of confusion. "She looks familiar. Is that…?"

The girl held up a finger in a just-a-minute gesture.

"Danny Cruz, from the *Respite*?" She was grinning when she looked his way again. "Yep. I'm going to teach her how to swim."

CHAPTER FIVE

ONE OF THE many things Aubrey loved about Tabbie's was that the owner, Lily, didn't blare music so loud throughout the pub that you couldn't hear yourself think—or talk to your friends. And the music she did play was a nice mix of country and classic rock. Except during the holidays when vintage Christmas tunes filled the air, like they did now.

It was a popular hangout for Coasties and local folks who were more interested in a sourdough bowl of seafood chowder, a couple microbrews and maybe the latest gossip than in forming a romantic liaison.

Aubrey was sitting in her favorite booth sipping herbal tea and listening to Bing Crosby dream about a white Christmas. Normally she would relish both but right now she couldn't enjoy either because Nina was busy explaining why her impulsive purchase of the county's iconic Quinley's Berry Farm was a good idea. Odd, how she'd been thinking about that place just yesterday. It was like, now that he was back, all things Eli had decided to rise up out of the depths and taunt her.

"This is perfect for me. I need to get out of the city. I need fresh air and space and the countryside." Nina smoothed her thick ash-blond hair over one shoulder.

"Pacific Cove isn't exactly a metropolis, Nina. Mayor Hobbes was just telling me last week how his worst fear is that we're never going to break that three thousand mark."

The coastlines of Washington and Oregon were dotted with small towns like Pacific Cove. In the summertime the population more than doubled. During weekends and holidays, tourists could swell those numbers manyfold. The nearest city of substantial size was hours away. There was a constant battle between the folks who wanted to maintain this small-town feel and those who wanted "growth." The proper way to foment that "growth," as well as acceptable manifestations, varied considerably depending on who you talked to. Although, luckily, most of the town seemed on board when it came to the Christmas competition. Pacific Cove pride was at stake.

"All we have here is fresh air. Unless you're down at the docks and then it can get a little fishy."

"I love pie," Nina countered as if this was also a legitimate argument for her relocation to the countryside.

"So…what?" Aubrey asked with a baffled shake of her head.

"Everyone loves pie." She jabbed a finger Aubrey's way. "Well…except you."

"I like pie. I just don't eat it because it has too much sugar."

"Yeah, well, as I was saying *almost* everyone eats pie. Therefore, they would love berries with which to make pies, right? Or muffins or jam or…compote or aioli or whatever the foodies are into these days. And smoothies—you eat those. I could sell them at the farmer's market in Astoria."

Aubrey stared blandly at her sister even as her heart clenched inside her chest. Less than a year ago her big sister, at the age of thirty, had been running her own wildly successful marketing company. She'd owned a three-million-dollar showpiece of a home in California and a vacation house in Aspen. That was before her world had imploded. Now she was going to retire to the countryside where she planned to grow organic berries and bake pies?

Nina met her eyes with a solid challenging gaze of her own. She was going to make her say it? Fine. If that's what it took to keep her sister safe, she'd say it. Aubrey accepted that it was her role in life to keep people safe— including her family.

"I don't think it's a good idea for you to be living that far out."

"It's twelve miles from town. I clocked it yesterday when I drove out there. That's hardly far out."

"You know what I'm talking about. You're way closer to civilization here."

"You honestly believe the Cove is civilization?" she quipped.

"You know what I mean." Aubrey stared, willing her sister to take this seriously.

Nina began fiddling with her silverware. "I haven't had a seizure in ages."

Her sister had been diagnosed with epilepsy when she was a teenager. Medication had kept it under control, an occasional seizure cropping up only now and then. Something had changed when her marriage began to fall apart. Stress, the neurologist hypothesized. Aubrey believed it; she couldn't imagine anything more stressful than the breakup of her sister's marriage to the lying, abusive Doug Halloren.

There was really no way to know for sure, but Nina had been through hell. Whatever the trigger, the result had been an increase in the frequency and intensity of her seizures. Changes in medication, dosages and counseling to manage her stress level had ensued in an effort to get her stable. To Aubrey's way of thinking, that stability had yet to be achieved and her city-girl sister moving even farther out into the country was not going to help matters.

"Six months and three days is ages?"

Brows scooted up onto the flawless alabaster skin of her sister's forehead. "You keep track?"

"Of course I keep track. You're my sister. I love you." And she did. Bottom line, the thought of her living so far out by herself scared her to death. "You know what? Forget about civilization. You're closer to me living here and that's what I want. Let's make this about me."

"That is so sweet. I don't know what I'd do without you—what I would have done without you all these months." Nina reached over and squeezed her hand. "But it's too late. I signed the papers this morning. I'm moving in this Thursday."

"Thursday! Without even talking to me about this first?"

She dipped her chin and looked up at Aubrey through her lashes. "I know you, too, Aubrey. Just as well as you know me. I knew you would try and talk me out of it."

No point in trying to deny that.

Nina gave her a beseeching smile. "Please try to understand, okay? I need something. I need… I don't know what I need, but this feels right somehow. Mom and Dad will be home for Christmas soon. I'm excited to show them how much better I am. Dad is so…judge-y. Especially when it comes to me. I want them to see that I can take care of myself again. I know they've had their doubts. And I can understand that. But I'm better now—you know that. I could really use your support here."

"Of course you can take care of yourself. No one doubts that. And Dad is not *judge-y*. He only wants you to be happy. But…a farm? How are you even going to…?"

A Santa-hat-wearing waitress stopped by to take their orders. Aubrey complimented her festive attire and requested another minute.

Nina reached down to the seat beside her and heaved a large three-ring binder onto the table between them. Giving it a firm pat with the palm of her hand, she added, "Don't worry, I have months to read up on how to be a farmer."

She had no idea what to even say to that. Did her sister seriously believe a notebook was going to teach her how to be a commercial berry farmer?

"Plus, I ordered three pairs of overalls from Amazon and the barn came with a pitchfork."

Aubrey snuffled out a surprised laugh.

"According to the Quinleys, buying in the winter is the way to go. Gives me plenty of time to get up to speed."

"Gives them plenty of time to get that humongous RV to Sedona in time to spend the holidays with their new grandbaby you mean?"

Nina let out a chuckle. "There is that." Something caught her attention in the direction of the door. "There's Alex! And, wait, is that…?"

Aubrey turned to look.

"Oh, my… Is that Eli? He looks…different. Wow. Even better."

Aubrey's pulse took off at a crazy flutter as the men strolled toward their table.

"Hey, ladies," Alex said, stopping in front of them. He removed a baseball cap to reveal his thick, brown thatch of unruly hair. It was the one thing about him that hadn't changed over the years. Unlike his once-stocky frame of muscle, which was rapidly softening toward plump. Of course, that was no surprise what with the atrocious eating habits Aubrey was constantly harping on him about.

He gestured happily at Eli. "Look who I ran into? Didn't think you'd mind if I asked him to join us."

Nina was already on her feet, moving toward him for a hug. "Of course we don't mind. Eli, hi! Alex told me you were back. It's been ages."

Nina was right; the years had been ridiculously kind to him. She'd always thought his sculpted and flawless features were unfairly beautiful. A thin white scar was now etched below his bottom lip and his olive-toned skin was a bit weathered from so much time outdoors. Soft lines were making a home around his eyes. The combination made him look less…perfect. And even more appealing, if that were possible.

Alex slid across the booth from her while Nina and Eli chatted. Her sisters had always adored Eli. Three years older than Aubrey, Nina had been away at college by the time Aubrey and Eli's romance began. Aubrey had never told her about it. Camile, being four years younger than Aubrey, had also been clueless. But then again, no one had noticed. They'd always been friends so it wasn't unusual for the two of them to spend time together. They'd been very aware that if her parents, especially her father, knew their friendship had blossomed into more, restrictions would be placed on their time together. They had planned to reveal the status of their relationship at the end of summer, when it was time for Eli to leave for the Coast Guard Academy.

But they didn't make it that long. Aubrey had never shared her heartbreak with anyone, not even her sisters. She'd suffered silently and persevered, focusing on swimming, school and her own career goals. The distance between them had been the perfect cover for their waning friendship.

Nina resumed her spot next to Alex. Eli slid in beside her. Why hadn't she thought to scoot over first? Because now his muscled thigh was pressing against hers and burning her skin. She felt a flush creeping up her neck and hoped no one would notice.

After another few moments of small talk, Nina flashed her a grin. "Let's ask Alex his opinion."

She shot her sister a wry look. They both knew very well he would support whatever Nina decided to do. He held himself partially responsible for Nina's disastrous marriage. He'd been the one to introduce her to Doug.

"Alex, you like pie, right?"

His eyes widened in surprise, as if she'd asked him if he liked to breathe. "Do I like pie? Remember how I used to have birthday pie instead of cake at my parties when I was a kid?"

"That's right!" Nina exclaimed. "I do remember that. Geez, your birthday parties were fun. I still remember that magician—the one who made your dad's plate disappear?"

He belted out a laugh. "I remember that. My mom was worried the guy was going to steal the china. My parties were epic."

Aubrey had to agree. Alex's parties had been legendary. The St. Johns would go all-out. Every year there'd been something new to look forward to—pony rides on the beach, a bouncy house or a magician. And Mrs. St. John would put together party bags so every kid would have a gift to take home. She and Eli used to discuss how the gift was always something more expensive than either of them could expect to receive for their own birthdays. One year they'd all gotten hand-held video-game systems.

Alex's dad, Carlisle, was a gazillionaire who'd only joined the Coast Guard because that's what the men in his family did—they gave back by serving their country. He'd been unusual in that he'd chosen to remain in the service beyond the requisite years before he'd retired to run his family's empire. Alex liked to joke that his dad's extra years entitled him to skip military service altogether. He made up for it by doing volunteer work and serving on the town council, which he loved. Aubrey believed he had political aspirations beyond the local level, although he had yet to confess as much.

"Remember your parents' Christmas Eve parties?" Nina asked. "Those were like… fairy-tale stuff. Do they still have those?"

Was it her imagination or did Eli tense beside her? And was it for the same reason that she was gripping her fingers together under the table so tightly they hurt? Thirteen Christmas Eves ago, with the scent of evergreen subtly floating on the air and soft Christmas lights twinkling around them, Eli had kissed her for the first time right beside the tree at the St. Johns' party. That kiss had marked the beginning of their romance.

"When she and Dad aren't traveling, they do. They've been wintering in the south of France for the last few years. They'll be home this year. I'll have to ask Mom."

Nina clapped a hand on the tabletop to indicate a subject change. "Eli, what about you?"

Eli, who had been studying the menu, looked up. "What about me?"

"Do you like pie?"

"Uh, no to pie."

Aubrey almost laughed at the stricken look on her sister's face. "What do you mean 'no'? You don't like pie?"

He hissed out a breath. "Sorry, no. Too much sugar."

Alex gave his head a mystified shake.

"You don't eat sugar?"

"Very little."

"Not another one?" She rolled her eyes. "Neither does Aubrey."

"Aubrey is a smart woman. She's always been smart. She obviously knows it's not good for her."

He winked conspiratorially and Aubrey couldn't help but share a smile with him.

Nina lifted one perfect brow and made a show of addressing Alex. "Neither is swimming in freezing-cold ocean water, but apparently these two haven't thoroughly researched the dangers of their chosen professions. Not to mention the recent increase in shark attacks worldwide."

Alex let out a loud guffaw.

She looked pointedly at Eli. "You do eat berries, though, right?"

"What, like blueberries?"

"Yes, and raspberries and strawberries."

"Yep, love berries."

Her sister grinned and said happily, "There, that settles it."

"Settles what?" Alex asked.

"Nina has decided to become a berry farmer. She's purchased—"

"The Quinley place?" Alex broke in excitedly. "I heard it was for sale. Nina, this is fantastic!"

She nodded happily while Alex beamed at her.

Aubrey felt a stab of pain behind her left eye as she willed Alex to think about what he was saying.

"This is great! Don't you think this is great?" He looked at her, his hazel eyes sparkling with sheer delight.

"She doesn't know anything about farming, Alex."

He waved a breezy hand through the air. "Well, she'll learn. I think it's perfect. It's gorgeous out there—all that open space. I can just see her in a big floppy hat strolling through the green fields..."

Aubrey stared, barely managing to keep

her jaw from gaping as he waxed on about "fresh air" and "the harvest." She wanted to ask if he was out of his mind. Didn't he realize Nina had already had enough dramatic changes in her life?

In a few days their parents would be returning from their annual southerly sojourn and all the Wynns would be back home in Pacific Cove. Eli was back in Pacific Cove, too. Alex was still in Pacific Cove. Aubrey knew she should be happy about this growing profusion of family and friends, but for some reason, between that and work and trying to save the pool, she suddenly felt as if the weight of the world had taken up residence on her shoulders.

And just when she'd finally started thinking that weight had begun to lighten, guilt immediately added its considerable heft. This was her family—and her friends. Or whatever Eli was. He was obviously too connected to not be a part of her life. Regardless, she should happy, she told herself, and not plagued with concerns.

Alex went on. "We'll help, right? At least, I will. Eli, remember that summer I worked for the Quinleys, too? That was such a blast. There's nothing better than fresh raspberries.

Man, we had some epic berry fights in those strawberry fields."

"We sure did," Eli said with a chuckle. They'd pelt each other with rotten and damaged berries. "Country kids version of paintball fights."

"How many years did you work for the Quinleys?"

"Five."

Eli had been Hank Quinley's permanent employee, but every person at the table had worked for the Quinleys at one time or another. The farm had always hired local kids during harvest time. He'd even gotten Alex a job after he'd been caught drag racing his father's vintage Mustang one warm spring night at the end of their junior year. Carlisle St. John had decided his son had too much free time on his hands and a summer job would curtail his "penchant for mischief." It hadn't really worked. The next summer Carlisle sent Alex on a mission to the Honduras to build homes for the poor. He'd hated it, but the situation had proved convenient for her and Eli because it had been much easier to keep their romance under wraps with him out of town. And as a bonus, Alex had discovered his love for engineering and construction.

"Probably about time to cut the blueberries

back," Eli offered, and there was no mistaking the nostalgia in his tone, either.

Aubrey glared at him.

Nina beamed and tapped on her gigantic binder. "Yes, that's what Mr. Quinley said, too. He gave me this notebook full of schedules and charts and instructions. It's incredible. It goes back for decades..."

Excited conversation ensued around the table as Aubrey's stress and incredulity grew. As soon as she could get a word in edgewise, she interjected, "Farming is also a lot of hard work, Nina."

Her sister gaped at her with a wounded expression. "I know how to work hard, Aubrey. I've worked hard my entire life, except for the last year, anyway. I miss it. I didn't know anything about starting my own business, either, until I did."

Alex and Eli were both giving her looks, too. Censorious ones. Additional weight seemed to settle in upon her. Why did it seem as if she was the only one who could see reason here?

CHAPTER SIX

THE SHOALS HOTEL was located on the outskirts of Pacific Cove on a long stretch of gorgeous sandy beach. The hotel was an institution on Oregon's coast, featuring a large Victorian-style lodge painted in charcoal-gray with white accents.

The hotel staff always decorated enthusiastically for Christmas, but they'd gone all out for tonight's crab feed. Lights glowed from the peak of the roof, all the way around the tall turret, and illuminated virtually every angle. An animated crab constructed of flashing lights skittered back and forth along the roof.

"Nice touch with the crab," Camile commented as they pulled into a parking spot in the already rapidly filling lot.

Aubrey had to agree, and she was thrilled. "Score points for creativity, decorations and Christmas spirit."

"I'll say," Nina added.

A couple of high school students were serving as doormen and handed them crab-shaped magnets as they walked through the entrance.

"Cute!" Camile exclaimed as she examined the keepsake.

A sign pointed upstairs, directing them toward the Driftwood Ballroom. The space took up nearly the entire second floor of the hotel. It was a popular venue for gatherings of all kinds: wedding receptions, reunions, parties and proms.

The sisters made their way up the stairs and entered through the tall double doors that stood propped open. A "race track" made out of wood had been assembled off to one side where a series of crab races would kick off the event and set the winning crab free.

The other end of the room was cordoned off where giant pots were already steaming. A buffet table had been set up near the front of the room. If it had still been light outside they would be treated to a stunning ocean view. Instead a lighted magical scene greeted them on the beach below. The crab sidestepping across the roof had only been a teaser as animated crabs and other sea creatures frolicked on the sand with their Christmas-themed friends. A snowman danced with a starfish while an elf rode a dolphin and a mermaid curled around an anchor.

A petite, curvy woman with silky black hair piled on top of her head hustled over to them.

"Aubrey, hi!"

"Gabby! Wow! I am speechless. No, I'm not. I am actually full of speech. All of it fantastic. You didn't mention some of these details and I am blown away. We are totally winning the food category. Remington's starfish-shaped pizza does not hold a candle to this." She motioned at the elaborate buffet table. Neighboring town and top competitor, Remington, had thrown an all-you-can eat pizza and movie night a few days ago. They'd rented a big screen and held it in their prized auditorium. Aubrey and Alex had gone to check out the competition. It had been well-attended and festive, but the pizza had been mediocre.

Gabby was beaming. "I am so stoked. Thank you for the last-minute help."

"Help?" Aubrey shook her head. "You mean the mailer?" She had called in a favor from a former high school classmate and had sent out postcards a couple weeks ago to advertise the event.

"No, I mean the cook." She pointed toward the cooking area. "Hailey Bennett was supposed help us boil, but she came down with some kind of terrible bug."

"Is that… Eli?" Nina asked.

Aubrey didn't have to ask. She'd already spotted him in the silly-looking white chef's hat that somehow managed to not look all that silly on him. He was so tall it would be difficult not to see him, even in a room full of people wearing the same hat. He was talking to the mayor, lifting a large pair of tongs above his head, and she couldn't help but admire the cut of his bicep. She immediately told herself this was only because she admired anyone who maintained peak physical condition. She knew herself how difficult it was to do.

"And the entertainment," Gabby added. "Eli's friend is a hoot."

All three of them turned to see Gale sashaying across the room, wearing a crab suit and throwing objects into the air.

"He's juggling," Camile said appreciatively. "That is awesome."

Gabby went on. "Eli called and said you told him about the event. He asked if there was anything they could do to help. Originally they were just going to help with the setup, but then Hailey got sick. And his friend

Gale... I don't know how that happened exactly."

Gabby, Nina and Camile continued chatting while Aubrey looked at Eli again. Their gazes connected and she took a second to enjoy the sensation before shaking her head as if to ask *What in the world?*

He gave her a warm smile, lifting his arms into a wide shrug. That's when she noticed his apron with a big red crab on the front. Above that it read Don't Pinch the Chef. Amusement and affection stole over her as she returned the smile with one of her own.

Eyes still trained on Eli, she tuned back in to the conversation in time to hear Gabby ask, "As sweet as Eli is, don't you think?"

"I think he's perfect, Gabby."

Nina snorted while Camile let out a yelp of laughter. Aubrey felt her cheeks grow hot and knew they were probably as red as the crab on the front of Eli's apron.

"I meant *it's* perfect. Everything is perfect."

"Yeah, well..." Camile added. "The way *it's* looking at you? I'm thinking *it* might agree that all of this—" she gestured at Aubrey "—is pretty perfect from his end, too."

Aubrey couldn't help but laugh herself. He'd asked if he could help, but this was so far above and beyond what she'd been expecting she didn't even know how to begin to thank him.

Just then Gabby made her way to the front of the room. She picked up a microphone, thanked the crowd and announced it was time for the crab races.

"HOW YOU DOING?" Gale asked Eli a short time later, wedging himself and his bulky crab suit into the space between the stove and the giant vat of live Dungeness crabs. "Did you see my crab take first place? I knew I picked a winner. There was determination in his tiny, beady eyes. He gets to go free now. It's a little strange when you think about it, though, right? Like hunger games for crustaceans."

"A little," Eli agreed. The winning crab was slated to be turned loose, back into the ocean. "You'll forget about it when you start cracking and eating, though. This is hands-down the best crab in the world."

"I cannot wait. I am so hungry."

"This one is done." With a pair of giant tongs, Eli fished a steaming crab out of the boiling pot. He dunked it into a tub of ice water beside him to stop the cooking process.

"You're like a pro."

"This is not my first crab boil, Kohen. But look who's talking…" Eli nodded at the bean bags Gale had been juggling. "With the mad skills I know nothing about."

"I got these in the gift shop. It seemed weird to just walk around in this crab suit and not do something."

"Yeah, that's the weird part."

Gale chuckled. "Amazing how approachable this suit makes me, though. I've met all kinds of people already. Bill Baxter owns the hardware store. Randy Noonan is the janitor at the school—that seems like the kind of job where you might hear things, huh? Al Cutler is an attorney. And June Tempe owns that new place, Bakery-by-the-Sea. She's a sweetie. I think she likes me. She offered me a free blueberry fritter if I stop by. But I think my biggest score is Lyle Smithers."

"Reverend Smithers?"

"Yep. He invited me over for dinner next week."

"He can't tell you anything. There's like a pastor-congregant confidentiality thing."

"He's not a priest, Eli. Besides, I don't expect to hear a confession. I'm just trying to get a feel for the town."

"That makes sense. Have you met Aubrey's sister Nina, yet? She might be a good source of information, too."

He scanned the room, searching for her,

but his eyes landed on Aubrey for about the hundred and eightieth time. She definitely didn't need a crab suit to be approachable, he thought as he watched her charm her way around the room. She just was. Of course, he knew how determined and relentless she could be when she wanted to win.

"I don't see her, but she looks a lot like Aubrey. Same blond hair, a little thinner, but you can tell they're sisters. They have a younger sister, too. Camile. But she looks different—smaller and really...cute."

"I'll find her. How much longer till you're done with these?"

"Another half hour or so."

"I'm going to go find Nina, and then introduce myself to the mayor and his wife," Gale said. "We'll plan on hitting the buffet when you're through."

Tons of people stopped by to chat and Eli enjoyed catching up with old friends. He was amazed by how many of them were married, and a little jealous of the ones who had families. He couldn't help but wonder if he and Aubrey would have had kids by now if they'd stayed together.

He looked up to find her watching him. Her smile went straight to his heart. He watched her walk toward him, keeping his eyes on her the entire time.

"Hey, you," she said when she approached.

"Hi. Looks like this is a huge success. Congratulations."

Her smile could rival the Christmas star for sheer brightness. "Thank you. Gabby did an amazing job. I helped her plan it, but I was just one of the support people on this one. I have to say, so far I've attended a pizza feed with Alex in Remington—no contest.

"Nina and I went to a salmon bake last week in Lewis Point. There was a decorated tree in the corner where you chose a souvenir Christmas ornament to take home, which I thought was a nice touch. But it did not compare to this. The mayor went to a clam chowder feed in Tiramundi on Wednesday night. The chowder made him and fifty-three other people sick. Of course, I wouldn't wish food poisoning on my worst enemy, but my point is—this is going to be tough to beat."

"I think you're right about that."

She reached out and laid a hand on his forearm. "Thank you so much, Eli. When you said you wanted to help, I didn't expect this… This is above and beyond what I expected."

One look at the expression on her face and Eli was pretty sure he'd do anything she asked of him. Their eyes met and held, twelve years falling away as spark-filled affection crackled between them. He'd always liked looking at her face. Especially when her moss-green eyes were brimming with happiness the way they were now. The sound of laughter broke into their bubble. They both looked up to see Gale in his crab suit standing off to one side of the ballroom juggling for a group of kids.

"Even I didn't expect that," Eli quipped and they chuckled together.

"Seriously, Eli, the fact that you'd do this for me… I mean, I know the pool is a good cause and everything, but I can't help think that…" She paused, a touch of pink tingeing her cheeks. "That you wouldn't be here if it weren't for me."

"You're right about that," he said, a cold blast of guilt immediately following. He didn't like the way it swamped the warmth that had only seconds ago been flooding through him. His answer was the truth, he reassured himself. He just wished it was the only truth that mattered.

AUBREY HOPPED OUT of her Jeep and raised a shielding hand to her forehead. Even with sunglasses, she found the need to shade her eyes from the dazzling sun. She'd slept for seven hours the night before and had woken up feeling great. The crab feed had been an unqualified success. She was ready to bring it with her "Visit with Santa" this weekend.

She took a moment to revel in the sight of the deep-green, tree-covered mountains. Winters in the Pacific Northwest meant days at a time where the sky was so utterly gray it could produce an almost physical yearning for the sun. So days like today kind of made her want to twirl or something. Like a ballerina. She might if she had any idea how to do that. The thought of one of the guys seeing her twirl made her smile. She circled around the edge of the tarmac toward the maintenance offices that were housed on one side of the building.

Wanting to chat with Senior Chief Nivens while he was in his office, she took a shortcut and noticed that the door to the records room was ajar. She stopped in her tracks. Why would someone be inside the records room, and why would the normally locked door be left open? She went inside and was surprised to find Gale standing in front of a file cabinet reading from an open file he held in his hands.

"This says the helo spotted two fishing boats headed south, thirty miles off the coast.

Why would they be out that far this time of year when…?"

His voice trailed off as he looked up and saw her. His lips stretched into a long, slow smile. "Hi, there."

"Hello, Lieutenant Commander Kohen."

Movement caught her eye. She swiveled to see Eli standing in front of the window, a scowl creasing his brow. "Good morning, Petty Officer Wynn," he said, his tone low and not unfriendly but not exactly warm, either. His thick arms were crossed over his muscled chest. He looked annoyed but maybe not with her.

The question spilled out before she could stop it. "What are you guys doing in here?"

"Don't worry. We have authorization to access some of the files." Eli's tight smile alerted her to her mistake. She probably shouldn't be questioning her superior officers.

"About SAR training procedures?" she asked anyway because she thought she might be able to save them some time and effort.

"Yes," Gale answered quickly.

She gave her head a gentle shake, confusion knitting her brow. "Well, you're in the wrong place then."

"How's that?"

"There's nothing along those lines in that

file cabinet, Lieutenant Commander. Those are all copies of reports called in to our station and followed up on by our teams—you know, like shooting stars mistaken for flares, UFO sightings, a whale in distress or 'there's a boat speeding in the marina, but I don't really remember what it looks like.' That kind of thing." She pointed across the room toward a bank of file cabinets. "And those are maps and maintenance records."

"Uh, we are…we were just…"

"Looking at maps and reports?" she offered calmly.

He lifted one shoulder into a shrug as his lips curled into a sheepish smile. She thought the reaction seemed odd. Like she'd found him reading her diary or caught him in a lie. But why would he lie about this? And why did Eli look funny, too?

Eli's response came out clipped, a little impatient. "We realize that, Petty Officer Wynn. I can assure you there is a reason for our presence here."

His rank called for the attitude and normally she wouldn't mind. Except this was Eli and she could tell when he was uncomfortable and edgy. None of this information was top secret or anything, except for the locked cabinets in the far corner containing old personnel records. They weren't anywhere near those. Like she'd mentioned, this room didn't contain any records relating to training procedures. So why would they be in here?

She paused, thinking. Something felt...off.

Eli's blue eyes bored into hers as she waited for him to expound on said reason. This was her domain, after all. When she wasn't swimming through frigid water to rescue people, or practicing how to rescue people, her duties included aviation and survival gear inspection and maintenance. Because she liked to stay busy, she also handled odd jobs and did the scheduling for Senior Chief Nivens. And because of her penchant for organization, she was unofficially in charge of this place, which was unofficially called the records room.

She lifted one curious brow. "Are you going to explain what that is, Lieutenant Commander Pelletier?"

"No, Petty Office Wynn," he drawled. "I am not."

"Oh," she said, looking around absently and noticing that they'd made a bit of a mess. Papers and files were stacked here and there and drawers had been left open. She couldn't help it—she stuck out a foot and nudged a wayward drawer shut. "Well, do you need help? I know where everything is in here."

"We've got it handled, but thank you for the offer."

Gale jumped in, "Don't worry about any of this. We'll restore order before we're through. Petty Officer Johnston informed us that you are kind of in charge of this place. And, uh, maybe a little particular about things being kept neat? Nice work, by the way, everything is immaculate."

She knew she'd been gently invited to leave, but she remained where she was, something nibbling on the edge of her thoughts.

"Thank you, but—"

"We're fine, Wynn," Eli cut her off rather sharply. He added a gentle smile but something in his eyes told her not to argue. "You're not on shift right now. What are you doing here?"

Why would he be keeping track of her shifts? Why did she feel like he was trying to distract her? She bit her tongue to keep from asking.

"No, I'm not. But because of the rescue there are some things I didn't get to that I wanted to take care of." Her normal schedule consisted of four to six twenty-four-hour shifts a month, which is how she managed to schedule other projects like swimming lessons and the Christmas contest.

"Right, uh, go ahead and get to that, then."

She opened her mouth to say something but she wasn't sure what.

"You're dismissed, Petty Officer Wynn."

Her jaw snapped shut. She nodded curtly and headed across the room toward her destination. It wasn't the first time in her Coast Guard life she'd had to bite her tongue at an officer's order, but it was the first time she made it bleed by doing so.

ELI BLEW OUT a pent-up breath as he watched Aubrey stride across the room and exit out the door. He wanted to laugh at the fire he'd seen in her eyes. He could tell she'd wanted to argue with him, but her training and discipline had won out. He could have fun with this superior officer thing, he realized. Of course, he wouldn't torture her in that way. He only realized Gale was watching him after he'd been staring at the door for too long after she'd gone.

He looked at Gale, who was wearing a goofy grin.

"She just has the whole package, huh? She seems friendlier than her sister, too. She's—"

"Off-limits," he snapped.

"What?"

"She's off-limits, Gale."

His friend let out a chuckle. "Last time I checked we were the same rank, Lieutenant Commander Pelletier. Now, granted, I may not have the admiral's ear like you do, but when it comes to women you can't give me orders. I think—"

"If you're *thinking* I will pummel you if you so much as touch her swim fins, then you're thinking is spot-on." Acid boiled in his stomach as he thought about seeing Aubrey anywhere near his unabashedly and unapologetically womanizing friend. Which was ridiculous. Aubrey was free to date whoever she wanted.

Gale laughed. "Her swim fins are off-limits, huh? What about her snorkel?"

Maybe not whoever she wanted, and definitely not Gale, but someone else. He didn't want to think about that right now. Or ever. And right now he had bigger things to worry about; he'd seen the look on Aubrey's face, the questions dancing in her eyes. He knew her. They'd grown up together solving mysteries that didn't need solving and executing missions that existed only in their fantasies. His tense tone had probably given her even more of a reason to wonder why they were in here.

He glared at his friend, who clearly wanted

to argue his own case. He shouldn't want to punch his best friend, should he?

Gale lifted his hands in a conciliatory gesture. "All right. Okay. I get it. I'll stay away from all of her, um, swim gear."

"Yes, you will."

"Although…being the detective that I've recently become, I'm going to deduce… From the way you were acting and the way she was acting? I'm guessing you two have a history that involves something more than friendship?"

"Yes."

"Yeah, I thought so. That explains you bailing out of the helo after her, huh?"

Eli shrugged a shoulder. He'd been waiting for Gale to bring it up.

He was surprised when his friend didn't push it. He didn't really need to, his smirk said enough.

"Go ahead. I know you want to say something."

"Not much to say that you haven't thought, I'm sure. Although, I could point out that she was staring at you like my sister used to stare at her poster of that one guy from that British boy band with the goofy name."

Even though they weren't finished, Gale was already tidying up the mess they'd made.

Aubrey had that effect on people. She made you want to do better—be better. And right now, Eli wasn't living up to that. He didn't like the feeling.

"What are you—?"

"She likes you, big guy."

For some reason those words were both welcome and not. Bittersweet. He'd never really understood that word. Never been able to describe a situation like that before. Until now.

"It doesn't matter if she likes me, Gale. I can't like her back."

"You can't?" He glanced up from studying the label on another file.

"No."

"Is she married?"

"No."

"Lesbian?" He said it doubtfully. Gale prided himself on his instincts in this area. "Obviously not. I can only assume you must have a really, really good reason not to pursue this?" He tucked the file away and picked up another.

Eli found himself shaking his head slowly, back and forth, just like he had the day his father had told him they were leaving Pacific Cove. He was in love with Susannah Wynn, he'd said, and he couldn't destroy her life by allowing the truth to leak out. At Brian's insistence, he was going to take a transfer, even knowing it would drastically set his career back.

After the transfer, his father had fallen into his worst depression ever. Eli had despaired of him ever recovering, even considering forgoing his own berth at the academy. His father had insisted he go, encouraging Eli to achieve what he'd been unable to. Halfway through his second year at the academy, his dad had retired.

"Her father is Brian Wynn." Then he forced himself to grind out the words—the title—that should have belonged to Tim Pelletier. "Captain Brian Wynn. Remember the guy who forced my dad's transfer?"

"Oh, shh…oot." Gale lowered the file he'd been holding. "I didn't put that together. Why didn't you say something sooner, man?"

Gale was the only person who knew the circumstances surrounding his dad's transfer, outside of him and his dad. And Brian Wynn. Yep, he knew it, too.

"It doesn't matter."

"Yes, it does. Is he still around?"

"Retired. But around, yes. He still lives here part of the year. Alex told me he'll be

home for the holidays. It's inevitable that our
paths will cross."

"What are you going to do?"

"I haven't decided yet."

CHAPTER SEVEN

AUBREY WAS INCREDIBLY grateful for the help when Alex showed up on Thursday with Eli and Gale in tow. With her, Camile, Nina, Jay and Osprey, Nina's move hadn't been nearly the ordeal she'd feared. Even with the entire contents of a large storage unit, furniture she'd had crammed in their parents' garage and the belongings Nina had brought to Aubrey's, the bulk of it was finished by late afternoon.

She had to admit the old two-story farmhouse was charming and the Quinleys had maintained it well. Nina had spent the last few days painting the inside. She'd opted for pale tones on the walls to accentuate the rustic antique furniture and colorful folk art she'd chosen for the décor. The results were nothing like the grandeur of her home in California. Thank goodness for that, Aubrey thought. She'd never been comfortable in that modern showpiece Nina had called home. But she could definitely get used to this.

The original wood floors, attractively scarred and toned with age, still held up in every room of the house. The Quinleys had buffed and polished them to a fine sheen before they'd moved out. Nina had purchased thick wool area rugs and placed them throughout to add comfort and warmth.

Aubrey's favorite features were the old stone fireplace that took up one entire wall in the living room and the ancient well-used butcher block that comprised one end of the island in the kitchen. The only new touches appeared in the kitchen where granite countertops had been installed along with gleaming stainless-steel appliances.

"Where do you want this one?" Jay asked, walking through the archway, his arms filled with a large box.

Aubrey had just headed into the living room to help Camile arrange photos and knickknacks on the built-in shelves along one wall. Nina and Camile had stayed behind at the house during the move to direct traffic to the various rooms where items belonged. Aubrey was amazed at the progress they'd already made unpacking.

"What does it say?" Nina asked.

"Um, it doesn't say anything."

"Really? Just set it here and I'll take a look. Thanks, Jay."

"No problem." He carefully lowered the box, smiled at the women and headed back out the door for another.

Eli and Gale were on their way with the final load of boxes from the storage unit, along with sandwiches they'd volunteered to pick up from Salmon Crackers.

Nina removed a pair of box cutters from the pocket of her overalls. She sliced through the tape and peeled open the cardboard flaps.

"Hey, look—it's Christmas decorations." She snatched a couple of items from the box. "These are the ornaments Grandma gave us when we were little."

Aubrey had bent over to inspect the contents when she heard a noise.

She glanced at Nina. "Did you hear that?"

"No, what did it sound like?"

"I'm not sure." She reached for a knitted stocking and paused. "There it is again."

"Ghost?" Nina asked with an excited gasp. "Do you think I could be so lucky as to buy a house with a ghost?"

Leave it to Nina to be excited about the prospect of a haunted house. "No. It's not a ghost. I think it's outside…" she drawled, waiting…

She pointed as Eli came through the door, his arms loaded with brown paper sacks from Salmon Crackers. A black-and-white dog trotted in beside him.

His face erupted with a smile. "Merry Christmas, Nina. I know it's a little early, but every farmer needs a dog, right?"

"Are you…?" Nina dropped the ornaments she'd been holding and hurried forward. "Kidding me, Eli? Oh, my gosh! She's beautiful."

The pooch was already wagging its tail and looking thrilled to be there. Nina wilted to the floor. The dog sank down beside her, whining enthusiastically, clearly reveling in the attention.

"Eli, I can't even believe this. Thank you. She's gorgeous. Wait, is it a she?"

"Yes, she's a she. A border collie. And she's actually a service dog. Trained for epilepsy." He tipped his head to one side. "Well, she's sort of a service dog dropout." He held out a card. "Grady Royce, a friend of mine, believes in her, though. He trains dogs and he's willing to work with you guys to get her officially certified if you want."

Aubrey narrowed her eyes in Eli's direction. "You got my sister a service dog?"

He winked. "Yep."

She turned to Alex. "Did you know about this?"

"Nope. But I wish I would have thought of it."

Me, too, Aubrey thought. Eli had always been thoughtful like this. And it was more than just being thoughtful; he always seemed to know what people needed before they did. Her included. Her especially.

"What's her name? Does she have a name?" Nina asked.

"She does, but Grady says you can change it if you want."

"Change it? That would be horrible. Unless it's something like Dummie or Ugly—then I'd be forced to change it. What is it?"

"Marion," he said.

Nina made a sound, part gasp, part squeal. "Marion? No! Way!"

Eli grinned and shot a questioning look at Aubrey. "Does this mean she likes the name?"

Aubrey shrugged with a grin of her own.

"I love it. It's totally meant to be," Nina explained, burying her face in the dog's silky fur. "Like a marionberry. I'm going to grow some. The Quinleys didn't grow them. But planting marionberries is going to be my first project and now—my first dog. Isn't that right, Marion, my love? You are such a beautiful girl…" She went on with a string of sweet, puppy-talk nonsense.

Aubrey was awestruck by the sheer joy radiating from her sister, and overcome with the kindness of the gesture. She could kiss Eli for his thoughtfulness. Not literally, though, of course. Because along with her appreciation and affection came the startling realization that she was in deep trouble. She absolutely could not allow her feelings for Eli to escalate beyond friendship. There was no way she could survive that kind of heartbreak again. A wave of anxiety followed. She needed some space, some air.

There were enough sandwiches to feed half the town or, in this case, a hungry moving crew. While the crowd oohed and aahed over the adorable canine addition to their group, Aubrey grabbed a roast beef and provolone and headed out the back door.

Nina had purchased a couple rocking chairs for the porch after declaring that all farmhouses had them or should have them if they didn't. The chairs had been delivered that morning in the midst of the chaos. As Aubrey settled into one, she decided Nina was absolutely right. She leaned back and closed her eyes, enjoying the soothing, rhythmic movement of the chair and the raspy sound it made against the old floorboards.

At the sound of a loud creak her eyes popped open. She discovered Eli watching her from where he now sat in the other chair. So much for that space she'd sought.

He smiled, blue eyes dancing with mischief. "It would be tricky to sneak up on someone on this porch, wouldn't it?"

"Were you trying to sneak up on me?"

"No, just checking on you."

"Checking on me?"

"Yes, I know you're not crazy about all of this." He gestured around.

"It's growing on me." Aubrey smiled and she couldn't help but pour her heart into it. "Eli, thank you. I can't believe you got her a dog. An epilepsy dog. Well, I can, actually. It's perfect. Why didn't I think of it?"

"Well, to be fair, it only came to me when my friend Grady called. He was in the area testing some puppies or whatever it is he does to see if he wants to train them. We met up, he had Marion with him, and it just felt like a good fit."

"A very good fit. However you thought of it, it was spot-on." She turned her head, focusing on the stunningly beautiful landscape because it hurt her heart to look at him. The gesture was too much. It reminded her too much of the Eli she used to know, or rather the way she used to know him, the closeness they had shared. Now that she was getting a taste of that again, she realized he was like a drug. Even a small dose of Eli left her wanting more.

The sun was just beginning to set, casting shades of red and gold and purple on the horizon. After two clear days, it looked like the rain was moving back in. A low-lying fog was blanketing the fields and the air felt heavy and thick.

"What a gorgeous evening," he said. "Probably rain tomorrow. It's nice to take a minute to enjoy it. I used to sit here on the porch with Hank sometimes while we'd go over the workday."

"Right now, I'm sitting here wondering why I've been so resistant to the idea of Nina living out here."

He stretched his legs out in front of him and turned his head to look at her. "That's an easy one. Because you're worried about her."

She tore a piece of bread from her sandwich and nibbled on it. "I've been told by both of my sisters that I worry about them too much. That I worry about everything too much."

"Your concern for others is a big part of what makes you who you are. It's also a huge reason you're such a great RS."

Aubrey managed a weak smile. "Thank you. That's a nice thing to hear." She took a proper bite of her sandwich, trying to ignore the feeling his compliment stirred up in her. She reminded herself that she didn't do warm and fuzzy, not where he was concerned.

His comment reminded her of the rescue, which she still hadn't heard anything about. The curiosity was getting to her. She swallowed and added, "Especially in consideration of your checking up on me the other day."

"Checking up on you?"

"Yeah, I know you and Gale went to see Danny Cruz. I figured you were investigating the rescue. When I didn't hear anything, I assumed that I was in the clear."

Eli's brow furrowed. "You went to see her, too?"

"Mmm-hmm." She nabbed a pickle slice hanging from the side of her sandwich and popped it into her mouth.

"Why?"

She lifted a shoulder. "I follow up with a lot of survivors after a rescue, especially if they've been injured. And extra especially if they don't know how to swim." She added a wink.

He rocked back in his chair and gazed up at the cedar-planked ceiling above them. His lips played with a grin. "Of course you do."

"Except for the criminals—the ones I know have broken the law. It might sound harsh, but I leave them to wallow in their misery."

THE CRIMINALS? Eli almost laughed. He wished he could tell her the truth. Her eyes and ears as an RS could be invaluable in making some headway into this investigation.

"The rescue is always so chaotic and crazy. Afterward, I like to see that they're going to be okay. Sometimes they don't quite know how to deal with the trauma they've been through."

He knew this was true. A brush with death could be incredibly life-changing for anyone. And if a loved one wasn't lucky enough to make it, the mix of emotions could really do a number on a person's psyche.

This was such an Aubrey thing to do—caring and worrying about people where others might not think to.

"That's really great…" He almost called her "mermaid," which would be a really bad idea. He was finding it difficult to be around her and not fall back into that comfortable familiarity.

He'd fudged a little about the dog. He knew she was worried about Nina and he'd wanted to ease her concern in some way. An epilepsy companion dog had seemed like a logical way to do that. He had called Grady to ask what breed he would recommend. They'd met up for coffee. Grady had just confiscated Marion from an incompetent "trainer" and the rest had worked out like he'd relayed.

"I wasn't checking up on you. It's a part of our job while we're here, to interview every survivor after a rescue. It's just one of the many ways we're evaluating procedures." These interviews were a part of the duties related to their "official assignment."

"Oh…" A furrow creased her brow. "I guess that makes sense."

He could tell the answer made her feel better. She fidgeted a little with the waxy paper her sandwich had been wrapped in, which made him wonder if she was picking up on his vibe. If she, too, was struggling with how they were going to work this between them?

First, he needed to clear something up. "I want to apologize for what happened on the base the other day. When you found Gale and me in your records room?"

She waved a casual hand through the air. "What are you apologizing for? I shouldn't have interrupted you or questioned you. And it's not *my* records room, I just like to keep it...you know, tidy and organized."

"I know that, technically. But I know I was a little, uh, short with you." He curled a hand around the back of his neck and squeezed.

"Yeah, I caught that."

The way she was nibbling on her lip told Eli she was thinking.

He went on. "I might be a bit more stressed about this assignment than I've let on. There's a lot riding on this job for me and I want to do everything right."

"I understand. It's fine."

"Are you sure?" He studied her with narrowed eyes, waiting for her to say more.

"Eli, I've been in the Coast Guard for a lot of years now. I'm used to taking orders, and I'm used to stressed-out officers and coworkers. This is a difficult and demanding profession we're in." She leaned back and stretched her long, shapely legs in front of her.

He could so easily entangle his feet with hers.

"Rewarding, too, of course. But hard."

"That it is."

"Although…" She paused, narrowing her eyes at him. "Never mind."

"What?"

"You guys shouldn't leave the door open when you're in there. A lot of those files are confidential and you shouldn't be careless about security and—"

"Duly noted," he interrupted with a grin. "The Coast Guard is lucky to have you, you know that?"

"Stop trying to distract me with compliments. I'm still wondering exactly what you guys were doing in there. It doesn't make sense. If there's something you need, some records, I can probably tell you where—"

"I know what I'm doing, Aubrey."

He reached out and slowly removed the waxy paper from her hands.

His sole purpose in doing so was to feel her soft, warm skin against his. He had to touch her even as he knew he needed to quit stealing these moments. He needed to find a place where they could peacefully coexist, one that didn't include touching her and wanting to kiss her lips. Lips that were now parted slightly as she watched him, her green eyes all soft and bright and full of questions and… And he knew he wasn't imagining the desire now swimming in their mossy-green depths.

Twelve years may have passed, but that was a look a man could never forget.

Her voice was low with that rasp it sometimes got when she was emotional, "Maybe you could give me some advice?"

Thankfully she cleared her throat and looked away because he didn't think he would have been able to break the contact. No surprise that once again Aubrey was stronger than him.

Eli hoped she wasn't going to ask something of him he couldn't give, even as a part of him desperately wanted her to. It would be easier if she'd take this out of his hands. Maybe tell him to stay away. Or suggest he come closer... Okay, he needed to get a grip. Just because there was clearly still an attraction between them didn't mean she had feelings beyond that. He definitely did. But why would she after the way he'd left her? He wished... Geez, what was he, a kid again? Wishing for things that couldn't be? He amended his thoughts and wished for the strength to resist her.

He quirked a brow. "I can try."

"I've been thinking about Danny Cruz. I don't know if she mentioned this to you guys, but she told me she's worried about her boyfriend, Brendan. She said Brendan's dad,

Brett, is over-the-top upset about the accident and the loss of his boat. *Enraged* was the word she used. Something about it just… bothers me. She's worried about Brendan."

Wish granted. Not only was she backing off, she was reminding him of his number-one task—his job. This was good. So why didn't it feel good? He followed her lead and leaned back in his chair.

"Really?" he said, trying to shift into the subject change. Danny hadn't mentioned this when he and Gale had interviewed her. But that wasn't really surprising—the fact that she'd be more open with a smiling and concerned Aubrey than with two imposing Coast Guard men in uniform. "Worried about what exactly, do you think?"

"I don't know… Maybe he's blaming Brendan for the loss of the *Respite*? Because his girlfriend was on board and he wasn't paying attention or…something? I'm not sure. I was wondering if I should follow up. Talk to him or recommend some family counseling or something? Now that I'm giving Danny swim lessons, we're becoming friendly. I feel invested in her happiness."

Her words flipped a switch in his brain, which was now humming along just fine with regard to the investigation.

"Hmm…" he drawled as if mulling it over. "Maybe. Let me think about it." He told himself not to overreact. He needed to calmly and rationally think this through. He needed to talk to Gale.

CHAPTER EIGHT

"So," GALE SAID as he pulled on a green-velvet coat with oversize lapels. "You know that guy we talked to yesterday? At the sawmill on Sparks Road?" He was standing in front of the mirror in the "staging area," which was actually the back room of Bakery-by-the-Sea. He tugged on the bottom of his jacket. "I can't believe this fits me. June said she would alter it, but I really thought it was hopeless. I think the last guy to wear it actually was an elf."

Eli and Gale had been researching sawmills. To start with, they'd compiled a list of mills within a seventy-five-mile radius, and the types of wood they processed. They'd been visiting them one by one. Sparks Road happened to be located on the way out to Nina's place, so they'd stopped on their way home after the move. They'd managed to visit three more the day before.

"Yeah?" Eli was arranging the neoprene Santa belly inside of his own costume. Yesterday, Pete Stahl, Aubrey's Santa, had come down with the same ailment that had taken out Hailey Bennett, the original chef for the crab feed. Pete's grandson, also down with the bug, was supposed to have been his elf. Eli and Gale had volunteered to fill in.

"He handles all different types of wood at his mill. He produces specialty wood on a per-order basis."

"Mmm-hmm."

"Do you remember the size of his scrap pile? It was tiny. All of the other mills had stacks of scrap wood, except the ones with wood chippers. But he didn't have a chipper. Not that I noticed, anyway. What do you think he does with his?"

Eli thought about it as he fussed with the fluffy white beard that would soon be attached to his face. "Sometimes these smaller mills will sell the scrap as firewood. It's illegal to burn it themselves, but that doesn't mean he's not getting rid of it that way. Although it would be tough to burn that much wood and not have someone see or say something about the smoke."

"What if someone is buying it for other purposes? Like, say, crate construction?"

"Interesting…" He also didn't see how in the world this beard was going to stay on his face. Nina was supposed to be helping, but she hadn't showed up yet.

"We need to pay him another visit."

"Couldn't hurt. There's something I need to run by you."

"What's that?"

"Aubrey said something that's got me thinking." He filled Gale in on her habit of visiting people she helped rescue, in particular her visit with Danny Cruz. "She's also teaching her how to swim."

"My goodness, your sweetheart is a... sweetheart, too, huh?"

Eli couldn't help his grin. "You have no idea. The kid? Brendan? His dad, Brett, the captain, was apparently furious about the accident. *Enraged* was the word she used. Seems a little out of place under the circumstances. He could have died, his brother, his teenage son and girlfriend all could have died. But he's in a rage about losing an old crappy boat?"

"Which was probably insured, anyway," Gale supplied. "I mean, upset? Yes. Devastated? Absolutely. Enraged? No, the situation does not call for rage, especially of a prolonged nature."

"Exactly."

"However, losing a hold full of drugs might cause a person to become enraged."

He liked it when Gale's thought processes so precisely mirrored his own. Lucky for him, it was a common occurrence. "Sure would. Kids can be dramatic, but I think we need to do a little digging on the crew of the *Respite*."

"I'm on it," Gale said and made a note in his phone.

He thought about Aubrey asking his advice where Danny was concerned. If they did have drugs on board, the girl might be the opening they needed to find out or possibly to even uncover other evidence. And with Aubrey giving her swim lessons, there was some relationship building going on between them. He just needed to figure out a way to capitalize on it and not let her know what he was doing. He ignored the jab from his conscience reminding him that this would give him yet another reason to feel guilty where she was concerned. She most definitely would not appreciate his using her to uncover information from Danny Cruz. But it couldn't be helped, he told himself. They needed to use whatever means at their disposal.

"I have an idea. But first, let's find out what we can about Brett West's finances and whether or not the *Respite* was insured."

He paused to look Gale up and down. "Man, you look so ridiculous. I wish I would have told the guys on the base what we were going to be doing today."

Gale glanced up from where he was now sliding his stockinged feet into a pair of black-satin slippers. The oversize toes curled up and over the ends of the shoes, while the bells decorating the tips jingle-jangled as he situated them on his feet.

He shrugged. "You could have told them. I'm confident in my manhood." He stood, bouncing up and down, causing a raucous round of jingling. "Besides, June said I will be an adorable elf." Standing to his full un-elf-like height, he threw his arms out to the sides as if to underscore how obvious June's assertion was.

Eli eyed him critically. "You know, I'm feeling like you enjoy this dress-up thing a little more than would be considered normal."

Ignoring the comment, he crossed his arms over his chest and gave Eli the once-over. "You think I look ridiculous? I don't see how you are ever going to pass for Santa Claus."

"Never underestimate the power of a woman," Nina said, coming through the door. She gestured at the vintage-style train case she was carrying. "Especially when she's bearing a suitcase full of makeup."

THE GAZEBO HAD been magically transformed for Pacific Cove's A Visit with Santa. Lights were strung from top to bottom and end to end, outlining the structure in a bright, cheerful glow. December on this portion of the country's left coast meant cold temperatures, rain and gusty wind for most of the month, so sheets of plywood and Plexiglas windows had been fashioned to cover the normally open-to-the-weather sides.

Thanks to the talented decorating committee, the inside had turned out even better than she'd imagined. The "windows" were lit, each one featuring an outdoor scene, so it appeared that you were looking out upon a snowy wonderland at the North Pole. Inside, there was a workbench with tools and partially completed toys as well as a small lighted Christmas tree. Santa had his own elegantly carved palatial chair complete with padded footrest to make it easier for the little ones to scale.

While winter scenes from the Pacific coast might not be favorites in a traditional collage of Christmas images, Aubrey thought the beach in winter held its own appeal. There was nothing like holing up somewhere and watching a storm roll in from the ocean and hit the beach. She and Eli used to do it all the time from their special spot—a cave on the cliff below the lighthouse. She hadn't been to the cave since she'd moved back to town.

She checked her watch. Parents and kids were already lined up under the eaves along the adjacent sidewalk, out of the soft misty rain, patiently awaiting Santa's arrival. Just a few more minutes and Santa would emerge from Bakery-by-the-Sea's storefront and make his way down the opposite sidewalk with his elf, "Elvin," beside him pushing a wheelbarrow full of the neatly bagged gifts she and the committee had stuffed the week before. A chorus of Christmas bells would accompany the entourage. It was Aubrey's job to assist the elf on duty and to pass out the stockings to the kiddos after they took their turn confiding in St. Nick.

Aubrey saw some movement and immediately realized it was Nina coming out of the bakery, her hood secured over her hair. She jogged toward the gazebo, slowing as she approached, one hand partially covering her smiling mouth. She ducked inside.

"How do they look?"

A giggle slipped out from between her fingers. "Not even in his early years could Santa have ever looked that good. Not to mention the elf with the…" Nina trailed off helplessly. "I don't even know what to call someone as good-looking as Gale. Even though the man gets on my nerves, I appreciate his enthusiasm. I did my best to transform them both."

Aubrey had despaired of being able to pull off the last-minute change. Two hot Coast Guard officers taking over for an elderly man and his elf-size grandson? But June had offered to alter the costumes while Nina had insisted that she could perform miracles as the "hair and makeup" person. She could only hope for the best at this point.

"How can you not like Gale?" Aubrey asked curiously. "What's not to like?"

"Exactly," Nina answered. "He's…too perfect and too charming. And just too…much."

"Huh. That's a lot of too's."

"I know," Nina said, as if Aubrey was agreeing. "His polished rich-boy charm reminds me of Doug." Nina peeked outside. "Here they come!"

She needn't have pointed that out because Aubrey was pretty sure the shouts and the accompanying cacophony of jingle bells could be heard at least two blocks away.

Outside on the set of covered risers, All in Tune, the first choral group of the day began

singing "Santa Claus is Coming to Town."
She joined Nina at the door and watched Eli
saunter along, waving and crooning, "Merry
Christmas!" and "Ho, ho, ho!" Elvin the Elf
trotted along beside him, smiling and pushing
his little wheelbarrow. Aubrey let out a laugh
of her own as he waved in their direction.

Excitement surged through the crowd.
Squeals of delight and shouts of "Santa!
Santa!" filled the air.

The Christmas-card scene couldn't be
more perfect, so of course that's when disas-
ter struck.

A small boy broke loose from his mother,
ran down the edge of the crowd and escaped
under the rope they'd hung to delineate the
queue. Aubrey and Nina both gasped as the
little guy then bolted into the street in that
shockingly fast way that only kids can do. A
high-pitched scream sounded above the singing.

Dropping her clipboard, Aubrey lunged
like a sprinter out of the blocks. All she could
see was the child running and swaying down
the middle of the rain-slick street. Straight
from her worst nightmare, a car rounded
the corner a short block away. It seemed to
be going way too fast and the child was so
very small. Waving her arms as she ran, she

shouted for it to stop, hoping the driver of the vehicle would see her and slow, even as she feared he or she would only be focused on Santa and his impossibly tall elf.

She was still several feet away when she saw "Santa" dash into the street and scoop the little guy up in his arms. The car slowed, skidding sideways like in a car-chase scene, before stopping. Relief jolted through her at the picture of Eli holding the boy securely in his arms. Aubrey hurried to them. While her own knees were weak, the little guy seemed oblivious to the near tragedy. A giggle rang out and she recognized him as one of the Paxon kids.

Emma Paxon was yelling, "Toby!" and running down the middle of the street. Aubrey knew Emma and Toby from the Little Swimmers program at the pool. Emma had five kids. Toby was the youngest, a precious, energetic child who strove valiantly to keep up with his older siblings.

Aubrey wrapped an arm around Emma when she stopped before them. "He's perfectly fine, Emma. Are you okay?"

She was nodding, tears streaming down her cheeks.

"Yes, thanks to you and Santa."

Eli was grinning at Toby, who was chortling with delight and hugging his shoulder, clearly elated from the ride he'd just enjoyed courtesy of Santa Claus. Aubrey offered a few more words of comfort to Emma. Toby patted Santa's beard as Emma took him into her arms. He waved and Eli ruffled the little guy's hair. After one more parting thank-you, they took off to rejoin the rest of their family in line.

"Phew," Aubrey said on a breath, walking Santa back across the street to join his elf. She kept her voice low so no one would hear. She didn't want to blow Eli's cover. "I'm so sorry."

"You're sorry?" he answered. "For what?"

"That could have been..." A shudder ran through her. "I should have gotten approval to have the road blocked off. Why didn't I think of that? I put up the cones to keep people from parking here, but didn't close the street." She gripped her temples.

"It's over and everything is fine. Kids do things, Aubrey. Unpredictable things."

"I know but—"

He stopped and turned toward her. His voice was gentle and soothing. "Listen, you can't prepare for everything. You know that. All you can do is the best you can do." He gestured toward the gazebo. "And from what I can see here, that's exactly what you've done. Now, stop worrying. It's going to be a great day."

"Thank you. I know you're right. It's just… I have this obsession to make everything…"

"Perfect?"

"Well, no, I realize perfection isn't possible, but I do like things a certain way and…" She glanced up to catch his teasing smile.

"Yes, okay. I am a bit of a perfectionist. I'll admit that. And sometimes I do, um, worry about things."

They stepped inside the North Pole Nook and Eli let out a low whistle. "Well, this looks about as perfect as it could be."

She studied the space with fresh eyes. It was pretty amazing. "Thank you for doing this. I don't know what we would have done if you and Gale hadn't stepped in."

"No problem. You and your committee have already done all the work."

"I don't know about *all* the work. I'm not wearing a Santa suit."

At that moment Gale poked his head through the door, looking both gorgeous and silly as an elf, complete with pointy ears and a pointy nose. Nina really was a genius with makeup.

Her lips twitched with laughter as she pointed at Gale. "Or that."

Gale stepped inside, clearly thrilled to be a part of it all. They were discussing the mishap when Alex joined them. He reached out a hand for Eli to shake. "Nice save, Santa. You and Aubrey looked like you were having a race from opposite directions. Funny how those instincts kick in even when we're not in uniform, huh?"

"Thankful for that," Eli said.

"Me, too," Alex said. "You guys ready? The mayor is thrilled and nervous as a mother hen. He's working the crowd right now trying to figure out who the judges might be."

Aubrey snickered. "I'll admit to being a little worked up over that myself, but I'm going to stay focused on those precious little faces out there like Toby's and enjoy the wonder of it all."

Alex grinned at her, snaking an arm around her shoulder and giving it a squeeze. "I like that. Hey, before I forget, can you guys come over for dinner Monday night? My parents are back in town and they're dying to see you, Eli. You, too, Gale—I mean Elvin."

"Ah, sounds great. I can't wait to see them."

"Sure," Gale said.

Aubrey's face split with a wide grin. "Yes, from me, too."

"Super," Alex said. "I already talked to

Nina and Camile—they're coming, too. As well as a few other people Mom and Dad thought you might like to see."

Nina peeked her head in. "Santa, Elvin, you guys ready? I don't think Mayor Hobbes and I can hold back the masses any longer."

CHAPTER NINE

"ELI, SON, IT'S good to see you." Carlisle St. John reached out a hand and clapped Eli on the shoulder with the other.

His hair was completely gray now but still thick and neatly trimmed. After his retirement from the Coast Guard, he'd made it a priority to maintain his excellent physical condition, and Eli was cheered at seeing him looking so well.

"Thank you, sir. It's good to be back."

"We certainly are proud of you around here."

Heather St. John wrapped Eli in a tight hug. "That's putting it mildly," she said. "Carl brags about you to everyone he knows. 'My best friend's son graduated top of his class from the Coast Guard Academy.' Like you were our own." She slapped her husband lightly on the arm. "I'm always telling him all the credit goes to Tim. He's the one who raised you all by himself."

"Your husband was a huge influence on

me, as well, Mrs. St. John. And if it wasn't for him, I'm not sure I would have gotten into the academy. That letter from Senator McChord certainly didn't hurt my cause."

Carlisle stood beaming next to his wife, who seemed even smaller than Eli remembered. But when she placed her hands on her hips and glared at him playfully he suddenly felt like he was thirteen again and getting lectured after some bit of trouble that he, Alex and Aubrey had gotten into.

"You can call me Heather, you know?"

Eli grinned. "No, ma'am, I can't seem to bring myself to do that. Thank you so much for inviting us tonight. Your home looks even more beautiful than I remember."

And it did. Eli had always marveled at how Heather had managed to make a beachfront mansion feel so homey. The open, simple design combined with her understated decorating style probably helped, he realized now. Two stories, fronted with glass, made you feel like you were on the beach instead of inside a house.

"You were always such a gentleman. I tried to raise Alex to be a gentleman. Where did I go wrong? How is your father? I wish he would come home for a visit now and then."

Alex guffawed. "Mom, come on, I'm standing right here. And what are you talking about? I'm an angel."

"Yes, of course you are, honey. Like a fallen angel." She patted him on the shoulder. "I'm kidding. You know we're proud of you, too. Very proud. Especially lately. But..." She gestured helplessly at Eli. "Eli is a Coast Guard officer and a pilot."

"Like Dad always wanted to be," Alex explained to Gale, who had walked over to join them.

Carlisle shrugged. "I've never kept that a secret."

Chuckles all the way around.

Gale added, "Can't say I blame you there, sir. That's all I ever wanted to be, too."

"Smart man. Eli tells us you're from Connecticut?"

"Yes, sir, I am. Grew up with the Coast Guard all around me. How could I resist?"

Gale graced Heather with his movie-star smile. "Thank you so much for having us over tonight, Mrs. St. John." He pointed at a distant wall. "I see that you're a fan of analytical realism. That piece is stunning. Is that a contemporary artist? I don't believe I've seen anything by that artist before."

"Why, yes, I am. And it is. Do you paint?"

"I don't. But my mother does and she..."

Gale's voice trailed off as they moved off to study the painting and presumably discuss art.

Gale fit in here, Eli thought. Which wasn't surprising. He was pretty sure the Kohens were even wealthier than the St. Johns. But then again, his friend seemed to fit in anywhere, from the seediest bar to the fanciest dress ball. His good looks certainly didn't hurt, but with Gale it was more than that. The guy could give Prince Charming a run for his money. He also possessed a resiliency that Eli envied; it reminded him a lot of Aubrey's now that he thought about it.

Carlisle had excused himself to greet other guests, leaving Eli and Alex a few moments to reminisce.

"Remember the time we made our own surfboards?" Alex asked.

They'd spent weeks sawing and sanding and gluing cedar planks that Tim Pelletier had left over from building a fence. They'd finally dragged their makeshift boards down to the beach to try them out, whereupon Alex had promptly caught a wave. And just as quickly fallen off. The board had conked him on the head, knocking him silly. He and Aubrey had then set about "rescuing" him.

"I think about that now and I cringe at

how easily I could have drowned. So lucky it didn't knock me out. And that you guys were right there."

Eli agreed. "That was quite a gash, though."

Alex rubbed the back of his head. "Ten stitches."

"All the stunts we pulled, we're all three so lucky we never fared worse."

"So true. Your friend Gale is a good guy, huh? He and Aubrey would make a nice couple. She needs someone who would treat her like a queen without being overwhelmed by her...moxie at the same time."

Eli followed Alex's gaze to where Aubrey and Gale appeared to be deep in conversation. Their heads were bent together and suddenly she broke into a bout of laughter. *Come on, Gale*, he thought. Lucky he trusted his friend. He was trying to figure out how to head that direction without being too obvious when movement beside Aubrey caught his eye. A man slipped an arm around her shoulders and kissed her on the cheek. She smiled at him, then spoke to Gale, presumably performing introductions.

The man turned. Eli froze. For the briefest second he considered slipping out the French doors behind him, jumping the deck railing and taking off down the beach. Like he and

Alex had done hundreds of times in their youth. But the feeling didn't last long.

Because he'd known this day would come. He'd prepared for it. He just hadn't expected it quite this soon, not tonight anyway.

There, standing in the foyer and assessing the crowd like the arrogant king of the world he believed himself to be, was Aubrey's father, Brian Wynn.

ELI MANAGED TO fake his way through dinner. Enough people had been invited—neighbors, friends, fellow Coasties—that Eli could avoid Brian at least temporarily. Thankfully he wouldn't have to stare at him over the dinner table. Heather had arranged a casual meal with the food served buffet style. People filled their plates at their leisure and then found a spot to eat at one of several small tables arranged for the occasion throughout the house's great room.

He fixed his plate and sat with Alex, Gale, Nina, Camile and Aubrey. Alex was on his game, entertaining them all with tales of town council chaos. No one seemed to pick up on Eli's tension, except maybe Aubrey, who kept casting curious glances his way. He breathed a sigh of relief when he saw Mr. and Mrs.

Wynn settle at a table on the other side of the room.

"Alex, no way," Nina was saying, as he tuned back into the conversation.

"Scout's honor," Alex replied, raising a hand. "It's against ordinance to use any outbuilding as a chicken coop within the town limits, so Ned Bittles built one inside his house. The inspector went in to take a look at it one morning and Ned shushed him because his 'chickens were still roosting.'" He added a chuckle and a shake of his head.

"So, Gale, what are you doing for Christmas?" Camile asked after the laughter died down. "Will you be heading home to Connecticut?"

"No, actually, I won't. My parents like to travel in the winter, too. They are in St. Croix and I have no desire to spend the holidays there. They don't really celebrate it, anyway, so I'm going to hang around here and see what kind of trouble I can get into. And Alex's mom already invited me here for her Christmas Eve party."

"Good," Camile said. "Then you can come over to our parents' place for Christmas dinner?"

"Thank you. I would love to."

Camile turned an expectant look on him.

"Eli, you're invited for dinner too, of course. I'm sure Aubrey has already invited you."

"Thank you, Camile. I'll let you know. Dad mentioned flying up, but I haven't heard for sure." Aubrey hadn't invited him. He almost laughed out loud at the idea of spending Christmas with Brian Wynn. Not happening. He could barely stand the thought of getting through the rest of this evening.

A couple of hours later he was thinking that he'd managed to do just that and was anxious to get out of there. While Gale went to say his goodbyes, Eli stepped out onto the deck for a breath of ocean air. He heard the door open behind him. Hoping Aubrey had followed him out, he turned to find himself face to face with the man he'd been trying to avoid.

"Well, if it isn't the Cove's very own boy from across the highway done good," Brian Wynn exclaimed, reaching out a friendly hand. Eli stared at it for a millisecond. He really didn't want to shake it. "Eli, how are you, son? Congratulations on your recent promotion. How does it feel to be back on your hometown turf-and-surf?"

But he did, he extended his hand, because this certainly wasn't the time or the place to have it out with the guy. Problem was, it likely wouldn't ever be. Not if he wanted to maintain any kind of relationship with Aubrey. And he did. At this point, he didn't know what that relationship would or could consist of, but he'd take whatever he could get.

"I'm doing well, sir, thank you. How are you enjoying retirement?"

"Honestly?" He reached inside his coat pocket and removed a cigar. He offered it to Eli.

"No, thank you."

"This is just between you and me, because I have a feeling you'll understand." He leaned casually against the railing next to Eli. "I miss the hell out of my job. I miss the ocean. I miss the wind, the sounds, the smell. There's nothing like the smell of the ocean, right?"

He produced a butane lighter and proceeded to fire up the stogie. He let out a puff along with a chuckle. "There's not even one decent harbor to be found in the middle of that desert. Don't tell Susannah I said that. She loves it down there."

He raised his voice a couple octaves and asked, "'Don't you love this dry heat?' And, 'Oh, this sunshine? I love it, don't you?'" He paused to chuckle at his own bad impersonation. "She's always asking me stuff like that and I want to say, 'Hell, no, I don't love this endless, blinding sunshine. I miss my gray skies. I miss the salty air of home. I miss the way my clothes feel damp even when it hasn't rained in two days.' But, she's been so patient all these years, so supportive. It's her turn now, right? She deserves it. So for that, for her, I'll tolerate endless, boring blue skies and dry heat that makes me feel constantly parched."

Eli stared, dumbfounded, at the man now trying to relight a cigar in the ocean breeze. He literally could not think of a single word to say. He used his hands to help shield the cigar and tried to pin some enthusiasm to his expression. This…geniality…wasn't at all what he'd expected. He'd been expecting… He wasn't sure now that he thought about it.

It dawned on him then—he didn't know.

It had never occurred to Brian Wynn that Eli was privy to the circumstances of his father's transfer. Which made sense now that he thought back on it. Eli had barely been eighteen. What father would tell his eighteen-year-old son that he was having an affair with his friend's wife? His would. Tim Pelletier was unusual in that way. Probably because it had always been just the two of them, he'd always been unfailingly honest with Eli. He wondered now if there was such a thing as too much honesty in a situation like this?

"I talked to your dad last week. I really need to get down there one of these days and go fishing."

"You talked to my dad?" How could Eli not know that his dad and Brian were still in touch?

"Yeah, before that I hadn't heard from him in a few months. He sounds really…good. I haven't heard him sound this good in a long time. I've worried over the years about his depression. I was so sorry to see him leave the Guard. I really tried to help him out…" He trailed off with a shake of his head. "But I've learned there's only so much you can do to help someone, right? I'm sure you learned that yourself years ago, tough as it is to accept."

And that's when Eli's defenses crumbled. What else didn't he know? Because, clearly, this was a man who loved his wife deeply. With few words, he'd conveyed how much he still cared about his dad and understood his condition, and even sympathized with Eli's struggles as his son.

After they'd left Pacific Cove, Brian Wynn had gone on to advance in the Coast Guard, eventually making captain. By all accounts he was a good man and a stellar officer who'd been decorated for bravery. Come to think of it, he'd never even heard his dad say bad things about him.

Eli tried to think back to that time. His father had always been prone to bouts of depression. He'd been in the midst of a particularly bad episode. Eli had been worried about him. One evening, after a couple beers, his father had confided that he was in love with Susannah Wynn. He was in trouble, he said, and he was being transferred ASAP. Eli had been under the impression that his leaving had to do with an affair. He'd said that Brian had arranged the transfer to get him out of Pacific Cove as quickly as possible. Could he have gotten it so wrong?

"You'll have to stop by and shoot the breeze with me. I'd love to hear about your SAR work during that flooding in Texas last year. Carlisle told me a bit about it. Susannah and I will be around through February at least. Best move I made hanging on to our house here. At least I get holidays and summers on my beach. Tell me about your assignment here in Astoria. Alex was saying…"

As he eagerly rambled on about the Coast Guard, Eli could tell how much the man loved it. He missed it, too, that was obvious. It occurred to Eli that he was one of those guys who should never have to retire. Was it possible that for twelve years he'd been harboring feelings for Brian Wynn that might not be completely fair?

Which brought him back to an earlier thought. What would have happened if he didn't know, if he'd never known, the circumstances behind his dad's transfer? What if his dad had never told him the truth? Scarier still, what if the "truth" he'd believed all these years wasn't entirely accurate?

CHAPTER TEN

"WHAT DO YOU mean 'disqualified'?" Aubrey stood in the marble-floored lobby of Pacific Cove's administrative offices gaping at Mayor Hobbes. "There must be some mistake."

"I'm afraid not, Aubrey." His voice held evidence of his own disappointment. His brown-black eyes were brimming with sympathy. She could see how difficult this was for him even as her shock began to morph into despair. "How can this be?"

"They got us on a safety violation."

"Safety violation? What safety...? We had all the necessary permits for the crab feed, plus a couple I don't think we even needed..."

The mayor executed a slow, sad head shake. "It was the Visit with Santa, when Toby Paxon jumped the line. The judges said you—we— *we* should have had the street closed. They extended us a courtesy by letting us know now in case we wanted to suspend our further scheduled events and activities."

She squeezed her eyes shut as the weight of

this news bore down on her like the pressure of a deep-sea dive. The judges were right; she should have closed the street. When she thought about what could have happened to Toby if Eli hadn't been there, it made her physically ill. She'd been going over and over the event in her mind; why hadn't she thought to close the street? Better yet, why hadn't she had Santa walk down the boardwalk instead?

"Jack, I am so sorry. This is all on me."

A fierceness transformed his handsome features. "No way, Aubrey. I will not allow you to take the blame here. I should have thought of this. Any one of the council members could have considered it. Plus, we have a lot of business owners on the committee. They could have spoken up, too."

In that moment she realized she was almost as disappointed for the mayor as she was for herself. He'd really wanted that commercial, believing it was the answer to their "stagnant population growth" and a surefire way to increase tax revenue for the city's skimpy coffers. She'd had her hopes up; aside from Toby's near-miss, the first two events had gone so well. Everyone had been talking about them, comparing them to events in neighboring towns. She'd been allowing herself to dream about the future of the pool.

Alex came rushing up to join them. "Aubrey, I'm so sorry. Jack told me what happened. This is my fault. I'm on the committee. As a member of the town council, I can't believe I didn't think of this. With all the events ASJ Engineering & Construction has done, I should have—"

"Alex, stop." She held up her hands. "Thank you, both of you, for trying to make this easier on me. The decorations in town are phenomenal. The crab feed couldn't have gone any better. And Santa's visit was…almost perfect. At least the kids loved it, and the parents, too, for that matter."

Alex asked, "Do you want me to cancel the treasure hunt and the variety show?" These were the last two events on the roster.

"No. No way. The prize shouldn't be the only reason we're doing this. Did you see those kids with Santa? It was worth all our hard work for that. We'll see this through and make this the best Christmas Pacific Cove has ever seen."

"Absolutely!" the mayor enthusiastically agreed. Aubrey adored him for it. Alex, on the other hand, looked skeptical.

"Aubrey, are you sure—?"

"I'm positive, Alex. This spirit of kindness and giving we've been seeing throughout the community is reward enough as far as I'm concerned."

ELI DROVE STRAIGHT to the pool when he heard about the disqualification. A bolt of relief shot through him when he saw Aubrey's SUV in the lot. Somehow he'd known she'd be here. Chalk it up to years of knowing her as well as he knew himself—better in some ways. The front of the building was dark, the ancient, glass double doors securely latched. He went around to the back to discover it was unlocked. "She should know better," he murmured and walked past the offices and headed to the pool area.

The only lights on inside the room were those illuminating the water in the largest of the three pools. A good third of those were burned out, he noticed. She sat on a bench with her back to him and didn't even look up when he approached.

"Aubrey?" He squelched the urge to add a term of endearment.

"Hey," she said flatly. "I'm guessing you heard?"

He came around and sat next to her. She stared into the water, clearly fighting tears.

She was always so strong. It killed him to see her like this. Telling himself he was simply comforting a friend, he slipped an arm around her shoulders. She allowed him to pull her close, resting her head against his chest. He placed a cheek on the top of her head, the silky feel and sweet vanilla scent of her hair poignant and so achingly familiar.

"Alex told me. I'm so sorry."

Her sigh nearly tore him in two. "I know. It's just… It probably sounds ridiculous, but I worked so hard on this competition. I've been planning and working on it since July. I mean, yes, I knew there was no guarantee we would win. But I was feeling confident. And to go out like this? It's… Ugh. I'm not used to losing, Eli."

He couldn't help but chuckle at that.

"And when I do lose, I can always rest knowing I gave it my all. And this doesn't just affect me. So many people in the community stepped up and worked on this. And the pool. The kids I teach… Especially the ones who I know probably wouldn't be here if not for this program. You should see them. Like little Eleanor you saw here the other day? When they learn to swim—the pride and confidence it builds, the satisfaction, the sheer joy."

He stroked the hair away from her brow.

"I mean, I know my time as a rescue swimmer is limited, but my time as a swimmer will last forever. My ability to teach these kids will last forever. How can I do that without a pool?"

Eli knew better than to spout platitudes and point out that there were other pools in neighboring communities. That wouldn't help in this moment. This place was a part of her and she wasn't ready to let it go. Plus, she was right. You couldn't beat the convenience, and one could certainly argue for the importance, of having a pool right here in Pacific Cove.

"What can I do?"

She shook her head. "Nothing. Right now, I just want to feel bad."

"But I don't want you to feel bad. I hate it when you feel bad. You feeling bad is worse than me feeling bad." Eli kissed her temple. He knew he was close to crossing a line here, but he ignored the warning.

They stayed like that for a long time and Eli knew he would have held her all night.

A long time passed before she sat up, inhaled a deep breath and tucked the hair behind her ears. "You know what? There is something you can do."

"You got it."

"I feel bad asking because you've already

done so much for me—the crab feed, Santa, Nina's move and getting her Marion… Although, I guess that was as much for her as it was for me."

That nearly constant and really annoying stab of guilt sliced at him. He countered by reminding himself that he was doing these things for her as well as for the investigation. There was no ulterior motive for helping with Nina's move or for being here with her right now. Why didn't that make him feel better?

"As long as it doesn't involve another fake beard. That thing seriously hurt when I pulled it off."

She let out a giggle and Eli felt a burst of joy at the sound.

"Not unless you feel the need to disguise yourself at the bowling alley."

"You want to go bowling?"

She grinned. "You know how I told you that Danny's boyfriend, Brendan, is having issues with his dad?"

"Yes." How could he forget? Especially when he and Gale's suspicions had only grown regarding Brett West and his brother, Billy.

"Well, Brendan's dad is on—was on—their bowling team. They have a big match tomorrow and he just up and quit the team. They need someone to fill in. I would do it except it has to be a guy. And I was thinking it might be a good opportunity for you to talk to Brendan. Let him know that he didn't do anything wrong."

"Of course I'll do it." He wasn't sure about the last part but he'd definitely capitalize on the opportunity to talk to the kid.

"Thank you. I will pay you back somehow, I swear. I'll pick you up at seven?"

"Make it six—you can pay me back by coming over early for dinner."

"You're going to cook me dinner?"

He realized that sounded an awful lot like a date, but suddenly he didn't care. He was going to choose not to think about the investigation or the situation with their parents, which he had yet to untangle, anyway. He'd called his dad for some answers, but he hadn't picked up. This wasn't unusual when he was out on his charter boat. There was rarely cell phone service.

Right now, Aubrey needed him. "Yep. I'm going to drown your sorrows with some food."

She pushed one shoulder up into a shrug, dipped her chin and grinned. "Sounds perfect. As long as there's a lot of it."

AND A LOT of it there would be, Eli thought as he set about cooking Aubrey one of her favorite meals. He whisked the buttermilk, eggs and melted butter, and added it to the flour mixture. He rinsed a soiled measuring cup and paused to look out the kitchen window above the sink. It was dark now, but from this spot in his and Gale's rented house he could see the ocean and the horizon.

It had been a gorgeous day; the sky a mix of every shade of gray with splotches of blue shining through. Rain showers had drifted through on the clouds all day, interspersed with long moments of colorful sky. Now he could see stars shining brightly in what would have been those blue-sky patches.

He couldn't help but think about Aubrey's dad. How much he clearly loved the ocean and, as he'd suggested, Eli did understand. There was something almost mesmerizing about the Pacific Ocean and its coastline. So wild and unpredictable.

Being back here seemed to soothe something inside him, too. Throughout the years, whenever Eli pondered the future, his thoughts always brought him back to Pacific Cove. Maybe even to Aubrey, if he was being honest.

Dinner with Aubrey and the means to do

some investigating about the case on the same night. He should be thrilled, and he would be if he could just squelch the guilt. Regardless, he owed it to the Coast Guard, the DEA, Gale, himself. He had to proceed. He had to follow this lead with the Wests.

Granted, it was just a suspicion at this point, but something was telling both him and Gale that Brett West's overreaction to the loss of his boat was worth following up on. And now, with Aubrey's connections to Danny and Brendan, Eli might have the means to get a sense of the West family.

Ultimately, he told himself, Aubrey would understand. She would, because if anyone understood the meaning of duty, it was Aubrey.

Except that he didn't really know how she would feel. He couldn't tell her, and he couldn't really go out with her. Not like he wanted. Not in the all-out, no-holds-barred, heart-on-his-sleeve kind of want that was currently tearing him up inside.

He was so stuck it wasn't even funny.

After preheating the griddle, he began spooning the batter into place. He'd just flipped the steaming pancakes and was removing the last pieces of bacon from the frying pan when a knock sounded on the front door. His palms were sweating and he couldn't remember the last time he had felt this kind of nervous buzz. He opened the door and the smile on her face propelled him back in time, dissolving much of the tension he'd been battling.

"Your feast awaits, milady." He gestured toward the kitchen.

She walked in and let out a happy gasp. "Eli! Buttermilk pancakes? Your dad's recipe? I'm so excited."

"Yep." He met her joyous smile with his own, relishing in the fact that he'd already managed to cheer her up.

Wielding a spatula, he removed the perfectly browned pancakes from the griddle. He handed her a plate with a fluffy, steaming stack. He dipped out a scoop of whipped butter and plopped it on the top.

Scooting two dishes toward her, he added, "I warmed up some peanut butter and sliced your bananas."

"I can't believe you remembered."

"Really?" he asked dryly. He turned to face her with one quirked brow. "You honestly can't believe that I remember how you like your pancakes?"

She swallowed nervously as she set her plate down and Eli couldn't help but enjoy that, too, because she was so cute when she was flustered. "Um, well…it's been a long time."

He leaned a hip against the counter, so close to her now that they were almost touching. "Aside from swimming, baseball is your favorite sport to play, football is your favorite sport to watch—although I would say speed skating is a close second, it's just not on television that much. You drink your coffee black, but you like your tea with cream. Broccoli is your vegetable of choice, and the only ones you won't eat are brussels sprouts and water chestnuts. Your foot is a size nine. Your favorite color is pink and you're afraid of frogs. The last two I always thought were slightly odd because you're such a tomboy, and frogs are amphibious. Like you." He lifted one shoulder. "But, hey, when I got to go swimming with you in that pink bikini, it was my favorite color, too."

OH. WOW.

That was all she had. Those were the only words Aubrey could seem to form in her brain. She was incredibly grateful they didn't escape from her lips as she stared into the dense ocean of blue that she always associated with Eli's eyes. His lips were curling at the corners and all she could think about was the way they used to feel pressed against hers. What was going on here? Whatever it was, she needed to halt it in its tracks.

"Ha, ha, ha." She squawked out something that sort of resembled laughter as a mix of nerves and confusion and desire churned inside her. "Remember that time you and Alex put the frogs in my rubber boots?"

His lips formed an official grin but his eyes remained glued to her face. "You have no proof that we did that."

"All these years later and you still can't admit it? You know, I still can't put on my boots without shaking them out first?"

"All I know is that you screamed so loud Mrs. Frampton called the cops."

They laughed together and this time it was genuine on her part. This was true. The Framptons had lived next door to the Wynns and the woman had indeed called the police upon hearing Aubrey's screams. Even now, she shivered as she recalled the feeling of sliding her sockless foot into her rubber boots while those frogs jumped and twitched and crawled on her bare skin.

He turned serious again, his expression searching.

"I'm sorry."

He softly uttered the two words Aubrey

had longed to hear for so many years. And even though he was apologizing for a child-hood prank, she knew they meant more. She couldn't stop them from sneaking right past the guard she'd so carefully constructed around her heart.

He reached out a hand and cupped her jaw, caressing her cheekbone with his thumb. Tilt-ing his head forward, his warm breath swirled around the shell of her ear, and she felt herself melting like the pat of butter on the pancakes before her. She started to grip the counter to keep from losing her balance, but he slid an arm around her and pulled her close.

"You smell so good," he whispered. "Like vanilla and chlorine. For so long after I left, even a hint of vanilla and I could stake my life on the fact that I would dream about you that night. It was pure torture…"

She watched his mouth descend toward hers. The movement was both too fast and too slow at the same time as fear and desire waged a quick battle inside of her. As soon as his lips touched hers, it was all over. *Champion desire*, she thought, as she returned the kiss with everything she had.

One hand slipped around the back of his neck while the other gripped the rounded muscle of his shoulder. Eli let out a groan as she pressed herself closer. She melded to him like water on dry sand. His hands and lips seemed to be everywhere at once but she still couldn't get enough.

Threading her fingers through his hair, she pulled him closer. He found her lips for another kiss, deeper this time, and Aubrey thought she might explode from wanting this. Him. So much.

Eventually he pulled away, leaving her completely breathless. That morning's set of fifty-meter freestyle sprints was nothing compared to this. She could hear his ragged breathing, too, as he kept her close and kissed his way across her cheek until his lips were nibbling on her neck.

"I have missed you every single day for twelve years," he whispered against her skin.

His words caused the sweetest rush, like a plunge from a high dive. She'd missed him, too. He'd taken a huge chunk of her soul with him when he'd left and it felt so good to have a taste of that again. But it also reminded her that once upon a time they'd shared these same kinds of moments and had dared to plan many more. Fear and regret followed, asking her why she had allowed this moment to happen because where in the world could it possibly lead? This was all too confusing.

"Eli, I, um… I'm not sure…"

"I know," he said. His sigh sounded completely contented and the crooked grin that accompanied it had Aubrey wanting to throw herself right back into his arms. "I'm sorry. That was moving a little fast, huh?"

And with those words Aubrey regained her senses, or enough of them that she was able to step away. *Was it?* she asked silently. She had no idea. Was too fast *and* too slow a possibility?

"Maybe a little," she managed to squeak out.

He reached out and gave her fingertips a gentle squeeze, which reverberated throughout her entire body, all the way to the tips of her toes. But it wasn't her toes she was worried about. Her toes she could protect.

It was her heart. It was her stupid, untrustworthy, mind-of-its-own heart that was the problem.

EXTREMELY CONTENT FROM the time he'd spent with Aubrey, Eli bowled his third strike in a row.

Accepting enthusiastic congratulations from his teammates, he took a seat next to Brendan and continued to analyze the encounter. He'd kissed Aubrey. Did he regret it? No.

Did this complicate matters for him? Absolutely. He'd seen the desire in her eyes, felt it in her body language. Somehow he needed to figure out a way to make this work. Problem was, she wasn't a woman he could have a casual romance with. With Aubrey, he needed to be all-in. He glanced over, across a few lanes, to where Jay Johnston was standing in front of her and Danny, awaiting his turn to bowl.

Aubrey hadn't mentioned that he was a member of the team. Out of the corner of his eye, he saw her laugh at something he said. They seemed to have such a natural and easy friendship. Was there something more going on between them? Were his feelings irrational and born of jealousy? Probably. He'd neither seen nor heard any real indication of romantic feelings. Jay was exactly the kind of guy Aubrey should be with and yet…

One of his teammates called out, "Hey, Johnston, quit flirting with the ladies. You're up next."

With a few parting words, he moved off to take his turn. Eli watched him bowl a split. The next effort resulted in his ball sailing directly down the middle of the lane, leaving the remaining pins untouched. He knew it was juvenile, yet he couldn't help but relish the surge of satisfaction; no question about who was the better bowler here. He hoped Aubrey was taking note of that, as well.

Beside him Brendan was talking to his friend and fellow teammate Tyler.

"You should see the new boat my dad just got, man. It is sweet."

The words *new boat* managed to shift his attention. Eli tuned fully into the conversation as Brendan, in an awe-filled tone, described the *Savannah Bound*, the fifty-foot Mikelson Luxury Sportfisher with a 1000-gallon fuel capacity.

"Awesome. Major upgrade."

"Yeah, really major."

"What are the chances he'd let us take it out?"

Brendan shook his head. "I doubt it. He's gotten really weird lately…"

He and Gale had learned that the *Respite* had indeed been fully insured, but Eli knew there was no way the insurance money had come through yet. Not to mention the amount wouldn't even come close to covering a boat that nice. He knew because it was nearly identical to the boat his dad had purchased three years ago.

IN THE END the Beach Bowlers crushed the Chinook Hooks, landing them the district championships. Eli had managed to rack up the second highest score on the team. He and Aubrey stayed briefly for the celebratory round of beer and pizza. They were both still full of pancakes, so they didn't eat. But Aubrey had fun watching as Eli was inundated with congratulations, thanks and extracted promises to fill in again in the future.

Finally, Aubrey drove him home. Thick, misty beach rain had begun falling. She pulled up to the curb outside his house, but kept the car on to prevent the windows from fogging.

"Thanks again, Eli. This was really nice of you."

"No problem. It was fun." He reached over and played with a lock of her hair. "Anything to spend time with you." His eyes seemed to be searching hers, asking something…? She wasn't sure what, but what she did know was that she wasn't one to live in a state of not knowing.

"Eli, what's going on here?"

"I'm not sorry I kissed you," he said. "If that's what you're wondering." And the way he was looking at her now, like he was about to do it again, certainly confirmed that assertion.

"I'm not sorry, either," she said. "I wanted

you to. And I feel like an idiot for saying this, but it meant something to me. I can't have you going around plying me with pancakes and kissing me while I'm weak. I think we need to…"

He let out a chuckle and when he spoke his voice was low and soft and so utterly sincere she found herself holding a breath.

"Aubrey, I'm pretty sure you've never suffered from a moment's weakness in your entire life. But I know what you mean. We need to resolve some things between us before this goes further. Before I ply you with pancakes and kiss you again, which I very much want to do, I need to prove to you that I won't leave you again. You need to forgive me for leaving the first time, and I need to earn your trust."

Wow, she thought, that was really good. Except… "Eli, I don't know if it's possible—"

"Aubrey," he interrupted, "just let me try, okay?" He leaned over and kissed her cheek.

Before she had a chance to think about it, and because she wanted it so very badly, she found herself agreeing with a simple, "Okay."

CHAPTER ELEVEN

"I THINK WE can safely assume that Brett West could not afford the boat now parked in his slip at the marina."

Eli couldn't shake the sensation that they were missing something. He and Gale had spent the morning reviewing the case. They were doing their best to cover every base, reviewing all Coast Guard drug seizures in the past two years, following up on every string of suspicion, while eliminating the ones they could. Gale steered his pickup onto the well-kept gravel road while Eli filled him in on the details of his bowling excursion, minus the parts about Aubrey.

Those parts he kept to himself as he plotted how to proceed where she was concerned. Should he get her a Christmas gift? Jewelry might be too much. Candy was out. He'd considered flowers, but he really wanted something more Aubrey-specific. And, he wanted to kiss her by the Christmas tree at the St.

Johns' Christmas Eve party, just like he had all those years ago.

"Eli? Hello? Did you check out on me?"

"Sorry, just thinking. How does he afford a boat like that? By all accounts the guy likes to spend his spare time at the casinos. Unless we missed him on the world poker tour, I'm guessing he doesn't have a huge savings account to supplement that insurance money he will be getting from the loss of the *Respite*."

"Hardly," Gale said.

Gale had done some investigating of his own. "His ex-girlfriend says he was always broke. Could never even manage to save enough to take her out for dinner. She claims she saw his bank statements when they lived together."

"How long ago was that?"

"They broke up right around the time school started. She moved out at the end of summer. She also confirmed that Brett has two hobbies—fishing and gambling. Said when Brett wasn't working, he was either at the casino or on his boat. 'I was not a priority. He never made time for me.' That last part is a quote."

"Huh."

"But get this—she also said that things seemed to improve for him financially after he started delivering parts with his boat. For cash. And remember Danny Cruz said the same thing—that Brendan told her they were delivering parts. I think we've stumbled onto a drug courier here, Eli."

"It's sure looking that way. We're going to need some hard evidence before we take this to Yeats, though. Getting a lead on those crates would be helpful."

They continued to discuss the strength of the circumstantial evidence until they came upon the sign pointing toward Coastal Wood Sources. They had decided to check out the sawmill again and take a look at that scrap pile. They'd opted not to call first, and Eli was glad to see a few cars in the lot, suggesting that the mill was running today.

After parking, they got out and strolled around, admiring the neatly stacked piles of lumber ready to be shipped. They were heading toward the building, which housed the mill, when Sam Turner emerged and gave them a friendly wave.

"He sure seems like a nice guy," Gale commented. "I hope he's not involved."

"Me, too," Eli replied under his breath.

They walked toward the stocky-built, engagingly jovial sawmill owner. Today he was wearing double-panel jeans that were ripped through both layers on one knee, revealing a pair of gray long underwear beneath. His red-and-black flannel shirt was faded to a dusty pink and gray. The silver hard hat on his head sported a serious dent on one side.

"Hey, Sam, how you doing?" Eli reached his hand out to shake. Gale did the same.

They made small talk for a few minutes before curiosity got the better of Sam. Eli couldn't really blame him.

"What brings you boys back here to my little neck of the woods?"

The first time they'd visited, they'd done so under the auspices of wanting to buy some lumber. They'd discovered that Sam didn't have a retail shop. He cut wood on demand, often breaking down larger dimensions into lumber for special projects.

"We were wondering what you do with your scrap wood. We were thinking maybe we could work out something where we could haul if off for you, sort out what we might need, then sell the rest for firewood, or give it to the school for their wood shop program."

Sam scratched his whiskered cheek with the back of one thumb. "Sorry, boys. I've already got something like that set up with a local guy."

"That's too bad for us," Gale said. "Good deal for you both, though, I bet."

"Yep, works out great for me. He hauls it all off, although I sure wouldn't mind seeing some of this wood used for furniture. It's so pretty."

"Me, too," Gale said. "It is gorgeous. I especially like curly maple and yew wood. I'd like to make my own kitchen cabinets out of some of that."

Sam flashed a satisfied grin and pointed toward the log house set back in the trees. "I just made my new cabinets from curly maple I cut right here."

"I'd love to see them."

"I'll show you if you have a few minutes."

They headed toward the house as Sam talked about the experience of building his home from the ground up. The house wasn't overly large but it was spectacular. He'd used an attractive mix of various types of wood for the floors, cabinets, trim and other creative accents. In the living room, Eli looked up and felt a course of excitement.

"This ceiling is sure pretty. What kind of wood is this?"

Sam followed his gaze. "Isn't that something? Turned out even better than I expected.

That's larch. I cut some with my mill last year."

"You don't happen to have any more of that lying around, do you?"

"Nope. Same guy hauled it off."

"Maybe we could buy some off of him? Any chance we could get his name?"

"Hey, yeah, that's a good thought. He's a great guy. He'd probably give it to you. He's a real big philanthropist around here. I know he's given wood to the schools in the past, probably still does."

"Sounds promising. We'll give him a call."

Gale had his phone out, poised and ready to enter a name.

"You might have even heard of him. His family has been around here forever. His dad owns a bunch of different businesses. He has his own business himself now, too. An engineering firm and a construction company. Name's St. John—Alex St. John."

It took every ounce of Eli's resolve not to react to this news. His brain raced, grappling for explanations, even as he somehow managed to finish the tour and make parting small talk with Sam.

A few minutes later they were in the pickup and headed back toward Pacific Cove.

They drove in silence for several miles before Gale spoke. "This doesn't mean he's involved. It could be, it probably is, someone from inside his business using the wood to construct the crates. From what I understand he has a lot of employees and subcontractors working for him. It could be any one of them."

"I know," Eli said, still trying to explain the coincidence away. Because it had to be a coincidence. It was not possible that Alex, his best friend since childhood, could be involved—not knowingly. "There are a lot of possibilities."

"Yes, and we'll look into this very carefully before we do anything," Gale said.

AUBREY'S CONTINUED DEDICATION to the Christmas competition in light of the disqualification was a huge source of pride for Eli. He could tell a lot of other community members felt the same. Sure, there had been some grumblings about the oversight concerning the street closure, but with Aubrey's reputation and standing in the town, grumblings seemed to be promptly and properly quashed before they amounted to much.

Eli felt an extra dose of satisfaction that the weather had cooperated so perfectly for the weekend's Coast Christmas Treasure Hunt.

Yesterday's windstorm had blown away every speck of cloud, leaving a sky the color of a robin's egg. It was an unseasonably warm sixty-four degrees and many people were strolling around on the beach in jeans and shirtsleeves. Even the surf was cooperating, with gentle waves lapping at the shore. He'd seen at least four kids with their shoes off.

Excitement, on the other hand, was raging like a storm. Early that morning, just as the tide was turning, handblown glass balls had been released into the breakers offshore. Now the waves rippled in, depositing the sparkling treasure for eager beachcombers on sand resembling an endless blanket of gray velvet.

"What do you know about Alex's work?" Eli managed to casually drop the question into the conversation he was having with Aubrey about chickens. Well, specifically eggs and what an exceptional source of protein they are.

"What do you mean? You know he's an engineer. His company does major construction projects, roads and bridges and buildings for the county and the town, as well as the Coast Guard. He has a great reputation, not to mention he's always donating to the community. Why?"

"Nina wants to have a chicken coop built.

I was thinking maybe I'd pick his brain about it, where to get the supplies and stuff. Then we could build it for her."

Aubrey stopped abruptly and looked up at him. "Eli, that would be amazing."

He shrugged. "Gale has volunteered to help. He's pretty handy with a hammer."

"Really? That is so nice."

"That's Gale. He's always helping people. Reminds me a lot of you, actually."

"And you." She winked and kept walking.

Eli could only wish his motives were as selfless as hers. They spotted several ornaments, but left them where they were in order to let enthusiastic treasure hunters find them.

"Aubrey!" A little voice squealed with delight just before a tiny girl launched herself onto Aubrey's person.

"Eleanor, hi! You made it." She bent over and gave her a hug. "I've been watching for you."

"Eli, I'd like you to meet Eleanor. Eleanor, this is my friend Eli. She takes swim lessons from me at the pool."

"Nice to meet you, Eleanor."

"Where's Sheila?" Aubrey asked.

Eleanor pointed. A family had placed chairs a ways up the beach. Eli couldn't blame them. It was a day to relish. Aubrey exchanged waves with a woman sitting in one of the chairs.

She looked back at Eleanor. "How's your day going, Dolphin?"

The little girl shrugged. "I'm having fun on the beach, but I haven't found a ball yet. I'm trying really hard, Aubrey, because you always say that we shouldn't give up if we want something really bad." The longing and bravery in her tone tugged at Eli's heartstrings.

"That's right." Aubrey nodded. "And if you keep looking and don't give up, I feel confident you will find one."

He wondered if she should be saying something like that to the obviously hopeful Eleanor. It seemed like the potential disappointment could be crushing to the kid.

"Really?"

"Yep. We'll help you. I think that stump over there looks like a good place for one to be hiding. Eli, will you take Eleanor over there to have a look?" She added a meaningful look and he suddenly suspected she had something up her sleeve.

"Sure," he said. He led little Eleanor over to the waterlogged stump half buried in the sand. They traveled all the way around it. Eli distracted her with examining the intricate roots. He pointed out a piece of white shell sticking out of the sand.

After a few minutes they returned to where Aubrey was waiting.

From the corner of his eye he saw a man and woman had stopped nearby. He was medium height and build, and wearing a baseball cap that shaded his face as he gazed out at the horizon. But the woman, plump and short with bright red hair, seemed to be surreptitiously watching them. Eli glanced up the beach. Eleanor's foster mom was still sitting in her chair while three kids played on a blanket in front of her. The couple's presence struck him as odd, and he wondered if the investigation was starting to get to him.

"Nothing?" Aubrey asked.

Eleanor shook her head. "We found a sand dollar." She held it up proudly.

"That's awesome. Have you looked around there?" She pointed to where a car-size rock jutted out from the beach. A large tide pool had formed around it.

They all moved toward the pool. Eli spotted the glass ball Aubrey had obviously squirreled away in her bag for just this occurrence. He found himself holding a breath as little Eleanor traveled the perimeter. The woman with red hair and the man in the ball cap moved closer. Eli kept an eye on them as he wondered if they were going to try to snatch the ball.

Seconds later Eleanor's delighted squeal split the air. "Look! There's one! I found one." She squatted and reached for the ball. She scooped it out of the water and held it aloft. Dancing from one foot to the other, she said, "Aubrey, look, it even has a dolphin on it. It's the most beautiful thing I've ever seen."

"No! Way! Good find, little one." Aubrey pretended to examine it. "It is gorgeous!" she declared.

They all spent some time admiring the prize, holding it up to the light and watching the silver dolphin sparkle in the blues and greens of the hand-blown glass.

Eli realized the couple had disappeared. A delighted Eleanor couldn't stop giggling and Eli found himself grinning from ear to ear as they delivered the exuberant child to her foster family. He was relieved when Sheila seemed genuinely excited for the child, hugging her close and telling her how proud she was.

After a few more minutes of visiting, they said their goodbyes and took off again.

"That was…" Eli searched for a word. "Incredible."

Aubrey grinned. "It was fun, huh? Sheila told me they were coming today, so I saved that one, hoping I'd run into her." She sighed. "I wish I could make her life that good every day. You should have seen her when she first started coming to the pool for lessons. I could see her wanting to be happy, but there was just this sadness weighing her down. Sheila and Dave have done so much for her, too, but even Sheila says that she lives for her swim lessons. I remember that feeling so well, and I had good, solid parents."

They strolled along, chatting and laughing. The next time he looked up, he saw Aubrey's mom, Susannah, approaching them with Camile. He added two barefoot adults to his tally.

"Hi, Eli! Aubrey, honey, this is just…so much fun! Look what I found." She held up a gorgeous glass ball in shades of red and gold. "Can I keep it?"

"Yes, you can keep it, Mom."

"I didn't know if it was against the rules or not, since you're in charge and all."

"This isn't my event, but it wouldn't matter, anyway. You're out here searching and enjoying the beach. That's the point of it all."

"Seriously gorgeous," Camile said, showing off her own glittering ornament in shades of blue and silver. "If Mom gets to keep hers, then I'm keeping mine, right?"

"Of course."

"I'm so excited. This really is amazing, Aubrey." Something caught her eye and she lifted a hand to wave. "There's Mrs. Green. I'm going to go say hi."

Eli followed her gaze. "Our English teacher, Mrs. Green? I loved her. I haven't seen her in years. Do you mind if I tag along?"

ELI AND CAMILE took off while Aubrey and her mom continued to walk and talk, enjoying the day.

"Mom, can you believe all three of us girls are home for Christmas this year? It's been... what? Four years?"

"Yes, all of my girls together under one roof for the holidays. The only thing that would make it better is if we had some grand-babies to join us..."

"Subtle, Mom."

Since Nina's divorce, their mom had been not-so-subtle about hinting that it was her middle daughter's turn to have a go at mar-riage. Which was odd, she thought, seeing as how Nina's experience had been such a disas-ter. It wasn't that Aubrey was determined to never get married, it was just that she hadn't found the right guy yet. Granted, she hadn't really tried that hard. Maybe that was because she'd found him once and then her instincts had proved to be so woefully wrong. Even though she'd been young, Eli had messed with her head. The notion slipped in that he might be doing the same thing again.

"I've tried subtle," her mom countered.

"I'll get to work on that. Just as soon as I find someone who is as great as Dad."

"Well, your standards are awfully high, honey. I've been telling you that for years and I—"

"Mom!"

Susannah laughed. "I don't mean it that way. I just mean that your father is not perfect. Not like you seem to think. He has his flaws. We all do. What I mean is, I think your constant strive for perfection is keeping you from settling down."

"I don't want someone perfect. I just want someone perfect for me. Besides, I don't expect anything out of anyone else that I'm not willing to deliver myself." It was one of her dad's favorite quotes.

Her mom stopped in her tracks, surprise and amusement stamped across her face. "Your sisters are right, you know? You are so much like your father."

"Thank you."

Susannah heaved a sigh and started walking again. "Honey, I'm going to tell you something and you're not going to like it."

"If you're going to lecture me about my love life, please don't. I have—"

She held up a stop-sign hand. "I'm not. Well, not directly, anyway. But I am going to tell you about mine."

"Please, if you love me, Mom, you will not do that," Aubrey quipped.

"Aubrey, I'm serious. I want to tell you this."

The stern edge to her mom's tone gave her pause. She stopped. "I'm sorry, Mom. What is it?"

Her mom stopped, too. The expression on her face was so grave it caused a jolt of nerves to flow through her.

"When you girls were younger..." Her mom paused to look up at the sky.

Aubrey waited.

She met her eyes again. "Your father and I almost got divorced."

"What? When?" In spite of her mom's use of the past tense, Aubrey felt her stomach knot.

"When you were in high school. Nina was already in college and Camile was in middle school. Let's see, that would have been what…your sophomore year?"

The same time she and Eli had been together. No wonder she hadn't seen it. She'd been so absorbed in her life, in Eli. Still, her family was close. She couldn't remember her parents ever fighting. Now that she thought about it, she did remember a time when her mom had complained that her dad worked too much, especially back then…

"What happened?" she found herself asking, even though she wasn't sure she really wanted to know.

Her eyes latched onto Aubrey's and she said, "I fell in love with another man. Well, I *thought* I was in love with another man and… I even considered having an affair. I thought I might want a divorce. Your father did not. He refused to even consider it. He didn't know that I was having feelings for someone else, although I don't think that would have affected his decision. You know him, he does not quit. Thank goodness." She added an appreciative smile. "You got that trait from him, too. You know, if you didn't look so much like me, I'd wonder if you really had half of my DNA."

"Mom… Um…" She didn't know what to say. It was so surreal. Was this something a daughter was even supposed to know about her own parents? What was she supposed to do with the information? How could her mom have even considered a divorce? Her dad was so great.

"I've grappled with telling you this for a while now. Because…"

Aubrey stared but somehow knew what her mom was thinking. "You were afraid I'd judge you?"

"I know how strong your opinions can be," she amended. "And I know how much you adore your father. Which is also why I wanted to tell you, because you are so much like him. The world is awfully black and white for people like you and your father. But people aren't all good or all bad, Aubrey. Relationships, situations, even people, aren't always as they appear. There is every shade of gray out there. And I just don't want you to pass up someone who might be a little gray but who might still be right for you. Is this making sense?"

"I think so."

"Good. Because in addition to your high standards, you can get so wrapped up in your work, or a project, or with saving the world, that you don't stop and see what is right in front of you. In spite of your expectations, or maybe because of them, you can also be a little oblivious and maybe a bit, um, hyper-focused? That's what happened with your dad and me. He was focused on a bigger picture and kind of forgot about me there for a while."

Aubrey listened as her mom filled her in on more details. By the time they caught up to Eli and Camile again, Aubrey was glad. She needed time to absorb what she'd heard. She wanted to talk to someone.

As IT TURNED OUT Eli didn't have to figure out a way to tell Aubrey about his dad and her mom. Fate, and Susannah Wynn, took care of that for him.

He and Aubrey stopped by her house after the treasure hunt to grab lunch before heading to the pool for a swim. They hadn't gone swimming together in twelve years. He didn't count the ocean rescue in their flight suits. He'd been looking forward to it, thinking about how much fun they used to have. Wondering if she still wore pink swimsuits and whether he could beat her in an underwater race now.

Until she said the words, "Eli, there's something I need to tell you…"

She went on to recite the details Susannah had disclosed. She added some more that strengthened Eli's belief that Brian Wynn wasn't quite as terrible as he'd believed for all these years.

"My mom says she didn't have an affair. Just that she wanted to. Do you think that's possible?" She threaded her fingers together and dipped her chin down to rest upon them. "Isn't that what people say when they want to admit something without feeling *too* guilty about it?"

Eli believed it. Because he'd been thinking about this a lot and he couldn't remember his dad ever saying they'd had an affair. He'd simply said that he was in love with Susannah, that he'd needed to get out of Pacific Cove, and that Brian had arranged a transfer for him. Looking back, he recalled how despondent his father had been. He'd seemed almost broken. Being so young, Eli hadn't questioned him thoroughly enough, he could see that now. He'd pieced together the rest and hadn't exactly done a bang-up job of it.

"My dad was gone a lot back then. I remember my mom complaining about that occasionally. But I don't remember any other man ever being around…"

Which gave him the opening he needed. "Except my dad?"

Her head snapped up and she froze, green

eyes full of shock as the truth hit her with all of its cruel and unrelenting force.

Her voice came out a hoarse whisper. "Your dad and my mom?"

Eli nodded.

"You knew about this? All these years you knew? And you never told me?"

"It wasn't my secret to tell. When my dad told me, he didn't know about you and me."

"Eli, that's unfair, and you know it. If the situation were reversed, you would have wanted me to tell you. You'd be furious that I hadn't told you."

This was true. He hadn't thought of that at the time, either. He'd been so concerned for his dad and the probable blow to his career. To Eli, on the verge of entering the academy and dreaming of his own career, the Coast Guard had been everything. The loss of his father's future had seemed like the end of the world.

"Maybe you're right, but…"

Aubrey folded her arms across her chest, her shock seemed to be morphing into anger. "I am right."

"I'm trying to apologize here, Aubrey. Even now, I'm not sure I should have told you. At the time I was sure they'd had an affair. I love your mom and I didn't want to hurt her. And your dad… I've spent the last twelve years hating him. Unfairly, I think now. I didn't want to be responsible for harming your parents' relationship, but mostly I didn't want to see you get hurt by it all."

"I think the only person responsible for that would be my mom. And your dad, too, to some degree. But why would you hate my dad? He seems to be the innocent one here."

Eli agreed. "He was—is. Except… Apparently he found out about them. I think that's what prompted my dad to take the transfer to New Jersey."

Her look turned sharp. "He said that?"

He thought for a second. *Had* his dad actually said that? Eli realized he really didn't know. "Back then I was under the understanding that your dad gave him an ultimatum—either take the transfer or he would expose the affair."

"That's not possible. My mom said my dad didn't know about another man, only that she was unhappy."

FINDING IT IMPOSSIBLE to sit still, Aubrey stood and paced the length of her small living room. The blood was now racing through her body, pulse pounding hard in her ears. Something else occurred to her and she stopped.

"Why are you telling me this now?" Even as she asked the question, the answer occurred to her. Was *this* why he'd broken up with her? This perfectly lame excuse had caused him to leave her? No matter the fine points, and in this moment she didn't really care about them, because her parents were still together and appeared happier than they'd ever been. Although, she realized now, Tim's transfer had probably been what had saved their marriage.

"Isn't that obvious?"

"Maybe. But I want you to clarify just in case I'm mistaken in thinking that you broke up with me not because of *me* but because of something going on with our *parents*!"

"Aubrey, calm down."

"What makes you think I'm not calm?" she asked much too calmly.

He swallowed nervously.

Good, she thought. *He should be nervous.*

He lifted his hands, palms down, fingers spread. "Yes. I left you—stupidly—I see that now. But at the time, I knew we couldn't stay together. I wouldn't have been able to keep this information from you. Think about it. We were so close. You were like a part of me. At the same time, I knew I couldn't ruin your life—your family. I could not do that to you.

"Instead of being angry with your mom and my dad, I channeled all of that toward your dad. All I could think about was that he was destroying my dad's career. His life. My life. But the worst part of it all was having to break up with you. It was like tearing my own heart out. That's why I didn't keep in touch. I couldn't talk to you, and laugh with you, and see you, and not…have you be mine."

She melted a little at those words and at the way he was staring at her, every inch of him seeming to plead for understanding. He looked incredibly frustrated and just…sad. And he was right; they had been close, so very close. She had no choice but to concede part of what he was saying.

They began speaking at the same time.

"I can see how you'd think that. And I…"

"Aubrey, I'm so, so sor-ry… R-r-really?"

His eager gaze latched onto hers, asking a question she was only too happy to answer.

"Don't get too excited. I'm still angry. You're right, it would have hurt me. It might have destroyed my family, and probably hurt your dad even worse than he was already hurting. Back then, I never would have been able to keep this information to myself." She was good at keeping secrets, but not this one. This wasn't a matter of keeping someone's confidence. This was information that affected a lot of people.

Suddenly chilled, she sidestepped to stand in front of the tiny wood stove that heated her house. "You still should have told me. You can't control what I get to know, Eli, in order to protect me. Just like you can't protect me from every physical danger that comes along."

He came forward and stood before her. "Aubrey…"

The way he whispered her name caused a sharp pang to shoot through her. For some annoying reason, hot tears began to roll down her cheeks. She dipped her head into her sleeve to mop them up.

He took her hand and led her to the sofa. He sat and urged her down next to him. She complied and he immediately cradled her against his chest.

Aubrey let the enormity of the situation—of his admission, of her mom's disclosure, of their discussion and the details of their breakup—sink into her.

"You're right. I was an idiot," he said. "I can see that so clearly now. We would have found a way to work it out. We shouldn't have had to suffer for their sins, whatever or however severe they might have been."

"Wow," Aubrey finally said. "What a mess."

Eli blew out a long sigh. "Yep."

"What are we going to do?"

"I have absolutely no idea."

"There is one thing I do know, though."

"What's that?"

She sat up and looked him square in the face. "In order for us to have a chance of making this—whatever this is—and I don't care if it's just friendship… But in order to make something work with us, you can't do this anymore. No more deciding what I get to know. And no more thinking that you need to protect me, okay? I am perfectly capable of taking care of myself. Do you think you can remember that, knight?"

He bent his head and brushed a soft kiss across her lips. "I will try, mermaid. I will try."

And then he kissed her again.

CHAPTER TWELVE

ELI REMEMBERED THE exact date he'd discovered the cave. It was the second of May, memorable because he'd just turned sixteen and gotten his license the day before. His dad had let him take his Jeep out for a drive. The afternoon had been bright and clear and he'd driven up to the lighthouse simply to enjoy the view. The year before, Alex had managed to steal a key and occasionally they'd let themselves inside and climb to the top.

But that day Alex hadn't been with him so he'd parked, deciding to take a hike along the cliff's edge. He'd walked for maybe a half mile and, although the weather had been sunny and warm, it was breezy like it usually was along the ocean's edge. A gust of wind had taken him by surprise, lifting his baseball cap from his head. It had sailed over the edge and landed about fifty feet down the cliff on a wide ledge of rock. He probably wouldn't have bothered except that the cap was his favorite. Aubrey had given it to him after she'd attended a Gonzaga University basketball game with her dad.

Studying the situation, he'd decided that it wouldn't be that difficult to retrieve. He'd carefully picked his way down until he'd reached the ledge. As he'd retrieved his hat and turned to face the cliff before him, he'd noticed a narrow crevice in the rock face. He doubted he would have explored further than that except that a butterfly had chosen that moment to flit by, disappearing into the space. Curious, he'd gone closer and discovered the opening to a small cave.

The next day he'd brought Aubrey back with him. They'd visited the cave regularly and, when they'd started dating, it became their "spot." The place they'd go to be together, to talk or to enjoy the ocean. He hadn't been back in twelve years and he found himself wondering if Aubrey had. He'd never shared the cave's existence with another living soul. By mutual consensus, they'd never even showed Alex, knowing that he'd never be able to keep it a secret. And later they'd wanted the place for their own. Even now, the idea of her bringing someone else here, to their place, bothered him.

With Aubrey in the passenger seat beside him, he drove past the lighthouse and parked.

Turning off the engine somehow revved up his nerves. What would she think about this? If she had any doubt about his intentions this would certainly steer her toward thinking he was serious.

She was staring out the passenger window. "I can't believe you brought me here." With her head turned away and her voice so soft, he couldn't gauge her reaction.

When she turned to look at him, her serious expression had him believing he'd made a mistake. At her next question he began to formulate an apology.

"You know what I've always wondered?" she asked.

"What's that?"

"If anyone else has ever found our cave." With a laugh she was out the door and running before he could grab his jacket.

He chuckled, his spirits lifting as he watched her heading down the trail. Alex was right, the girl really could move like lightning. He slipped into his jacket and set off after her.

"I'm still faster than you," she teased. She was waiting for him by the giant rock that they'd always used to mark the place where they descended to the ledge below. It was steep, but they both remembered the route to get down and several minutes later they were on the ledge and entering the cave.

Aubrey removed her phone from her pocket, tapped on the screen and pointed it up. "Look, it's still there."

Eli had surprised her once by bringing a paint pen and writing Knight loves Mermaid on a large, flat piece of rock that made up a portion of one of the cave walls. It was the first time he'd told her he loved her.

He stepped closer, wrapping his arms around her. He nuzzled the side of her head, burying his face in her hair. She pivoted in his arms so that she was facing him and put her phone back into her pocket. She slipped her arms around him, one hand cupping the back of his neck.

He took a few seconds to enjoy the feel of her hand on his skin. They were close enough to the entrance that light still made its way inside. He could see that her lips were parted slightly, playing with a smile. Her green eyes glowed with laughter, joy and affection that he hoped he wasn't imagining. She was the most beautiful thing he'd ever seen, and by far the best person he'd ever known.

"You know what?" he found himself asking.

"What?"

"It's still true," he whispered just before his mouth covered hers. "I've always loved you, Aubrey. There's never been anyone else. There could never be anyone else."

AUBREY FELT LIKE her heart might explode, and not just because Eli was kissing her. Yes, she wanted that, and him, but it was the way his touch was combining with the movie reel of emotions now flickering through her brain— desire, affection, relief, love, fear, anxiety... They all expanded inside her, leaving her chest tight and aching.

She didn't want this moment to end even as she wished it wasn't happening. Because rising to the top of her consciousness was the fact that he'd told her this twelve years ago. He'd told her he loved her and she'd believed it then, too. And she'd loved him. They'd loved each other. But it hadn't been enough. Or maybe he'd loved her too much, she realized now. So much that he felt like he had to protect her. He'd always tried so hard to protect her. Maybe that wasn't such a bad thing, though. Sometimes. And he did seem to realize now that breaking up with her, while noble and selfless in a way, hadn't been the solution.

The bottom line was that he was trying. She wanted to try, too.

She was in love with him, too, she knew that. She always had been. She could only hope that, this time, their love would be enough.

"I FEEL LIKE a jerk," Eli said to Gale the next morning. He stood up from where he'd been sitting at the dining room table in their rented house. "Am I a terrible friend for even suspecting Alex could be involved?" Stretching his arms over his head, he let out a groan. "I can't believe I'm already stiff from that workout." He and Aubrey had gone to the gym that morning.

"Well, yoga isn't normally a part of your workout plan." Gale chuckled. "Next thing you know you'll be wearing tights and taking spin classes. And, no, you're not. I suspected him, too."

Alex's company was using the wood from Coastal Wood Sources, all right. They were using it for projects in home construction for a charity organization. One of Alex's many worthy causes was building homes for needy families.

"We've been to his warehouse, his maintenance shop, his office and four building sites so far. Where else can we look?"

Gale ran a pen down the list of locations they'd compiled. They'd visited each one, searching for crates or evidence that someone in Alex's organization was constructing them.

"The problem," he added, "is that it wouldn't take much space to make crates. A person could do it in their garage. They could be sneaking pieces home and making them."

"Exactly," Eli agreed, exhaling a frustrated sigh. "We need…something."

"Nothing else from the West kid?"

"Nope, not yet. Aubrey has another swim lesson with Danny tomorrow. I'll see her tomorrow night, so if something comes up, hopefully I'll hear about it. And then she's back on duty for a day."

Gale eyed him, a half grin curling his lips. "You two have really been spending some quality time together, huh?"

"We have," Eli answered enigmatically.

They'd managed to see each other every day for the last four days, including the day he'd taken her to the cave. As bad as he felt about the disqualification, Aubrey's loss had been his gain. Now that she didn't have quite as much pressure from the Christmas contest weighing down on her, he'd been able to capitalize on her free time. Of course, she was still Aubrey, which meant she was virtually unable to sit still for longer than it took to eat a meal.

"What's the status with you two?"

He paused, not yet sure how to answer the question. Things were going incredibly well. They'd taken a hike along the beach, gone rock climbing at an indoor wall, and driven down the coast looking at Christmas lights. Tonight they were having dinner at Nina's.

"You know, your lack of information in this regard tells its own story."

"Oh, yeah? So does that bag over there stuffed with tennis balls and dog toys." Eli pointed across the room to where a shopping bag from the local pet store Sandy Paws was sitting.

"Those are for Marion. You know how much I love dogs. Border collies are a very energetic and playful breed. They need a lot of stimulation."

"All right. I'll buy that. But what about that book on the coffee table on how to raise free-range chickens? Is that for Marion, too?"

Gale's lips twitched as he tried not to smile. "Hey, I'm going out there tonight, too. I'll have you know that Gwyneth Kohen would be appalled if her son arrived at a dinner party without a gift for the hostess."

"I'll have you know, Mr. Old Money Connecticut, that around here we don't call them dinner parties. It's just dinner. And we bring things like wine or a dessert."

"Right," Gale said, turning serious. "Anything else I should know?"

Eli belted out a laugh. "I have to say, I never thought I would see this day."

"What day?"

"The day that Gale Kohen was nervous about a girl."

"Yeah, well, Nina Wynn is not your average girl."

"At least you've already made friends where her dad is concerned. Clearly, Captain Wynn likes you."

"In spite of what you told me about him, he seems like a good guy. And he seems to like you, too."

"I know," Eli said. "Weird, right?" He was still reeling from learning that Brian Wynn wasn't the monster he'd believed him to be for all these years. Yet, now that he'd had time to think it all through, something still felt off about the scenario.

He had questions. He felt like his dad held the answers, but he'd only spoken to him a couple of times since the conversation with Aubrey.

He'd been working long hours with his fishing business and, each time, the conversations had been brief. His dad had sounded happy and Eli hadn't wanted to bring the subject up seemingly out of the blue and spoil his dad's good mood. He was beginning to wonder if he ever wanted to. Why not just let it go? Aubrey seemed fine. The Wynns seemed happier than they'd ever been. He didn't see how anything could be gained from dredging up this subject with his dad, and yet, something kept telling him to pursue it.

MARION GREETED HER and Eli as they walked through the door of Nina's house. Aubrey liked the sound her doggy paws made as her nails tapped lightly against the wooden floor. She barked once and then sat like a perfect lady before them. Aubrey bent and scratched her ears. Eli took a knee to greet her properly and all semblance of ladylike behavior flew out the window as Marion flopped over onto her back to give him access for a belly scratch.

"Hey, guys." Nina came out of the kitchen, long blond hair twisted on top of her head, wearing an apron covered with snowmen that she somehow managed to make look stylish. "Thanks for coming out. I'm so excited you're here."

In keeping with Nina's impeccable taste and creative bent, the decorations looked like something from a country living magazine.

"This place…" Aubrey gushed, moving into the living room. "Looks spectacular. Your tree is gorgeous." A lighted Christmas tree stood in one corner and she recognized many of the vintage ornaments that had belonged to their grandmother.

"Thank you. Alex brought it out for me. And then helped me decorate it. I hope you don't mind that I put your ornaments on there from Grandma, too?"

"Of course not. I'm happy to see them being displayed like this." Christmas was less than two weeks away. "I'm not sure I'll get a tree this year, anyway. I've been so busy and I go back on shift tomorrow. It's nice to be able to enjoy yours and Mom's, though."

"Aubrey, you have to get a tree. Even if it's just a small one. Once you start letting traditions slide, you're this close—" she pinched her thumb and finger together for emphasis "—to skipping midnight mass and eating Rocky Road ice cream and drinking peppermint schnapps while watching *The Christmas Story* twenty-four-hour marathon."

Aubrey barked out a laugh. "I've only missed midnight mass one time in my life and that was because I was on a rescue. I don't drink, and I don't like Rocky Road, so I think we're safe there."

"Okay, maybe that was me I was talking about. The dark holidays, I like to call them. But you get the idea. Trust me, no tree is *no bueno*." She added a breezy laugh.

Aubrey laughed with her, even though she knew her sister was referring to the years surrounding her divorce.

"Hey!" Gale's voice sounded from behind them and Aubrey watched the flicker of mortification pass across her sister's face. It wasn't like Nina to get embarrassed. She embraced her quirky side and relished her own eccentricities.

Aubrey watched Gale, who only had eyes for Nina. His expression seemed to be a combination of concern and amusement…and admiration?

Hmm, she thought.

"Merry Christmas," he said. He leaned over so he had one hand on Marion's head, who was already glued to his side, gazing up with lovestruck eyes. He handed Nina a gift bag. "For the hostess," he added with a shy grin. He fished something out of the other bag, a plush reindeer, and offered it to Marion. "This is for the hostess's assistant." He knelt and gave the toy in his hand a little squeak. Marion barked joyfully and a game of tug-o-war ensued.

Nina seemed uncomfortable with the attention, which she knew was Doug's fault. Her sister hadn't even considered dating since her divorce. She'd love to have it out with Doug someday. In the meantime, she couldn't help but think about how wonderful it would be for Nina to have someone in her life. Someone kind and thoughtful who appreciated her exactly as she was.

Her parents and Camile came through the door, interrupting her thoughts. Alex was only steps behind. They visited briefly before Nina herded them all to the table.

For dinner she served a thick Irish stew and fresh-baked oatmeal bread. The meal was delicious and she was smart to warn everyone to save room for dessert. She brought out a fresh-baked berry pie that looked too beautiful to eat.

With a flourish and a "tah-dah," she plopped another bowl on the table between her and Eli. "Fruit salad drizzled with a bit of raw honey for those among us steering clear of refined sugar."

"Thank you. How thoughtful," Aubrey said.

Camile scooped out ice cream for the pie. Aubrey caught Nina's shy smile as Gale accepted a giant helping of pie with a double scoop of vanilla bean ice cream.

The evening was wildly successful, especially if noise volume was any indication. The Wynn family didn't do silence. Stories were told, interspersed with plenty of teasing and an abundance laughter. For Aubrey, the event made it easy to forget about what had torn her and Eli apart all those years ago. And, unlike then, he didn't make any effort to hide his feelings for her, holding her hand and curling an arm around the back of her chair. Oddly enough, no one commented or seemed surprised.

Camile went around the table refilling drinks and when she was finished, their dad stood to make a toast.

"I just want to say that I couldn't be prouder of my girls. Nina, the stew was delicious, and this pie might be the most delicious I've ever tasted. And I believe this farm is the best thing that's happened to this family in a long time—to you and to your mom and me, for sure. Because even though Camile is at college, she's not far away. And Aubrey is here for at least two more years, give or take."

He raised his glass. "To family, and to good friends who feel like family. There's nothing on this earth more important than that."

CHAPTER THIRTEEN

THE MAYDAY CALL came in while Aubrey was in the eighteenth hour of her twenty-four-hour shift. They'd already been called out once on a minor issue, but she hadn't been deployed. This report relayed that the *Angela Sue*, a fishing boat twenty-five miles off the coast, was taking on water and the vessel's bilge pump was not functioning. One of Aubrey's capabilities as a rescue swimmer was to board stranded boats via a cable hoist with the assistance of her flight crew. She could then assess the boat and the crew and render aid as needed.

She was suited up and heading toward the helo to board when she saw Eli jog up to the pilot who was standing beside the aircraft. Lt. Cdr. Vincent would be piloting this mission. She loved flying with Vinny because in a profession full of cool heads, his was one of the coolest.

"Threading the needle," as hoisting an RS down to a vessel in need was sometimes called, could be tricky. In the midst of rough seas, bad weather or wayward rigging, it was downright perilous. Luckily, they were facing light winds and relatively calm seas this morning. But still, as the human needle hanging on the end of that line, she was always glad when he was piloting.

A quick conversation ensued before Eli and Vinny shook hands. Vinny headed back toward the hangar while Eli climbed into the helicopter.

Vinny jogged past her to go inside.

"Hey, what's up?" she asked.

"Lieutenant Pelletier is taking this one. He and Lieutenant Commander Kohen are going to assess."

A surge of nerves buzzed through her. All personnel had been briefed that this might happen. She'd assumed they'd have a warning before it was executed, that Eli and Gale would schedule the flights beforehand. Springing this on her felt like a pop quiz. She hated pop quizzes. Not to mention that after the *Respite*, she wasn't sure how she felt about working with Eli.

"You okay with this?"

He shrugged a shoulder. "Sure. Not like I have a choice. I'm going to take a nap. With the way things are going, I wouldn't be surprised if something else gets called in."

Aubrey climbed on board and buckled herself in. Johnston was the flight mechanic, which meant he'd serve as the hoist operator. Also good news. It was easy to trust him with her life.

Once airborne, Gale informed them that the original Mayday had been canceled, but they were continuing out to observe the scene. The first mate of the vessel had called in the initial report, stating there were three persons including the captain on board. The captain had radioed back, canceling the call, but without confirming that the problem had been alleviated.

With a flight speed of 180 miles an hour, it took them twelve minutes to reach the destination.

"We have a visual on the vessel. Wynn, you want to take a look?"

It was pitch black outside. Aubrey donned the night-vision equipment. "Looks fairly simple. It's smallish, but that's a nice clean spot right there on the stern if I need to go."

"That's what I'm thinking, too," Johnston chimed in.

They discussed their strategy for a moment before Gale came back on. "The captain is now requesting assistance. Command Center got this one right, huh?"

Eli addressed her, "After you board and assess, let us know the situation. If you can't get their bilge pump working, we'll lower the portable down to you."

Aubrey agreed.

Johnston shifted around to prepare the hoist. As she removed the night-vision glasses she felt Eli's hand on her arm. He gave it a quick squeeze. She glanced up and he mouthed, "Why do we do this?" She couldn't help the smile that lit her face, the warmth that filled her chest. As kids they used to ask each other this precursor to the rescue swimmer's creed before every wild jump off practically every single cliff or crazy plunge into ocean or pool alike.

"So that others may live," she mouthed in return, hoping this was his way of conveying his confidence in her.

After adjusting her helmet and visor and checking her gear, she got into a seated position in the doorway. She and Johnston made quick work of the deployment and safety procedures and soon she was attached to the hoist and headed down to the boat.

Adrenaline surged through her as she neared the vessel. With Eli piloting and

Johnston both aiding him with verbal direction and operating the hoist, she was able to land in the exact location they'd chosen on the stern of the boat. She released the cable, flashed the hand signal that she was all right, and headed for the cabin.

The second Aubrey entered the space she was struck with a bad feeling. A paunchy man with an angry scowl introduced himself as the captain. Two crewmen stood off to one side. Tension coursed through the group, which wasn't unusual in such high-stress situations. In emergencies, people often disagreed on the best course of action, and she knew a distress call had been made and then canceled.

She quickly introduced herself and asked, "How are you guys? Do you have any injuries?" She looked from one man to another, waiting for each to respond.

A tall, muscular guy with a red face was the only one wearing a life vest. It was too small and stretched tightly across his dirty red coveralls.

"Are there other life jackets on board?"

"Uh, yeah," the captain said, glancing around nervously.

"Could I get you and your crewman to put those on for me?"

The other crewman was toothpick thin with a neatly trimmed goatee and a bucket hat on his head. He disappeared into the forward cabin below the bow and returned with two life vests. He tossed one to the captain and slipped the other on.

"What seems to be the problem?"

"We're, uh, leaking," the captain explained. "We have a lot of water below."

"Do you know where it's coming from?"

"No."

"Boat's been leaking for a long time," Coveralls offered.

"Never this bad," the captain snapped.

Bucket Hat mumbled something unintelligible.

Coveralls looked at him. "What? This never would have happened if we could have taken the *Savannah B*—"

"Shut up," the captain said angrily. To Aubrey, he explained, "It's leaked a little, but the pump always keeps up."

"Okay, we can talk about all this later." Aubrey refrained from lecturing them about taking a leaky boat miles out into the ocean in the dark. They all looked plenty nervous as it was, especially Coveralls.

"I'll take a look." She moved back toward the stern and studied the situation. Bucket Hat was kind enough to hold a flashlight. Basic solutions—flipping the switch, checking for loose wires, examining the fuse block— didn't help. From the state of the old and dirty parts she could see, she could make guesses about the cause of the problem; a hull fitting had gradually corroded, the pump intake was clogged with debris or the float that operated the switch was stuck. Of course, she couldn't know for sure amid all the high, dirty water.

"Are there any other pumps on board?"

"Two portable bilge pumps," the captain answered.

"I think we should abandon ship," Coveralls said, his gaze focused on the deck. She imagined he was waiting for water to start gushing up from below. "How many can you fit in the helicopter?"

"That's not necessary at this point," Aubrey said. It wasn't unusual for people to get panicky in these situations, especially inexperienced boaters. But it was part of her job to try and save the boat as well as the people on board.

"But, don't worry, we have plenty of room if need be." She'd once been on a rescue where they'd recovered a group of eight hikers who'd become stranded in a snowstorm. Along with the standard crew of four, it had been cozy inside the helo that evening—cozy and joyous.

"Why aren't they going?" she asked, referring to the pumps.

"We were trying one and couldn't get it started when you showed up."

"Where are they?"

"In the cabin."

Aubrey removed her radio and contacted the helo. "The bilge pump is not working and is inaccessible at this point. I'm going to get a spare pump working. Requesting a boat from Cape Disappointment to escort or tow this vessel to port."

"Roger, that," Eli said. "Let us know if you need anything."

"I'll keep you advised." She clicked off.

"To port?" the captain snapped, wild-eyed and disbelieving.

"Yes, sir. This is only going to be a temporary fix. Your bilge pump is irreparable at this point."

"I don't think that's necessary. Can't we just use the spare pumps and have this one fixed when we get to our destination?"

"Unfortunately, no." Aubrey didn't have time to negotiate. "If I can get a pump working, you should be fine until the boat arrives. The pumps are in here?" She pointed, heading forward. She could hear the captain whispering heatedly to the crew as she entered the cabin.

The place was a mess, stacked with mildew-scented rain gear, coolers, boxes, bags and junk. Immediately in front of her on the floor was a pump, discharge hose attached; obviously the one they'd tried to get going. She picked it up and headed back out. "This will take a few minutes. Can one of you find the other while I get this one going?"

The two crewmen entered the cabin where she'd just been. She assumed they were going to retrieve the second pump. She placed the pump, secured the discharge hose over the side of the boat, and quickly connected the wires at the bilge pump fuse block. Turning back to see the pump working, something caught her attention off the bow. Coveralls and Bucket Hat were standing starboard and tossing something overboard.

Concern and irritation shot through her. "Hey," she called. "What are you doing?"

The captain emerged from the cabin and answered. "We were thinking it would be helpful to dump some of our heavier gear overboard. You know, make the boat lighter."

A blast of cold fear flooded through her as she looked at the crew, all three of whom were now staring guiltily back at her. The captain wore an insolent "What are you going to do about it?" expression. Coveralls looked ready to jump overboard. Bucket Hat stood off to one side, eyes darting around. She knew then that they had tossed something illegal, but she didn't know if it was guns or drugs or what. Certainly it was some kind of contraband. Her mind began to spin.

One woman—granted, one tough woman— against three desperate, possibly dangerous men. She knew she needed to proceed carefully here. Showing no fear, she pretended to buy their story.

"That's not necessary, guys. I know they show that kind of stuff on television, but in this case it won't help much. These pumps are your answer."

At least the captain had found the other pump. Working as quickly as possible, she set it up, wired it for power, and soon had it running. She waited a few minutes, checked the water level, and then radioed the helo.

"Two pumps are working and gaining ground. There's plenty of capacity. All should be well until help arrives, as long as the engine is running."

A quick conversation ensued with the captain, making sure he fully comprehended the situation. He said he understood and then informed her his crew was going to stay with the boat.

Aubrey looked at the two men. "Are you both comfortable with that?" She focused on Coveralls, who she could tell desperately wanted to go. He glanced at the captain, who was glaring daggers his way.

"Uh, yeah, I guess I'm staying."

"Okay, we'll be hanging around until your escort from Cape Disappointment arrives, just in case. We'll be in communication. If anything goes wrong, or anyone changes their mind, you let us know."

"Sure thing," the captain said. "Uh, thank you, Officer."

She called for the cable and headed out to the stern. After the hoist had lowered and the ground line hit the deck, she attached the hook to her V-ring and signaled to be brought up. As far as she was concerned, she couldn't get off of that boat quick enough.

After entering the helicopter, she donned the ICS and highlighted the events, including the part about the crew throwing something overboard as well as their odd behavior.

"Any clue what it might have been?" Gale asked.

"Negative. I was focused on getting those

pumps going. But something is shifty with this crew."

"We'll be here until the forty-seven arrives. If they're planning to dump something else, we'll be watching."

Gale then radioed the command center to fill them in. The Cape Disappointment guys were going to have a boat to inspect after they hauled it to port.

NERVE-RACKING DIDN'T begin to cover his reaction to the experience. Eli glanced at his aching hands, knuckles still white from clenching the controls. A sheen of sweat dampened his brow and his skin felt itchy. He'd never had a problem putting the mission first, but where Aubrey was concerned, all bets seemed to be off.

He knew very well how capable she was, how skilled every RS and the entire flight crew had to be. But that didn't help him in the moment. He'd spent the entire time she was deployed thinking about all the ways it could go wrong. He'd once had an army doctor tell him that after spending two tours as a medic in combat, he'd passed out while his wife was giving birth. He assumed he was experiencing a similar phenomenon.

At least she was safe now, he told himself

as he listened to her relay what had transpired on the boat below them.

The Coast Guard boat arrived and all he could think about as he flew the helicopter back to base was how much danger she'd been in. So many ways she could have been hurt or killed…

After landing and disembarking, Aubrey gave them a step-by-step accounting of her experience.

When she was through, she added, "These guys are shady. Something is not right. They don't know anything about boats." She explained how the crewman told her the boat had been leaking for a long time. "But the captain had no idea how to use the portable bilge pumps. They are not that complicated. They come with instructions. The whole experience was odd. I don't know what they threw overboard, but I'd be willing to bet it was something illegal. They claimed they were fishing, but there was no sign of that, no poles ready, no bait or gear visible."

"What else did you see?" Gale asked.

She gave her head an absent shake. "Besides a cabin that looked like the inside of a storage unit? These guys are slobs, I can tell you that."

"Tell me what you saw in there—exactly."

Eyebrows knitted, she brought a hand to her face, massaging her brow. "Um, let's see…coolers, boxes, duffel bags, a tool box, garbage bags…"

"Were there any wooden boxes or crates?"

She nodded slowly, analyzing the picture in her mind. "Yes…" she said. "There were a couple boxes that looked like fruit boxes or something. You remember, Eli—the boxes Mr. Quinley used for berries sometimes? With the top on them? Why would you ask that?"

Eli felt a rush of excitement and knew Gale must be feeling it, too.

Gale ignored her question and followed up with a few more of his own. "That's all we need for now. Nice work, Petty Officer Wynn."

Eli watched her walk out the door.

As soon as she was gone Gale said, "They were tossing drugs off that boat. What are the chances they got them all overboard?"

"We'll find out soon enough."

"I can't wait for the Cape D guys to get back with that boat."

Eli turned toward the window. His initial reaction to Aubrey being deployed was hard enough. That was before he realized she had likely been lowered onto a boat full of drug dealers. Lifting a hand to his jaw, he saw that it was shaking. He looked up to find Gale studying him with narrowed eyes.

"You okay?" he asked.

"Yeah, just tired."

"Tired?" his friend repeated doubtfully. "You're tired?"

"Uh, yeah," he drawled, feeling the knot of tension finally begin to unwind inside him. Aubrey was safe and that was all that mattered right now.

"I've seen you stay awake for thirty-six hours straight, take first place in the Candleman Triathalon, and come out looking fresh as a daisy."

Eli chuckled at the happy, pain-filled memory. He'd done that last year after he and Gale had spent two days on a volunteer SAR mission after some horrific flooding in Texas. They'd helped to evacuate thirty-six people trapped by floodwaters that weekend.

"What I have never seen you do is fidget while flying a helicopter. What was wrong with you up there? If I didn't know better, I would have thought it was your first solo flight. Ever."

"I was, uh—"

"You were worried about Aubrey. And now that you know she was lowered down there into a nest full of vipers, you are ready to lose your mind."

Eli stared, trying to think of something to say. Denial seemed pointless. Gale knew him too well.

"On that same track, I don't think I need to point out to you that we now have two boats with suspected involvement in drug trafficking where Aubrey has been the RS on both of them."

"I am aware of that."

"Good, because I'm afraid it's going to be an issue."

"Surely you're not suggesting that she's involved?"

"No." Gale pursed his lips as his head swayed to one side. "But…"

"But what?"

Gale met his steely stare with one of his own.

"It's a coincidence. Even if she was involved, how could she possibly know that those boats would get into trouble on her shifts? And why would she let us know they'd thrown drugs overboard if she was somehow involved?"

"She wouldn't *know* they were going to get into trouble. And she would mention it in case someone from the helo saw it, too.

If the drugs are gone, it doesn't matter what she says she saw. She'd be covering her butt at that point."

"Gale—"

"Look, I don't think she's involved, either. I'm just asking you to think about this. Johnston told me she basically does the scheduling for Nivens. She writes it up and he signs off. She could easily put herself down on the days when the drugs are being moved, as a precaution in case things do go wrong. Or maybe someone else is making sure she's on when they are being moved."

"Why would they do that?"

"I don't know. I'm just telling you the way it might look to someone else. Yeats, for example. She's going to be looked at, Eli, especially if Alex is involved."

A vein began to throb uncomfortably hard in his neck, and he made an effort to relax. He wanted to get mad at Gale, but there was logic here, too. If he were in his place, he'd be saying the same things. How long before someone else figured this out, too?

"Let's go get some breakfast while we wait."

They headed to the Boatsmen, a hole-in-the-wall café Gale had discovered in his quest to ingratiate himself with the locals. They'd just finished the Whaler's Breakfast—a delicious combination of eggs, sausage, peppers, onions and hash browns, all fried and served in one big heap with a dollop of country gravy on top—when Gale's phone rang. He picked it up.

"It's Cape D," he mouthed, indicating they were calling with news about the *Angela Sue*. "Yes, I'll make sure it's taken care of... Yes, we would... We'll be over there soon." He hung up and said, "Aubrey was right, wooden boxes found in the cabin. All of them empty, but what do you say we go take a look?"

IT WAS APPROXIMATELY a half-hour drive to Station Cape Disappointment, the Coast Guard's boat station located across the Columbia River in Washington. Within the hour Eli and Gale were examining the wooden boxes discovered in the cabin of the *Angela Sue*.

"It's not larch," Eli said, looking closely at the wood. "But the construction of the box looks the same. These were put together with an air gun, too."

Gale agreed. "Let's call Yeats. We can have the DEA use their forensic guys to examine them."

This was all the proof Eli needed. He knew there had been drugs on that boat. This was good from a professional standpoint. Chances were that this would reveal some clues that would get them closer to solving the case.

On a personal level, this was the worst possible news. Icy-cold tendrils of fear ran up his spine as he broke out into a sweat. What was he going to do?

Aubrey had been on that boat.

LATE THAT AFTERNOON Eli sat in his office and stared out the window. He'd made a decision. He didn't have a choice, really. He knew this was going to hurt. This might even rival the hurt he'd caused her twelve years ago when he'd broken up with her. He'd felt in his heart it was the right thing to do then, just as he did now. Apparently it was his destiny to hurt the only woman he'd ever loved. And not just once, but over and over again.

Frustration tore through him. He hated this feeling of helplessness. He wasn't used to it. He was the type of person who fixed things. The DEA would bring these guys in for questioning and hopefully get some more evidence. But in the meantime, he needed to do what he could. Regardless of Aubrey's reaction.

He knew Aubrey. No, he hadn't spent time with her these last twelve years, but he had spent time with her nearly every day in many of the preceding years and in the last couple weeks. He knew she wasn't involved in this drug ring. But, as Gale had suggested, he also knew how it might look to someone who didn't know her; like an awfully big coincidence. And if Alex was involved, it might look even worse for her.

There was only one way to keep anything like this from happening again. He picked up the phone and hit the line that would connect him to Daphne, the uncommonly efficient office manager assigned to both him and Gale upon their arrival.

She picked up immediately. "Yes, Lieutenant Commander. How can I help you?"

"You can connect me with Senior Chief Nivens."

He knew this was going to make it worse, but that couldn't be helped. He'd sacrificed their relationship once before for Aubrey's happiness. This time he was doing it for her safety. Because, in spite of what she maintained, she couldn't always take care of herself. Sometimes circumstances were beyond her control.

Thankfully, in this case, they weren't beyond his.

CHAPTER FOURTEEN

At APPROXIMATELY 8:00 A.M. the next morning Aubrey climbed out of the pool and picked up her towel. She hadn't seen or heard from Eli since the incident on the *Angela Sue* the day before. So when her phone rang, she grabbed it, thinking it might be him.

She had some questions for him regarding the crates he and Gale had asked her about. It hadn't escaped her notice that Gale had glossed over her inquiry. She knew better than to push it while they were on duty, but she intended to see if Eli could disclose anything off the record.

She answered only to discover it was Daphne letting her know that Senior Chief wanted to speak with her. She offered no clue as to what it might be regarding.

Huh. It wasn't unusual for him to contact her when she wasn't on duty, but it was odd for him to request a face-to-face meeting.

She planned to go to Nina's later, so to save time she drove to the base first before heading home to shower and change. Senior Chief was working his mechanical magic at a workbench when she found him.

"Hey, Senior Chief. Daphne said you wanted to see me?"

Senior Chief Wyatt Nivens looked up, an unreadable expression on his face. He had gorgeous brown eyes with lazy lids and lashes so thick it was difficult not to stare at them sometimes. This morning his sleeves were rolled back to reveal lean, muscled forearms smudged with grease. He was a gifted mechanic who resisted being promoted any further because he didn't want to relinquish control over the shop. He was also a super boss and an all-around great guy.

"Hey, Wynn. How are you doing?"

"I'm doing well, sir. How are you?"

He crossed his arms over his chest and shifted his weight from one foot to the other.

Nervous, she thought as he went on, "Good. I'm good. High winds in the forecast for tonight, but it sure is a gorgeous morning, huh?" He gestured out the window.

She squinted in that direction. In an overly enthusiastic tone, she agreed. "Yes, the weather is just delightful."

He gave her a sheepish grin.

"Seriously, why are we exchanging pleasantries and discussing the weather as if we don't see each other all the time?"

He seemed to study the ceiling somewhere above her left shoulder. "All right, Wynn, because..." He muttered something under his breath before finally making eye contact. "I hate having to tell you this."

Her stomach dipped. "Tell me what?"

"You're benched."

"I'm... What?"

"You're off the schedule."

"Off the—" Anger shot through her so fast and hard it made her breath catch. "I'm suspended?"

"Technically? I'm not sure. I'm sorry. Obviously you know this wasn't my call. Lieutenant Commander Pelletier—"

But she already knew who was behind it. "Am I being investigated for something?"

Nivens tucked his hands into his back pockets and shook his head. "I don't know. He didn't give me any details. He just told me that you were to be removed from the RS rotation—effective immediately. He's got some kind of special power right now and I..." He trailed off with a frustrated shrug.

Special power? Assessing SAR procedures didn't give him the *power* to remove her from duty like this. But she couldn't argue and she certainly couldn't react in front of Nivens. She couldn't let on how much this bothered her on a personal level. But she couldn't not say anything, either. "This is a mistake. I haven't done anything wrong."

He nodded. "I know that, Wynn. I reviewed the log. I talked to Johnston."

"Thank you for believing in me, Senior Chief."

"I'll do whatever I can to get you back on duty."

She marched to Eli's office only to find that he was gone. She texted him.

What's going on? Chief says I'm suspended.

She waited. A text came through almost immediately.

Sort of. I have some safety concerns.

Safety concerns? She studied the words. *He* has safety concerns. About what? She tapped out a question.

What does that mean? Am I being investigated for something?

I'll explain what I can later. It's more of a judgment call.

A judgment call? That could only mean *he'd* done this. Eli had made this decision without even talking to her. Without giving her a chance to defend herself. And defend herself against what? She didn't even know what she'd done wrong.

Her skin felt hot and tingly. She couldn't remember the last time she'd been this angry. Of course, if she had done something wrong, she'd expect to be called on it. But he'd clearly implied that he was responsible for the decision.

With her brain fogged over with a thousand questions, she headed home, trying to think this through. How could he do this to her? *Could* he do this to her? Obviously the answer to that was yes or else Senior Chief wouldn't have let it stand. She gripped the steering wheel tightly and forced herself to inhale a series of deep, calming breaths.

The Coast Guard was her life. Even when she was cleared to go back on rotation, this would surely leave a mark on her record. Even if it didn't go into her permanent file, people would remember. And they would wonder what she had done wrong.

After returning home and taking a shower, she was scrambling some eggs when her phone buzzed on the countertop. She picked it up and read another text from Eli.

I need to talk to you.

A cynical laugh escaped her. She said to the empty room, "You need to do more than talk, big guy."

Chewing her eggs, which felt like rubber in her mouth, she was trying to compose a response when he sent another.

I'm on base now. Can't talk here.

She stared at the display. What was that supposed to mean? That seemed as cryptic as Gale telling her they couldn't disclose what might have been in the wooden boxes. She knew this had something to do with the rescue yesterday, she just didn't know what. But something was telling her this was a whole lot more complicated than she'd been led to believe.

Her phone buzzed again.

Remember we have plans tonight. We'll talk then.

"Maybe," she said. "Then again, maybe not." She tapped out a message.

Will we be talking about how you made an error in your "judgment call" and I'm back on duty?

He responded immediately.

I can't do that.

Am I being investigated for something?

Tonight.

"Oh, now it's tonight, period. Sans question mark. Arrogant…" Fuming, she thought about responding with her own NO, period, or maybe even a NO, exclamation mark. Instead she headed upstairs and began shoving necessities into her duffel bag—toothbrush, underwear, socks… She'd already planned to spend the day with Nina. They were going to do some hiking. But now she was thinking she'd go ahead and stay the night. Eli would have to settle for his arrogant self for company tonight. She slung the bag over her shoulder, grabbed her hiking boots and headed back out to her SUV.

There was a reason why people who had a personal history shouldn't work together, she thought as she drove the miles toward Nina's, willing herself to calm down. She tried to think things through rationally. She started by trying to remind herself that Eli was just doing his job. But how could that be? There hadn't even been enough time to conduct an investigation. No one gets suspended or removed from duty or whatever he was calling it mere hours after a successful deployment. What job was he really doing here exactly? And what did any of it have to do with her?

She turned onto the picket-fence-lined drive leading to Nina's house. Even in her altered mental state she couldn't help but admire the flat-out beauty of the place; dormant fields stretching far on either side and the two-story, pale yellow house with white trim perched on the gentle rise. Two outbuildings had been painted with the same lovely scheme, while a big red barn sat farther back from the house.

As she closed the distance, she smiled when she saw that Nina had hung icicle lights across the front of the house. She was also glad to see her car parked in front of the garage. They'd made these plans a couple of days ago and Aubrey had texted before she'd left her house, but hadn't heard back. She'd hoped it was because her sister was working somewhere on the property and not because she'd forgotten and decided to go somewhere else. Although that didn't really matter at this point, because she was going to be hanging out here for a while, anyway. Unless she heard some very compelling reason from Eli not to.

The door was unlocked so she went inside. The house was silent. She called her sister's name. She didn't hear Marion's bark or the tapping of paws, so she assumed they must be outside. She headed out the back door.

Fifteen minutes later she'd checked every outbuilding, including the barn, and found them empty. As she walked back toward the house she scanned the horizon. She could see across the flat expanse of farmland for a long way. If Nina was out roaming the fields, she should be able to see her. Unless... Tamping down the bubble of worry spreading through her, she headed inside. This time she took a moment to study the surroundings. The kitchen still smelled like coffee. An empty oatmeal packet and unwashed dishes in the sink told her that her sister had eaten breakfast that morning.

Aubrey sent her another text. Hey, I'm here. Where are you?

The fact that Marion was gone, too, lent her an extra bit of comfort.

Then she spotted her pills. Nina had one

of those dispensers where you measured out your medication for the entire week. Today's pills were still in the container. Not once in all the months that she'd lived with Aubrey had she missed a dose.

Concern jolted through her, leaving her scalp tingling.

She noticed her hands shaking as she picked up her phone again. This time she dialed Alex.

"'Sup, buttercup," his deep voice answered on the second ring. Background noise told her he was at the marina. He'd been working on some kind of job down there lately.

"Hey, have you by any chance talked to Nina today?"

"Yep, this morning."

Yes. Good, she thought. "What time?"

"Um, let me check." Aubrey heard talking in the background and what sounded like a boat motor. "Just after nine. She said she was going to hike around her entire property to get a feel for the agricultural empire she now owns." He barked out a laugh. "Wait, are you there now?"

"I am, and she's not here. At least, I can't find her. Maybe she forgot I was coming…"

"No, Aubrey, she didn't." Alex's somber tone set her on edge. "She told me you were heading out there today. She was excited and planning to hike with you. Did you check outside?"

"Yes." Aubrey had been walking as they talked. "I've been all over, even the raspberry patch." She stepped into the master bedroom and froze in her tracks. The room seemed to tilt as she stared at the lovely ornate antique nightstand by the bed. She reached a hand out to the wall to steady herself.

It registered only vaguely that Alex was still talking. "Aubrey, are you there?"

She couldn't speak, couldn't take her eyes off the nightstand—more particularly what was lying on top of it.

"Aubrey?" Alex's voice shouted out of her phone.

"I'm here. Alex, I just found her phone. I'm trying not to panic." She explained about the medication. "What do I do? I'm not sure what to do. What if she went for a walk that turned into a hike? It's not really that far to the state forest. What if she went too far and got lost or had a seizure?" The property bordering Nina's was owned by the government and full of hiking trails leading up into the coast range mountains. Hiking trails—and rivers and cliffs and rocky bluffs to fall into or off of…

Crushing fear was squeezing her lungs. "I'm… I don't…" she wheezed.

"Aubrey, breathe, okay? Hold on. Stay there. I'm on my way."

She slumped onto the bed as the line clicked off.

But she didn't stay there. She sprang to her feet and started moving because she wouldn't find her sister by crying on the bed.

She began by checking the entire house one room at a time. Then she expanded her perimeter, starting with the barn because a few days prior Nina had been talking about getting some horses. Horses. Aubrey could only stare blandly when Nina had told her that one. "Trading in my sling-back heels for some boot heels," she'd joked.

Aubrey ignored the ominous creaking sounds coming from the faded gray ladder as she climbed up to the second story hay loft. Smelling vaguely of hay, she could see the space was empty save for two old bales and a few dozen fruit boxes tucked off to one edge where the roof sloped down from the peak. She stepped into the space and took a quick look around anyway. She counted six openings along the edge of the floor where it met the wall so hay could be dropped directly down into the stalls. Aubrey looked into each one. She returned to the ground floor, checked every stall, the old tack room and another space with floor-to-ceiling shelves that appeared to have been used for storage.

She moved on to the canning shed. The building was approximately twelve by fifteen feet. The stone walls were at least two feet thick, ensuring the inside stayed cool. It smelled like potting soil and was lined with floor-to-ceiling shelving. The Quinleys had left some canned goods. She was on her way out when something on the far side of the room caught her eye. The floor seemed to be uneven…

She approached the spot, bent down and discovered a rusty metal latch nearly flush with the floorboards, like a hatch. She reached out and pulled, surprised by how easily the door gave way. She swung it all the way and found herself staring down at a stone staircase leading into a pit of blackness.

"Nina?" she called, even though she knew her sister wouldn't be down there with the door closed. A shiver ran through her as she closed it.

She hurried back outside. The sun had wrestled its way through the clouds, mocking her with its cheerful brightness everywhere. She gave her eyes a moment to adjust and spotted a glint speeding up the drive. Alex, she realized along with a rush of relief. She jogged toward the house to meet him.

Them, she realized as three bodies emerged from the vehicle. Eli. Her heart soared with relief and gratitude, her worry for her sister trumping her anger and frustration with him.

Eli and Gale were already pulling their packs out of the trunk when Aubrey approached.

"Tell us what you know," Gale said as he adjusted the strap around his waist.

She didn't waste a second in relaying everything that had occurred.

After the recap, Gale asked, "Any idea or feeling where she might have headed? Anything she may have said in the last couple days that has stuck with you?"

"No. The fact that she didn't take her medication with her and left her phone bothers me the most. The house was unlocked, breakfast dishes still on the counter. Like she left in a hurry or… I don't know. I want to say it's not like her, but Nina can be a little impulsive sometimes… She is this unusual mix of creativity and free spirit combined with get-things-done. But she's also easily distracted."

"But no Marion?"

"No. No sign of either of them."

"Alex told us she likes to hike."

"She does. We had planned to go hiking this afternoon. I wasn't supposed to get here until around noon, so I'm hoping she headed out for a short hike and just got carried away and forgot her phone." And her medication, and to lock her door, and to do her dishes…

She smothered a fresh wave of worry. She needed to stay calm in order to think clearly.

Eli laid out his plan. "Gale, you and I are going to head east. The parking lot to access the Tyee Forest borders Nina's property. There are several trailheads there leading into the mountains that we've all hiked. Alex can walk the property lines and the creek. Aubrey, you can stay here in case she comes back and—"

"What? No! No way, Eli. I'm not staying here. I'll go crazy. I'm searching, too." He might outrank her at work, but she didn't have to take orders from him here, and especially not where her sister was concerned. "You might be able to stop me from rescuing other people, but not my own sister."

"Aubrey—"

She looked at Alex. "Alex, can you stay here?"

"Of course." He gave Eli a look that told

her maybe they'd had this conversation already. Which wouldn't surprise her.

Alex would know that she could never sit still in this situation. Of course, Eli should know that, too. It dawned on her then that he didn't know her. Not anymore. And she certainly didn't know him. Because the Eli she knew never would have suspended her without proof of some wrongdoing or tried to keep her on the sidelines where her family's well-being was concerned.

Eli sighed and gave her a curt nod. He clearly wasn't pleased, but he didn't waste time arguing, either. No one in this party needed to voice that, when a person went missing, time was of the absolute essence.

"When was the last time anyone spoke to her?"

"According to her phone, it was 9:04 this morning when she talked to Alex."

Eli punched some buttons on his phone and Aubrey knew what he was doing—noting the time. The police normally waited at least twenty-four hours before following up on a missing person. But she knew there were exceptions. One of them was when the missing individual had medical problems. Aubrey planned to play that card as soon as she could. She prayed she wouldn't need to.

"We won't be waiting twenty-four hours to call this in," he added, his thoughts obviously paralleling hers. "What about your parents? Have you told them?"

"No. They are in Seattle for a couple days visiting our aunt. Camile went with them."

He nodded. "Let's wait for now. Until we know…more."

"I'm going to get my stuff," she somehow managed to say.

She ran toward the house, unable to hold back the tsunami of fear now threatening to swamp her. As she gathered her gear, she allowed the sensation to run through her, willing it to pass quickly. It did, but the force of it left her shaking. She regularly and knowingly jumped from helicopters into frigid water, was lowered onto sinking boats in twenty-foot swells, and recovered stranded hikers from the edges of cliffs while dangling from a cable, but never once, in all her years of being an RS, had she experienced this degree of terror.

CHAPTER FIFTEEN

THE THREE MEN stood in the driveway and watched Aubrey disappear into the house. Shifting into his SAR mind-set, Eli assessed the conditions. A bank of menacing gray clouds out over the ocean was creeping toward them. It felt like rain; the air was heavy and thick with moisture. But the wind was Eli's biggest worry. The weather report said a storm was moving in from the west with high winds predicted, seventy to eighty miles per hour and gusts of 100 plus.

As if to underscore his concern, a breeze ruffled his hair and sent some wind chimes tinkling madly in agreement from their home on the porch. Winds that most other places excitedly referred to as "hurricane force" were common along the Oregon Coast, and usually referred to by locals as "pretty windy." But most folks also knew to hunker down when a real windstorm was coming. Because winds like this regularly toppled hundred-foot trees, brought down limbs and knocked out power. It was no time to be out hiking.

"Do you really think this is a good idea?" Gale's question interrupted his thoughts.

He knew Gale wasn't referring to the weather. He was talking about Aubrey. Eli knew it wasn't smart to allow the family member of a missing person to search with him.

"No, but what choice do I have here? She'll go off by herself if I don't let her come with me. Then I'll have two women to worry about."

Alex chimed in helpfully, "He's right. She will. I'll stay here. I don't mind."

Gale nodded, looking grim. He didn't know Aubrey well, but he'd probably learned enough by now to believe what they said.

Eli could see his concern for Nina mixed with his anxiousness to get going. "You take Alex's route. If we don't find her in the next three hours, I'm calling Grady and have him bring his dogs."

"Who? What kind of dogs?" Alex asked.

"Grady Royce, he's a friend of mine. He trains dogs, mostly companion and search-and-rescue dogs. He's the guy I got Marion from."

"Oh, um…" He scratched his chin. "Yeah, that would be good."

Aubrey emerged from the house carrying her backpack, strapping it on as she hurried toward them.

A couple hours later he and Aubrey had zigzagged their way across Nina's property. They'd discovered no sign of her and no fresh indication that a person or dog had been through the area in quite a while.

They scaled a fence, jumped the ditch and emerged onto a road. They walked to where it ended at a gravel parking area. A large sign read Tyee Forest Trails with a colored map outlining a series of hiking routes you could embark upon from that location.

He called Grady, who he learned was on an SAR case in South Bend. He agreed to head this way when he'd wrapped it up. He'd just hung up when he received a text from Gale.

Call me.

He tapped on the screen. Gale picked up on the first ring. "I'm back at the house. I've got nothing. No tracks. No one has been through there recently except for some deer." It had been raining on and off for nearly a week, so fresh tracks should be easy to spot. "Where should I go from here? I mean, if she was going to walk her property lines, it would make sense that she'd stay along the fence line. Unless..."

He continued talking while Eli watched Aubrey walk around the parking lot, questioning people and showing Nina's photo. A young couple descended one of the trails into the parking lot. She approached them. After a moment she handed her phone to the young man. Nodding, he appeared to study it for a few seconds before passing it to his companion. Aubrey retrieved her phone and exchanged handshakes with the couple. She turned and jogged his direction.

Gale was saying, "When I got back to the house, I started looking for anything that might give us a clue as to where she went. Alex has been doing the same. We've been careful." He didn't need to say that specifically they'd been careful about tampering with anything that could possibly be evidence. "Now I'm looking at some aerial photos. They are older. They were in that big notebook she's been packing around. The one Quinley gave her?"

"Yeah."

"The photos show that there's another building on the property. It's quite a ways from the house, but Alex says he thinks it's part of the original Quinley homestead. Probably not much there anymore but a pile of stones. He thinks there's an old orchard there, too. Ask Aubrey how likely she thinks Nina would be to go check out something like that by herself."

"I'll ask her, but I can tell you right now I think the answer is yes." Nina and Aubrey were alike in that way—adventurous. Aubrey was fearless when it came to herself, even as she worried about others.

She stopped before him and he filled her in.

"Yes," she said, her head bobbing before he'd even finished explaining. "We have to cover every base. She knows it's there. She's mentioned it to me. I told her I would go with her. She seemed focused on getting the house shaped up first, but you know Nina. She gets a whim and off she goes."

Eli agreed and said into the phone, "Go ahead and check it out."

He explained about Grady and hung up. Aubrey hurriedly informed him, "That couple I was talking to thinks they might have passed Nina on the trail. She was headed up toward Daisy Vale Lookout. We need to head that way. Nina loves the lookout. We've hiked to it dozens of times. And they have this book where you can sign in with the date and time.

She loves to do that, and see who else has been up there."

"Why do they think it might have been her?" He knew how unreliable eyewitnesses could be. Makeup, a different hairstyle, smile, no smile—even clothing could alter a person's perception. He knew very well how hopeful people could get with even a hint that their missing loved one had been spotted. Even with her SAR training, Aubrey wasn't immune to this. She was too close. He reminded himself that he would be the same way if Aubrey were the one missing.

"I showed them her picture. The guy says he thinks yes, the wife says maybe. He said the woman they passed wasn't very tall, and his wife agreed. Nina is tall, but..."

He approached the green, late-model crossover SUV the couple had climbed into. He quickly confirmed what Aubrey had said, and gathered an additional important detail.

"You're sure the black-and-white dog with her was a border collie?" he asked the woman.

"Positive. I grew up on a sheep farm outside of Roseburg. We had border collies my entire life. At first I thought it was an Australian shepherd," she said. "Then I noticed the tail—black with a white tip."

Eli nodded, waiting for more.

"Border collie tails aren't docked," she supplied.

But he was already convinced. In his experience with search and rescue, eyewitness information was different where dogs were concerned. Because people who loved dogs usually remembered them better than they did people.

WHY HADN'T SHE thought to ask if the woman had had a dog with her? Aubrey's pulse was racing. It had to be Nina. But why wouldn't she have taken her phone? If she'd forgotten it, surely she would have noticed by now and headed back. Especially since she knew Aubrey was coming out to see her...

She forced herself to calm down and listen to Eli's questions. The way he asked them seemed to elicit more details. Ones she hadn't thought about. Apparently this woman was wearing a green scarf and carrying a camera. She was struck by the thought that he'd make a great detective.

He seemed to be wrapping it up and Aubrey was ready to take off when the man offered another fact, this one not nearly as helpful as the others. "You guys know about the weather, right?"

"What about it?" Eli asked.

"Rain and a high wind warning."

"Yeah, thanks," Eli said. "Heard about that. We've got our rain gear. Hopefully, we'll be out before those high winds kick in."

"That's good," he said. "The trail is washed out in some places. It depends on which way you head at the fork, but it can get a little dicey in spots if you decide to head up to the lookout."

It went without saying that "dicey" didn't scare either one of them. They thanked the couple and started up Daisy Trail. The path followed Daisy Creek for two miles before it veered east and looped around the base of a large monolith. It met up with the creek again where you could either continue to Daisy Creek Falls or cross a suspension bridge that would take you deeper into the Tyee Forest. Backpacking country, Aubrey thought, which meant enough gear to stay overnight in the woods. No way Nina would have taken off for the night without telling her. Although she knew at this point she needed to rule things out with evidence as well as her thoughts.

They stopped to put on their rain gear because along with the wind, droplets of rain were now falling. The path up to the lookout was long and considered steep for most hikers. Nina enjoyed the challenge, often grousing good-naturedly at Aubrey when they reached the top because she would be barely out of breath while Nina would be struggling.

Aubrey glanced up. She'd been okay, relatively, up to this point. Because she'd been moving. Doing. Solving this problem. But now the familiar trail suddenly looked daunting and felt ominous. What would she do if something terrible happened to Nina? She'd never be able to forgive herself. She'd known it wasn't a good idea for her to move out to the farm by herself and...

Next thing she knew Eli was standing in front of her, his hands lightly gripping her elbows. "Aubrey? Are you okay?"

She tried to swallow but her mouth was too dry.

"Let's take a second."

Tears boiled behind her eyes but she managed to contain them. He handed her a water bottle. How did he know what she needed? He always seemed to know what she needed. She took a drink.

"I'm fine. We need to get going. We need to keep moving..." She heard her voice crack and tried to cover it with a cough.

Before she could protest, his arms were

around her, holding her tight. "We'll find her," he said, his breath warm in her hair. He sounded so positive.

"I want to believe you," she whispered. "I do. It's just that… None of this makes any sense to me. Nina can be impulsive but she's not stupid. She's actually really smart and I… Eli, I am so scared."

She knew she should move away from him, but she couldn't. It felt too good to be wrapped in this cocoon that he had created for her, if only for a minute or two. Her anger at his removing her from duty didn't compare to the love she felt for her sister. Besides, here he was, helping her, searching with her. That was enough for now.

THEY CHOSE THE route based on what the couple had told them. The woman who might be Nina had mentioned the lookout, so they headed that way. The rain was now falling in fat, pelting drops. Fog had formed in reaction to the cold wind and visibility was severely limited in places. They moved much slower than she would have liked. The trail was muddy and slick in places and the guy in the parking lot had been right—they had to skirt around a few spots where the footing had washed away. In places, Aubrey could see the cliff plunging off to their right. Every step took them up, increasing the distance, and the potential fall, to Daisy Creek below.

It seemed like days before they finally emerged into a small meadow. The old cedar-planked cabin was just ahead. Before she could run around Eli and sprint the remaining distance, he stopped and turned to face her.

"Don't fight me on this. I'm going to go inside and look around. Stay here."

He took off before she could argue. The fear crept over her again, weighing on her with the force of a million pounds. She knew why he didn't want her to go with him—what if Nina was in there and…not okay.

Despair nearly overwhelmed her. She considered letting her tired body sink to the ground. Instead she forced herself to study the area, looking for any sign that Nina or Marion had been there. Walking back and forth across the grass, she analyzed the tracks. There were canine prints, but she quickly realized they were much too large to belong to a petite border collie.

The remains of an old fire sat at one edge of the clearing. She could make out a half-burned Graham cracker box among the gray, soggy ashes. Not long ago, someone had been having fun here, roasting marshmallows and making s'mores. Not looking for their lost epileptic sister…

Eli came out of the cabin. He held his phone up to his ear and seemed to be looking for her. She wondered if he was talking to his dog friend or to Gale or Commander Pence or worse…

His eyes latched on to hers. He lifted a hand and headed in her direction, but she couldn't read anything on his face.

"Perfect. Thanks, Gale. Yeah, I'm going to tell her right now." He clicked off the phone. "Nina's been found. She's fine. I mean alive, but…"

She bent at the waist and placed her hands on her kneecaps. *Alive.* Her head felt light as relief blasted through her. *Wait…* "But?" she repeated.

"She's mostly fine," he amended quickly.

The words felt like a brand-new punch to the gut. "What do you mean 'mostly fine'?"

"She's alive. Injured, but alive."

"Injured? Where is she?"

"She's at the hospital. Gale found her."

"Found her where? Hospital? How is she injured?" She could hear her voice all shrieky and shrill. "What aren't you telling me?"

"She was in a car accident. She's in and

out of consciousness. She has a head injury, a fractured wrist and some broken ribs. They're checking for internal injuries, but it's her head that they're most worried about."

"Where? Where did he find her?"

"He decided to walk along the road. He heard barking and spotted a pickup over an embankment. Any idea why she would she be driving a pickup?"

Aubrey lifted her hands to squeeze her now-throbbing temples. "She mentioned she was going to buy one because that's what farmers drive, but she hadn't told me she'd bought one yet. Probably planning to surprise me. I'm getting really tired of her surprises, by the way. In and out of consciousness?" A bout of nausea threatened.

She paused to swallow it down. "Head trauma can be a trigger for seizures. Was she wearing her epilepsy bracelet? Is there any sign she had a seizure? Who is with her? Where's Marion?"

"Yes, she was. Marion was lying beside the pickup. That's how Gale knew… The neurologist hasn't seen her yet. Gale and Alex are both there. Alex called your parents. They're on their way home. Apparently, Camile is already in Pacific Cove. A friend picked her up in Seattle this morning and she's on her way to the hospital. And Marion is with Carlisle and Heather."

Aubrey's entire body started to shake. She began nodding as she thought aloud, "Okay. Okay, that's good. Camile will stay with her until I can get there. Let's go. We need to get going."

She took a few determined steps toward the trail. Eli reached out and placed a hand on her shoulder.

"Aubrey, I don't think we should."

"What do you mean?"

"It's already getting dark. We both heard the weather report. This wind is going to get way worse before it gets better. Way worse. Gusts of one hundred miles per hour plus are possible." He gestured around them and she realized the light was already waning. "Trees are going to blow over and limbs will be falling. If that happens at the wrong moment while we're on that ridge trail?

"Our best bet is to stay here in the cabin until it passes. It's dry in there. We have plenty of food and water."

As much as it pained her, she knew he was right. Even now, she could feel the force as the wind shoved and jostled her backpack. She could hear it howling and snapping branches in the surrounding trees. Although… They were both extremely fit. She had a headlamp in her pack and a powerful flashlight. And extra batteries. She chewed on her lip and tried to think this through. It was the first time she'd ever questioned the logic of her search-and-rescue training.

Eli stepped closer, threading a hand around the back of her neck. "Hey," he said. "Look at me."

She did.

"I have my phone. We have service. I have a portable charger. If anything changes, Gale or Alex will call. There's nothing you can do for her right now." Something in his tone, in the feel of his hand on her skin, managed to soothe her. His next words convinced her. "And there won't be anything at all you can do for her if you try to hike out of here and get injured yourself.

"Let's just rest and eat something. We'll see how it looks in a few hours, okay?"

She gave him a reluctant nod and he led the way to the little cabin.

Eli was right. It was dry and significantly warmer out of the wind. Aubrey removed her pack and took off her rain shells. She gave the jacket a shake and stretched it, along with her pants, over a broken chair lying on the floor. She rummaged in her pack for her spare fleece top, which she slipped on over the layers she already wore. As she settled on the floor, her back against the wall, she realized how exhausted she was. Why was emotional fatigue so much more draining than physical hardship? A half-mile swim in the freezing surf was nothing compared to this.

She watched Eli rustle around for several minutes, no doubt checking every nook and corner for anything that could be useful for them.

"What are you doing?" she finally asked.

"I'm going to light us a fire."

"Where?"

He gestured at the little potbellied wood stove in the middle of the room. "Here. Then I'm going to fix us some soup."

She couldn't help but smile at his optimism. "What are you going to burn? Everything is soaking wet."

"Energy logs." He pointed across the room. "I'm guessing park staff or hikers stashed them in anticipation of a repeat visit. They probably won't be happy we're using them, but I think this officially constitutes an emergency." He added an eager grin and said, "I have chicken noodle."

Aubrey didn't argue. A warm fire and a cup of something hot sounded like heaven on earth.

CHAPTER SIXTEEN

GRATEFUL FOR THE tinder he kept in his pack and the dry cardboard box someone had left in the cabin, Eli soon had a hot fire burning in the wood stove. He kept an eye on Aubrey, but couldn't read much in her expression. She was good at keeping her feelings contained. Coast Guard training would do that to a person. Any military training helped with that. And Aubrey had always been skilled in that area, anyway.

As a teenager, he hadn't even known that she'd had a crush on him. Not until his own feelings had welled up to the point where he couldn't stand it one second longer. He knew exactly when things had shifted for him; the first day of school his senior year. Aubrey had been a sophomore. Somehow over the course of the summer between ninth and tenth grade she'd turned into this…this siren.

Walking down the hall, he'd been looking for her to tell her he'd arranged his schedule so he could have study hall with her and

Alex. And he'd seen it—her—standing by
her locker. Tall, with those long, toned legs
encased in snug jeans, she'd been laughing,
talking to a friend. As he'd neared her, she'd
turned and smiled at him and he'd been struck
by her beauty. And he'd already known her,
worshipped her in a way, and knew the inside
was even better than the outside.

Problem was, it seemed that every other
guy suddenly saw her, too. He'd made it his
semisecret mission to thwart every romantic
attempt by his peers. The scheme had been
semisecret because Alex had helped. They'd
agreed that no one was good enough for her.
Eli had kind of included himself in that notion, not wanting to admit his crush to Alex.

He'd managed to keep his feelings under
wraps until Christmas Eve that year. He still
remembered what she'd been wearing that
night; a silver dress, fitted at the waist, with
tiny, delicate straps over her swim-sculpted
shoulders. The skirt had swirled around her
knees, shimmering at her slightest move.
She'd worn her hair up, silver threads intri-
cately woven into a complicated twist. El-
egant, he remembered thinking, like some
kind of Christmas angel. He remembered
marveling over the fact that she rarely wore

fancy clothes, yet when she did she pulled it off like a veteran on the red carpet.

When he'd found her alone downstairs in the family room at the St. Johns' house, he hadn't been able to help himself. He'd kissed her by the Christmas tree. Expecting shock, possibly even a slap, he'd been overjoyed when, without hesitation, her hands had slid around his neck and she'd kissed him back.

Those months they'd been together had been the best of his life. Of course, he'd been young. Too young to realize how just wanting something—or someone—wasn't enough. There were those things that happened in life that made your own wants and needs take a backseat. There were also those things that completely and entirely obliterated them. That's what fate had done to them. He hoped that wasn't happening again now with this investigation. Had he done the right thing by removing her from duty?

He had planned to tell her tonight. As soon as he'd called Nivens, he'd known he was going to tell her. He was going to tell her about the investigation, leaving out their suspicions about Alex for the time being.

Studying her now as he waited for the water to heat, he could see the sadness tugging at her features. It killed him to think that he'd probably contributed to it, even though he knew she was focused on Nina right now. He had to believe she would understand why he'd done it.

"Soup's on," he said as he handed Aubrey a steaming cup.

"Thank you. Can't believe you managed this. Mmm, delicious," she added after taking a sip.

"Amazing how dehydrated vittles can taste like a five-star entrée under the right conditions. Something to be said for keeping these search-and-rescue packs updated, right?"

He was treated to a warm smile. "I, for one, am grateful for your anal retentive behavior."

He chuckled as he retrieved his own soup and settled on the floor beside her. He'd taken three sips when his phone buzzed in his pocket. He fished it out and studied the display. "Message from Gale." He read it quickly. "Good news. Camile is there. And…the neurologist said she has an excellent chance of making a full recovery."

Aubrey squeezed her eyes shut and kept them closed for a few seconds. Eli imagined he could see a bit of the worry lift from her weary features. She opened her eyes and asked, "Is she awake?"

Eli tapped out the question and hit Send.

They waited in silence until the phone buzzed again. "Not right now. She's been in and out. She doesn't remember much from the accident, but the doctor says that's normal after what she's been through combined with the pain meds." He reached over and gave her knee a gentle squeeze.

Aubrey nodded slowly, as if absorbing it all. She hissed out a long breath.

"She's going to be fine, Aubrey."

"You don't know that, Eli. You do know how much I despise platitudes, though." She softened her words with a sad half smile. "I appreciate you trying, though. I really do."

"I do know the second part. And, as for the first—you know I wouldn't do that. If I didn't believe she was going to completely recover, or if I doubted it, I would say so. But the circumstances, including the information we have from the doctors at this point, are telling us that she will, in fact, eventually be fine."

She patted his hand. He was pleased to hear her chuckle, hoping this meant her worry had lessened to a degree.

"Finish your soup."

"Don't boss me. We're not on duty."

"Please finish your soup. You—we—need our strength."

Keeping her eyes glued to his, she raised the metal cup to her lips and drained it.

"Thank you," he said, his own lips twitching with humor. "Do you remember the time we went camping with Alex's family over by Sun River in eastern Oregon?"

Laughter erupted from her along with a shake of her head. "Still can't believe they called that camping. I love the St. Johns, but a six-bedroom cabin on the Deschutes River with a hot tub is not camping. Remember how we brought all our backpacking stuff? You had your propane burner and I had my new water filter, and we both brought sleeping bags?"

"There was maid service."

They reminisced about the camping trip that had turned into three days of playing tennis, shuffleboard and swimming at a nearby resort, and how Alex hadn't bothered to inform either of them that they'd need something suitable for a dinner at a five-star restaurant.

"We went shopping, but we couldn't afford anything from those boutiques."

"Hey, you rocked that dress we found at Second Time Threads or whatever that place we finally found was called."

"Second Time Around," she corrected in a

wistful tone. "The clothes in there were more expensive second-hand than what I usually had new."

He grinned. "I was all set to wear my cargo shorts and baseball T-shirt, but you wouldn't let me."

"And you were glad."

He tipped his head back and rested it against the wall. "I was. You were always looking out for me."

She tucked her chin and looked at him over her shoulder. "That worked both ways," she said softly.

He considered telling her about the investigation but quickly changed his mind, not wanting to add to her burden right now. As soon as they got back and she could see for herself that Nina was okay. Then he would tell her.

"I hate that it's dark already and we have hours to kill. I'm going to go crazy."

He went to his pack again and began digging around. "How about a rematch?"

"A rematch?"

"Alex and I were talking about how you used to beat us at that game." He joined her again and held out a deck of cards and a flashlight. "Now that I'm a skilled helicopter pilot who has been repeatedly promoted for all my awesomeness, I think I can beat you."

"Ah, speed trap. Yes, of course I remember."

"That's it, speed trap. Couldn't remember the name."

She swept her palms together eagerly, "Bring it on, Lieutenant Sloth Hands."

A FEW HOURS and innumerable card games later, Aubrey rightly declared herself the champion.

"Well, you might be a passable helicopter pilot, but you still can't play cards."

"Winning three games out of fifteen against you makes me a champion in my own mind."

"I suppose we all need to be winners somewhere, huh?" she teased.

The wind was still bombarding the little cabin, rattling the windows so forcefully a few times she wondered if they would hold. He stowed the cards and returned with a small fleece blanket that he draped over them both.

Aubrey resisted the urge to scoot closer to him. She longed for the comfort she knew he could provide. But she also knew, when it was all said and done, that it wouldn't change anything. It would just be a temporary fix and one that would end up messing with her head. Again. And she'd already gone too far down that road with him as it was.

She focused on Nina, trying to send good vibes her way. That was something Nina would do—the vibe thing. Aubrey was so anxious to see her she could barely sit still.

She could do this. She was strong. She'd always been the strong one in her family, her sisters and her mom relied on her emotional support. She was the one who always kept it together. She was also the one who moved, who acted, who problem-solved and who made bad things better. Somehow, she promised herself, she would make Nina better.

"Stop fidgeting." Eli wrapped an arm around her and pulled her close.

"You—"

"Don't argue, please," he urged. "Just try to get some sleep. I will wake you when the wind dies down."

"I'm too tired to argue, but this doesn't change the fact that I'm mad at you."

"Believe me, that's not something I can forget."

"Eli—"

"Aubrey," he interrupted, suddenly sounding tired himself, "we will talk about your... temporary break from duty later, okay? I will explain the situation as best as I can as soon as I can. Just get some sleep."

"How am I supposed to sleep after that cryptic comment?" she asked grumpily. "You and Gale are like a couple of spies lately."

His answer was to hold her tighter. But then he sighed and said, "You know what? You're right."

"I am?" she asked brightly.

"Yes. I realize how difficult this must be for you. So, for now, I can promise you it's not as bad as you are thinking. You didn't do anything wrong and you aren't in trouble. But, the underlying situation that forced me to make this decision is also probably worse than you're thinking. That's all I'm going to tell you right now. Trust me. Please. Believe me when I tell you I had to do this."

A part of her wanted to badger him for more information while another was relieved to hear even that much. Still another was irritated that he hadn't told her that from the start. Although, she supposed he might have been trying to when he was texting earlier. Or he was going to tell her when he saw her, but then Nina… Yes, Nina. She closed her eyes and refocused on those vibes for her sister.

She finally drifted off. She didn't know how many hours she'd slept when she awoke

CHRISTMAS IN THE COVE

to discover that she was clinging to Eli like a desperate vine of ivy. She was lying mostly on top of him, chest to chest, her cheek resting near his shoulder. She stayed still a moment, listening to the slow, hard thump of his heart.

In the ensuing hours, he'd somehow managed to scoot them both down onto the floor. He was using a portion of his pack as a pillow while she'd apparently used him as a mattress. Her muscles were screaming in pain, so she knew his had to be, too, since his body was also absorbing the cold hard floor.

Moving slowly, careful not to wake him, she attempted to push herself up with one arm. Realizing her arm was asleep she shifted her weight more evenly. That hurt, so she brought up one knee, transferring some of her weight there. Essentially holding a one-armed push-up with Eli beneath her, she was deciding the best way to stand when his arms tightened around her.

"Good morning," he said, his voice thick with amusement.

Her eyes darted to his to find his amused blue eyes staring into hers. His mouth was curling with a smile.

"How long have you been awake?" she asked flatly.

"Long enough to enjoy this little yoga routine you've got going."

She released her arms and let her weight fall on top of him.

He whooshed out an "oomph" along with a chuckle. She sat up and glared at him.

"You slept." He sounded pleased.

"Apparently. What time is it? Has there been any news?"

"It's four-thirty. Nina is awake. Or she has been awake enough to talk."

"That's great…" But something in his tone, in his expression, didn't sit right. "Isn't it?"

"There's something I need to tell you."

"What?"

"The police are coming in to talk to her later this morning."

"The police? Because of the accident?"

"Yes," he answered.

"Well, that's normal, right? Any time there's an accident, the police get involved…"

He raked a hand through his hair. "Nina said, and the police believe, that her pickup was forced off the road."

"It… What?" The cabin began to spin before her eyes. The sensation reminded her a lot of the time she'd been hit by a piece of driftwood on a training mission. The initial pain was different but the aftermath was the same. They both left this confusing bout of fuzziness.

"What are you…?"

"She says a big SUV came up fast behind her while she was driving. It sped up till it was beside her, turned into her and forced her vehicle off the road. She hit the brakes, but there was a patch of gravel and she slid over the embankment."

Aubrey began shaking her head. "This makes no sense. Why would someone want to hurt Nina?"

"I have no idea. But Gale said she's mentioned Doug's name."

"Why would he try something like this now? They're divorced. They both have plenty of money. Even before it was final Nina told me that she'd removed him as the beneficiary on her life insurance policy. It doesn't make any sense. He wouldn't be that stupid, would he? I mean he would know that people would suspect him. If they knew he was in town and Nina got hurt."

"How well do you know him?" He handed her a protein bar.

She ripped it open and took a bite, chewing thoughtfully. "Not that well, really. He visited Mom and Dad with Nina a few times after they were married when I was there. He

was charming and polite, but also kind of…
smug. Like he was better than us provincial,
working folk, yet amused by us at the same
time. He's really pretentious."

"So you two were close?" he quipped.

"Very," she said with fake enthusiasm. She
finished her protein bar and downed a bottle
of water. Then she added, "I think there was
physical abuse along with the mental. Nina
never said for sure, but…sisters can sense
these things. Needless to say, no one was
heartbroken when they divorced."

She watched Eli tense as she relayed this
information.

"Poor Nina," he said tightly. "I had no
idea."

"It was worse than any of us knew. I've
learned a lot this past year and pieces are still
coming out."

She pulled her pack on over her shoulders.
"Ready?"

CHAPTER SEVENTEEN

ALEX WAS WAITING in his Range Rover when Aubrey and Eli emerged at the trail head. They climbed in and he headed straight to the hospital while he filled them in on Nina's condition.

"Your mom and dad arrived last night, but I'm so glad you're here. Nina's been asking about you."

Aubrey understood. She'd be asking for her sister, too. There was something irreplaceable about sister love in certain situations. Life-threatening injuries fell into this category.

"How is she?"

Alex let out a chuckle. "Tougher than boiled bat wings, as my grandmother used to say. And bossy. But, you know, it's in that Nina way. She's not mean. She's just...specific about her demands. One of those repeated demands has been for me to bring you to the hospital."

"Feisty. I feel like that's a good sign."

"Feisty? Feisty doesn't quite cover it. She

ordered Gale to go pick you up in a helicopter."

She laughed. "That's our Nina Nothing-is-Impossible Wynn."

Alex glanced over at her, his expression sobering. "I need to warn you about something, though. The doctors say that she looks even worse than she is, and she looks really, really bad. I mean like someone beat the living hell out of her."

Aubrey hadn't even thought about how she might look. It was thoughtful of Alex to remind her.

A short time later she rushed into the hospital room to find her parents and Camile seated around Nina's bed. Her parents moved back to let her in, and as she closed the distance, she realized that Alex's warning was more than thoughtful. It was practical and it kept her from crying out.

Horrible didn't even begin to describe her sister's state. Her face was so swollen Aubrey might not have recognized her, the skin discolored in innumerable shades of blue and purple. A long line of stitches ran across one side of her forehead and up onto a strip of now partially shaved scalp.

Aubrey reached down and held her hand. "Nina?"

Her eyes fluttered open. "Aubrey." Her name came out along with a choked sob.

"I'm so sorry that it took me forever to get here. Stupid windstorm. How are you feeling, sweetie?"

"I hurt. I'm not going to lie. They're generous with the pain meds, but you know how sick they make me."

"I do." She dipped her chin and tried desperately not to cry as her eyes traveled over her sister's bruised, stitched and battered body. "You'd be a terrible drug addict. No self-respecting junkie wants to hang out with someone who pukes every time they try to get high."

Nina let out a sound—part laugh, part groan. "Don't make me laugh. It makes me hurt all over, especially my ribs. Camile has been doing that, too."

Aubrey smiled. "I'm sorry. I'll try not to. But that's one thing we have in common, huh? Making each other laugh." She reached out and tucked some hair behind her ear. She found a spot that was less discolored than the rest and lightly caressed her brow there. "For the love of…" She sighed. "Why are you so busted up, sister of mine?"

She mumbled something.

"What?"

Aubrey felt her mom squeeze her shoulder as she said gently, "Aubrey, don't…"

"Don't what?" she asked even as her stomach took a plunge.

"It's okay, Mom," Nina said. Aubrey thought she might be wincing, but it was difficult to tell with her face so messed up. "I wasn't wearing my seat belt."

"Oh…" Aubrey resisted the urge to react. "Well, that explains why you look like a pile of rotten hamburger."

"Aubrey!" she heard her mom gasp.

She heard her dad chuckle as Camile burst out laughing. Nina giggle-groaned again and then her face formed what was clearly a grimace. "Ouch, I told you not to do that."

"Sorry," she said loud enough for their mom to hear. She dipped her head and kissed Nina on the forehead. She lowered her voice and whispered, "Not sorry. We'll talk about that stroke of idiocy later. Right now, I'm just so, so glad you're going to be all right."

Nina heaved a sigh as her eyes fluttered closed. She seemed inordinately relieved by Aubrey's response. She knew she could be rigid when it came to certain things—important things like matters of safety.

She thought about the conversation with her mom, that black-and-white thing. Did decision-making and strong opinions make a person judgmental? It broke her heart to think her sister had been lying in a hospital bed fearing that she'd be mad at her because she hadn't worn her seat belt.

Camile rose from the chair she'd been sitting in and stood across the bed, so Nina was between them. She looked at Aubrey and said, "She's been so keyed up waiting for you to get here. Every time she wakes up, she asks where you are and when you're getting here." She reached down and caressed Nina's puffy cheek with the backs of her fingers. "I feel like she'll be able to rest now."

"I hope so."

They stayed where they were for a long time; two sisters listening to the soft sound of their big sister's breathing while the beeping of the machines assured them she was alive.

THE WYNNS ESTABLISHED a pattern of sorts over the next few days. Their mom and dad would take the overnight-till-morning shift, Camile would come in late morning and stay through lunch, while Aubrey took the afternoon-till-evening shift. This gave her time to work out in the mornings, teach her swim lessons and help with Marion. Poor dog. Aubrey and Camile had been keeping her close.

The police had determined that Doug hadn't been involved in the accident. Nina didn't even remember mentioning his name. The doctors said it wasn't unusual for someone with a head injury like she'd suffered to make statements that didn't have any bearing on the accident. But that they could be a manifestation of other fears brought out by trauma.

Forensic analysis did confirm her report that a vehicle had run her off the road. They'd found paint transfer and a broken turn signal lens. The police seemed to favor the notion that it was kids fooling around. There had been several reports of vandalism along that same stretch of highway in recent weeks; mailboxes destroyed, driveways torn up, even some items reported missing.

On the fourth day, Aubrey walked into the hospital and headed to the café to fetch Nina a container of her favorite Greek yogurt. As she entered the cafeteria, she saw Eli sharing a table with an older man. So sweet that he and Gale had visited Nina almost every day. It was the only time she'd seen him in the last few days and they hadn't yet had a chance to talk about her suspension.

She walked over to say hi and it wasn't

until she was almost upon them that she recognized the man.

"Mr. Pelletier? Hello! Eli didn't say you were for sure coming home for Christmas. Well, I guess this isn't home for you anymore, is it?"

Already on his feet, he engulfed Aubrey in a huge hug. "Hi, sweetheart. Eli didn't know. I told him I might make it on Christmas day. Then a big fishing party that had me scheduled for the entire week canceled. A buddy of mine works for one of the airlines, so I headed to the airport hoping without much hope I'd get on a standby flight. But I'll be darned if it didn't work out and here I am."

Aubrey was smiling. "I'm so glad you did. I hope you'll be able to make it to the St. Johns' party tomorrow night." She couldn't believe Christmas Eve was the next day. They were planning to release Nina in the morning. Even though she would have to miss out on the party, at least she wouldn't have to spend the evening in the hospital.

Something occurred to her then. "Why in the world are you guys having dinner in the hospital instead of a restaurant?"

"Also my fault. I rented a car at PDX. I called Eli when I got on the road and asked him what was going on. He said he was here, and filled me in on what happened to Nina. I pulled in here and surprised him."

"He sure did," Eli said with a warmth to his tone. "He just got here about an hour ago."

Aubrey felt bad about interrupting. "Well, I'll leave you two to—"

"Actually, I'd like to talk to you, if you have a few minutes? Dad is going to go up and see Nina. Your mom and Gale are upstairs with her right now."

"She would love that," Aubrey said. "She's getting so bored. A sure sign, I think, that she's ready to get out of here."

Tim hugged her again and left the cafeteria.

Eli motioned for her to have a seat.

She did and, without pausing, he said, "There are some things I'm going to tell you that you're not going like, and that you're probably going to find very difficult to believe."

EVEN AS HE spoke the words, Eli wondered if he was doing the right thing. Because instead of telling her part of it, now he had to tell her everything.

"As you've probably suspected, Gale and I aren't really here to evaluate rescue procedures."

Her head tilted as her brows drifted up. It

was more a sardonic look of confirmation than one of genuine surprise. All that was missing was a sarcastic "no kidding?"

"We are part of a joint task force with the DEA and the Coast Guard..."

Aubrey listened silently as he recited the details of their assignment. From the look on her face, she hadn't expected anything quite so dramatic.

"Wow," she said when he stopped talking, giving her a moment to absorb it all. "I knew something wasn't right. When I found you guys in the file room and you wouldn't tell me..." She trailed off thoughtfully.

"I couldn't tell you, Aubrey. We couldn't tell anyone."

Her face formed a thoughtful scowl. "Obviously. I understand that. So, why are you telling me now?"

Inhaling a deep breath, he plunged ahead. "There's more. I believe, and Gale concurs, that Alex might be involved."

"What? Alex? *Our* Alex? Are you out of your mind?" The shock didn't surprise him. He hadn't expected anything less. He was still having a difficult time believing it himself.

"I know this is hard for you. I'm still struggling with it myself. You know that I value his friendship as much you do."

"Then how can you...?"

He explained about the wood from the crates.

"So? That doesn't mean he's the one making them or using them."

Her thoughts were mirroring his and Gale's. He understood that she needed time to absorb the information. "He is, Aubrey. We found crates in an outbuilding at his company headquarters this morning. What we don't know is the extent of Alex's role in the operation—yet." The wood didn't match, but the construction did, right down to the nails that had been used. In a stroke of brilliance, Gale had thought to bring a sample of the nails with him from California.

"Maybe someone stole the crates."

"Who would steal wooden boxes?"

"I don't know. A drug dealer maybe?"

"That seems unlikely."

"So does Alex's involvement," she shot back.

"I know." He ran a tired hand across his cheek.

"How are you going to figure this out?"

"We're going to keep digging and we're going to watch him. The DEA is sending some agents to help us with surveillance." He glanced at his watch. "They should be here anytime. All we can do is hope that his involvement is minimal."

"He would never do this. He must be doing someone a favor. He's probably giving the boxes away or something. There's no way he knows anything about any drugs."

"That possibility has occurred to me," Eli conceded, knowing he had to be careful about the way he responded. "That his big heart may have gotten him into some trouble."

Her anguished expression had him wishing he could take her into his arms and make it all better. But he couldn't. Not yet, anyway.

"There's something else."

"What?"

"About your suspension."

He watched a range of emotions play across her face as the realization sank in that she wasn't being investigated.

"If you're not here to evaluate us, then I'm not being investigated for safety violations… So, why am I suspended?"

"Like I told you before, that was my call."

"I got that part," she said dryly. "But why?"

"For your safety."

"My safety?"

"Yes, we also have reason to believe the *Respite* as well as the *Angela Sue* were involved in drug transport."

ALONG WITH THE shock of what Eli was telling her, several other revelations crystallized in her mind at that moment. None of them good.

"So," he said when he finished, "you can see why I didn't tell you any of this."

Aubrey stared into his earnest blue eyes and tried to decide which of the numerous issues to address first.

"No," she countered much more smoothly than she was feeling. "I can see why you didn't tell me *part* of this, which includes the details of your assignment and Alex's alleged involvement. And I say alleged because he's not involved, Eli. There's no way. I can't believe you could even think he would do something like this. I can't believe you would think this about our friend."

"But you can see that I had no choice, right? To remove you from duty? With the kind of danger you were in?"

"Wow," she drawled sarcastically, "you must be shocked that I've managed to survive the last twelve years without you."

"Aubrey—"

She felt like her head was going to explode with the way her pulse was throbbing in her temples. "Let's talk about these choices you say you didn't have. How about the one where you could have chosen to trust me? Or the one where you…oh, I don't know, chose to believe in me? In my abilities and my judgment as a highly trained and skilled rescue swimmer?"

He looked baffled by the notion.

Anger flamed to life inside her, anger that she now realized had been smoldering since she'd learned the details of their breakup. Eli had been protecting her then, too, and deciding what she should and shouldn't know. Making decisions about her life and what was best for her, all without ever consulting her. And he'd done it again. Even after she'd specifically asked him not to.

That was the worst part. That's when another realization hit her, and it hit so fast and hard she could barely take a breath.

This was never going to work.

She and Eli could never work. He didn't trust her, not in the way she needed him to. And, clearly, he didn't respect her, not really. Not professionally. The fact that he'd removed her from duty because *he* wanted to protect her? That was proof. And it was also so… presumptuous.

Not to mention high-handed and…arrogant. "You can't just relieve me from duty to protect me from some imagined danger you think I may or may not be exposed to."

He frowned. "Yes, I can."

"No, you can't. And if you don't reinstate me immediately I will go to Commander Pence, or the DEA, or your buddy, Admiral Schaefer…or someone. I will go to them all if I have to and file complaints. This is unfair and wrong on so many levels."

Now he was starting to look frustrated, too. "This isn't about me believing in you and your abilities or whatever it is you're thinking, Aubrey. This is about me trying to protect you."

"Why didn't anyone else get suspended?"

"What do you mean?"

"What about Johnston and Oliver? Jay was involved in both of those rescues, too. Why didn't you remove either of them from duty?"

"Because—" He stopped himself and she thought he might finally be getting the idea.

She answered for him, "Because it's me. This is personal."

He didn't argue so she went on. "We haven't even discussed the fact that I am needed here in my position. I save lives, Eli. That's what I do and I'm good at it." Disappointment and frustration clogged her throat, but she forced it away. "It's what I live for. I seriously believe it is what I was put on this earth to do. It's not right for you to keep me from doing my job because you *think* I might be in danger. I know you think you're keeping me safe, but you're crushing my spirit in the process. What about all the other lives that might be in danger out there on the water every day? Lives that I could help save?"

"But you *are* in danger right now," he countered softly. "And I... I can't handle that. If something happened to you, I would never forgive myself. Especially considering where we've been heading. I've been hoping that we...that maybe we were starting over again."

As she stared into those gorgeous blue eyes brimming with honesty and sincerity, she felt some of the tightness loosen inside her. Because that statement was incredibly...sweet. His desire to protect her was kind of endearing, as well. She would want to protect him, too, under certain circumstances. She wanted to protect her family. She wished she could have protected Nina. It managed to deflate some of her anger. But only a little because it didn't change certain facts.

"That's never going to happen if you don't trust me, if you don't believe in me."

He threw his hands up. "I don't even know what that means. I don't see how my wanting to keep you safe means I don't believe in you."

"Well, then, you need to think about this.

I am in danger every single day in this job and you know it. Boaters get drunk, boaters use drugs, they get mean, some are just stupid or unprepared and, yes, some of them are even criminals or murderers. I never know what I'm getting myself into when I go out on a rescue. None of us do. But I am no different than any other AST. And I shouldn't be treated any differently."

Now he looked defensive. "But—"

"Fix this," she said. "If you really care about me, you will fix this. You will give me my life back, Eli."

Folding his fingers together, he dipped his head onto them as if in prayer. After a few seconds he met her gaze again. "Fine. I'll have Nivens put you back on the schedule, but I don't want you giving Danny Cruz swim lessons anymore, taking her out for coffee, going bowling, or just generally hanging out with her at all until this is over."

She met his glare with one of her own. "Are you kidding me?"

"No, I'm not. The West family is involved in this, too. We just don't know to what extent and exactly which family members."

"So, what, you think Danny is a drug dealer, too? Or wait, maybe she's Alex's right-hand girl?" She knew she sounded snarky, but clearly the situation called for it. He was being paranoid and ridiculous.

"No, I don't," he returned patiently. "But I do think there's a chance Brendan might be, or he may know something—something that could get him hurt. Or worse."

"Worse? What is this, an episode of some cop show? People are getting killed now?"

"People get killed over drugs every single day in this country. You know that. The Coast Guard deals with it all the time."

"Eli, this is Pacific Cove, Oregon!"

"Come on, Aubrey, you are not that naive. In the short time Gale and I have been here, we've spent a lot of time out in the community. You wouldn't believe some of the stories we've heard. Some of the crimes people in this town have committed. I've talked to—"

"You're right. I'm not. Because something else just occurred to me, too. You and Gale? All the Santa, chef's hat, crab cooking, do-gooder, elf-juggling crap? Helping out with the contest and stuff? That was all for the investigation, wasn't it? That's why you guys have been so social and so curious about everything. And Gale charming everyone in town?"

She paused and then let out a gasp. "And

you, with the bowling and Danny and Brendan…"

"No, Aubrey. I…"

She narrowed her eyes menacingly, daring him to deny it.

"I mean, yes, some of it may have had a dual purpose, but I still would—"

"A dual purpose? I am such an idiot." She laid a hand on one flaming cheek and let out a dry laugh. "I thought you were doing all of that for me."

"Will you please let me explain?"

"By all means. Explain. I would love to hear an explanation counter to the one I'm sitting here thinking."

He looked surprised, opened his mouth, closed it. Then opened it again and offered a measly, "Please, try and understand this from my perspective…"

She barked out a harsh laugh. "That's the only perspective there is as far as you're concerned, isn't it? In pretty much everything you do, it's your way or nothing."

Gathering her bag, she slipped the strap over her shoulder and stood. "Even if you're right about the drugs and the danger and the Wests and the…the…stupid crates." She couldn't even bring herself to say Alex's name in relation to Eli's outrageous theory about their friend.

"You can't protect me, Eli." She leaned over so her face was only inches from his. "You. Can't. Protect. Me. And, you know what? Even if you could, I wouldn't want you to. Whatever this—" she flapped a hand between them "—is, was, whatever that we *were* doing? Now we have a name for it. It's called *over*."

He looked miserable—angry and hurt and disappointed. Well, too bad. So was she. But she couldn't care about that right now, not for him and not for herself. What he'd done was wrong. His heart might have been in the right place, but his actions had been way off base. And those actions had hurt her so very badly.

CHAPTER EIGHTEEN

GALE CAME THROUGH the door on Christmas Eve while Eli was putting the finishing touches on his project.

"Well," he said, resting his hands on his hips and surveying the mess now covering nearly the entire surface of the dining table. "Looks like someone has been spending a little too much time on Pinterest, huh?"

"Funny," Eli said as he glued another string on the knight-shaped game piece he'd found. He dropped it. "Ouch, this hot glue gadget gets really, really hot. Have you ever used one of these? There's a reason why they call them glue *guns*. I'm pretty sure the military could weaponize them." He gestured at the ornaments scattered across the table. "What do you think?"

"It looks good, I guess... It's an interesting theme, that's for sure. 'Under the Sea' meets... Medieval Times? Is this for the tree I saw in the back of your pickup? All these years I've known you and this is the first I'm seeing of your crafty side. I've gotta say, I'm liking it. Any chance I could put in an order for a tea cozy while you're at it?"

Eli grinned as he peeled some dried glue and burned skin from his thumb.

Gale picked up the mermaid tree topper. "Pretty."

"I know," he said. That had been a score. "It's an angel mermaid. I had no idea they even made them."

"I didn't know such a delightful creature even existed," Gale commented dryly.

"It's for Aubrey. She'll understand. I'm taking all of this over there tonight before the party, after she leaves for Nina's, and setting it all up."

After a sleepless night of agonizing about what had happened with Aubrey and how it had all gone wrong, which he still didn't quite get, he'd set about trying to figure out how he could make it right. And then it had hit him.

He'd taken off early in the morning on a shopping trip. He'd never been so happy about quirky beach shops in his life. The mermaids had been no problem. They were everywhere. The knights had taken some innovation. With an inordinate amount of help from an enthusiastic saleswoman at the craft store, he'd purchased what he needed and then some. He'd stopped at Ike Clairmont's tree lot on the way home and picked up the tree. He couldn't believe it when he'd found the nearly perfect blue spruce sitting in the corner of the lot behind an overly bushy Shasta fir. Blue spruce was Aubrey's favorite.

"Okay, but why don't you just take it to her now? Decorate it together? Chicks love that kind of thing."

"She's not talking to me. Well, she's not talking much." After three phone calls and an embarrassing number of texts, she'd replied with a single response.

Please stop. I can't talk to you right now. Have fun with your dad at the Christmas Eve party. I'm spending the night with Nina.

That last part had stung. He'd been looking forward to spending Christmas Eve together again at the St. Johns'. He may have been fantasizing about re-creating their first kiss by the Christmas tree.

Gale winced. "I take it you told her about the investigation and Alex?"

"Yes, there's that. And, it didn't take her long to guess the ulterior motive for our, um, enthusiasm with the contest. She thinks we were only helping out because of the investigation."

"Sorry." He made an apologetic face. The community-involvement angle had been his idea.

"It's okay. It was a good idea on more than one level. The worst part was when she realized why I removed her from duty. She can't understand how I did it for her own safety..." He trailed off with a shake of his head. "I don't know. She totally overreacted. She said it's over. I refuse to accept that. As soon as she's had time to think about it, she'll understand. This tree will remind her why I did it."

"Mmm..." Gale's tone was doubtful. "Maybe."

"What do you mean 'maybe'? I had the power to keep her out of danger. Why wouldn't I use it?"

Gale nodded slowly and heaved out a breath. "You know, for someone as brilliant as you are—you're an idiot when it comes to women."

"What do you mean? No, I'm not. I..." He probably was. Since his first breakup with Aubrey, his focus had been on his career. Life in the Coast Guard usually meant moving every couple years, anyway, which would mean a relationship would take more effort than he'd been willing to give. Until now. "You're saying you wouldn't have done the same?"

"Nope, buddy, I wouldn't have. Not even a little bit."

"But—"

Gale lifted a hand and interrupted. "Hold on. Think about it this way. You're on duty in the middle of a huge storm. A call comes in, Aubrey is your superior officer, and she's the one handing out assignments. You're supposed to be piloting, but she calls you off because the storm is too big and scary and she's afraid you might get hurt. You're saying that would be okay with you?"

Eli stared at his friend as he recited the ridiculous scenario. "This is different."

"How? Danger is danger. Who are you to decide where or what the most danger is? Look at what happened to Nina. I don't think farming is exactly a high risk profession and she's the one who ended up in the hospital."

"But…" Eli froze as the implications of what he'd done sank in. The Coast Guard, flying—that was his life. It was more important to him than anything—anything except Aubrey. He'd do whatever he could to protect her and keep her safe. But in trying to protect the most precious thing in the world to him,

he'd taken away the most important thing to
her. How could he have been so shortsighted?
Because he loved her, was the answer that
immediately sprang to mind. Gale was right.
Aubrey was right, too; just because he loved
her and wanted to keep her safe didn't mean
he could. Not always.

"Uh-oh." He scrubbed his hands over his
tired cheeks and mumbled under his breath,
"I think I seriously messed up."

"Yep. You did."

Even after the conversation about their
parents, where she'd told him he shouldn't
make decisions about her life without consulting her, he hadn't really understood. Sure,
he'd come to realize that's exactly what he'd
done in that situation. And it had been easy
to say he wouldn't do it again. But when the
time had come for him to make a similar
decision—this one about her safety—he'd
plunged head-on right into the same mistake.
No, not the same. This one was even worse.

"I have to get her back, Gale. How can I
convince her to give me another chance?"

Gale pointed at the table. "This seems like
a pretty good start."

"I hope so," he said with absolutely no con-
viction. Because he felt none. His shopping
trip, the hard work, the tree, seemed paltry

now when weighed against the magnitude of his screw-up.

Gale let out a chuckle. "Listen, you can't give up." He moved around the table, taking a seat across from Eli. "Yes, you royally messed this up. But it's not a lost cause. I've seen the way she looks at you, the way she talks to you. She gets all soft around the edges. She doesn't talk to anyone else like that. Except her sisters, and they don't count because they're women and related."

"Thank you for the pep talk, coach. But I need some specifics."

"What I'm saying is, it might take more than one *tree*, so to speak, but the main thing is to show her that you respect her. That you have faith in her intelligence and judgment. And that you believe in her skills. Just like you would with a colleague. One that you don't want to...well, you know, always keep safe or whatever."

She'd said that, too. Of course he had faith in her skills. He always had. He thought she was the most amazing person in the world; intelligent, courageous, strong, athletic, kind, funny... He felt lucky to even know her. Her very existence on this planet ensured his happiness. That was obvious. Wasn't it? Why else would he try so hard to protect her?

"I'm guessing that you guys aren't going to the Christmas Eve party?"

"I'm still going. Dad wants to go. Nina isn't up to it so Aubrey is going to spend the night with her out at her place."

"Speaking of Nina… If you want to stop feeling sorry for yourself, I'll give you my news now? It might cheer you up."

Eli picked up the hot glue weapon and waved him on.

"You're not going to believe this, but the pickup Nina was driving? She bought it from Alex."

His focus returned to Gale. "No way."

"Yep. Don't you think it's odd that in all this time, and in all the conversations we've been having, this hasn't come up?"

The implications were obvious, but could it be that simple? Could someone have been after Alex instead of Nina? It made sense. If he'd lost not one but two drug shipments to the sea, that could conceivably anger someone awaiting drugs or payment. The windows were tinted on the pickup. It would be an easy mistake to make.

Another pressing question occurred to him. "Why hasn't Nina mentioned it?"

"I have no idea. But I think we should ask her, don't you?"

"I do." He glanced at his watch. "You have time to run out to the farm before the party."

Gale winced. "I was afraid you were going to suggest that."

"You don't want to do it?"

"I do. It's just that Nina…she is…"

"Well," Eli said, sitting back and crossing his arms over his chest. "This is a first. And after all your sage advice about women."

"Yeah, believe me, I know. But… Nina is different. She doesn't like me."

"What do you mean she doesn't like you?"

"It seemed like I was making progress before the accident, but now it seems worse. We've been going backward."

Eli belted out a laugh. "Now you are cheering me up. A woman who doesn't like you?"

Gale was shaking his head. "It doesn't matter what I do or say, she just gives me this steely look and says, 'Stop trying to charm me, Kohen. Your pretty words won't work on me.' Then I don't know what to say… I've never been tongue-tied in my life, but somehow she manages it. She, uh, she intimidates the hell out of me."

"Well, you know her ex was a first-rate charmer who turned out to be an abuser, right? And from what the doctors say, this ordeal seems to have caused some of that old trauma to resurface. That might explain some of her, um, reluctance."

He watched the play of emotions on his friend's face and thought, *Uh-oh*. He wouldn't want to be Nina's ex and run into Gale in a dark alley. "I knew she went through a bad divorce, but I didn't realize…"

"I didn't, either. Aubrey told me a bit about it when we were up in the cabin."

Gale went to change and returned a few minutes later wearing a suit and a grim expression. He picked up his keys. "I'll meet you at the party. We are a pair, aren't we? Going on about our business just fine for years and now both of us suddenly and totally distracted by the women in our lives?"

"At least it's not Rocky Road and peppermint schnapps." Aubrey handed Nina a plate containing a sourdough bowl filled with steaming-hot seafood chowder. Apple slices and a chunk of Nina's favorite sharp cheddar from Cove Aged Cheeses rested on the side.

"Lucky for me, Lily is open on Christmas Eve, huh?"

"Hey, I could have fixed something. Granted, it wouldn't have been nearly this good, but I could have done it."

"You're missing the party and midnight mass. I feel terrible."

"Please don't feel bad. I don't want to go to the party anyway." She really didn't. She wasn't ready to see Eli. The thought of spending Christmas Eve at the St. Johns' where they'd shared their first kiss just depressed her further. "And don't worry, I can go to mass with Mom and Dad tomorrow night."

They both turned toward the front of the house as a thumping sounded from the porch. Marion leaped to her feet and let out a woof.

"Good girl," Aubrey encouraged. "Do you think Gale forgot something?" Gale had been leaving just as Aubrey arrived.

She got up to check it out, but the door opened before she could get there.

"Merry Christmas Eve!" Camile came in and stood on the entry rug, soaking wet, blond curls dripping. She removed her jacket and hung it on a peg by the door. "It's really coming down out there."

"What are you doing here? Why aren't you at the party?" Nina asked.

"Because my sisters are here. I didn't really want to go anyway. And after I realized Mom didn't really care if I went with them, it was a no-brainer. Is that seafood chowder from Tabbie's? Please tell me there's more?"

"Yes and yes. We're so excited you're here."

Aubrey went into the kitchen, fixed another plate and brought it into the living room. She handed it to Camile.

"Thank you. Is Eli coming? I'm not eating his food, am I?"

"Um, no-oo," Aubrey drawled, settling herself on the other end of the sofa. Nina was in the recliner; the only place she could manage to sit somewhat comfortably with her cracked ribs.

Aubrey looked up to find both of her sisters staring expectantly at her.

"Oh, I thought you two were, um, you know…?" Camile scooped up a bite of chowder and blew on it.

She sighed, knowing it was pointless to avoid the subject. These were her sisters, after all. The two people who knew her better than anyone else. Eli not included because…because he didn't know her like she thought he did.

"I don't know. Maybe we were there for a second. But it won't work. He's just… We're just… We're better off just being friends."

Nina set down her glass of tea. "He's just what?"

"He's…controlling."

"Controlling? Eli?" Nina returned doubtfully.

"In a manner of speaking, yes."

Camile tore a piece of sourdough from the edge of her bowl and dunked it in her soup. "What manner is that?"

Aubrey thought of a way to explain without explaining. "He's always done this thing where he *saves* me and *protects* me. He tries to swoop in and help me when I don't need it. He thinks he knows what's best for me, so he sort of makes decisions on my behalf and…"

Her sisters remained still, waiting, confusion on their faces as they no doubt wondered what in the world she was getting at.

"You guys, he removed me from duty because he thought I might be in danger."

"Were you?" the ever-intuitive Nina demanded. "Are you in some kind of danger?"

She shrugged. "My job is dangerous. You guys know that. He thought he had reason to believe that there might be some…extra danger involved. So he had me removed from the schedule."

Camile let out a gasp. "How dare he?" she asked in a sarcastic tone. "How dare he care about you in that extreme manner? Unacceptable. It's almost as if he loves you or something."

"Camile, it's not that simple."

She winked at her and slipped a chunk of bread to Marion who was sitting politely at her feet. "I'm sure it's not to you, Aubrey, but it sounds pretty simple to me. All I know is that you've got yourself a man like Eli and he cares that much about you. I would love to have that."

"What did she say?" Eli asked Gale after he arrived at the party.

"She said it didn't occur to her to mention it."

"In her state I think I can buy that. But what about Alex? Why hasn't he mentioned it?"

"My thoughts exactly."

"If you're guilty of something, I can see how this would be a tough one. Saying something could arouse suspicion while not volunteering the information does the same."

"If it were me, I'd take my chances and not mention it. And it almost worked. The police didn't even ask her where she bought it or how long she'd owned it."

Eli's gaze found his dad across the room where he was deep in conversation with Alex.

This was such a nightmare. Having to bust his best friend. Alex was good to his dad, too, just like he was to everyone else. Even visiting him in Florida a few times. From three thousand miles away, he'd helped his dad find the best boat for his charter business for the best price.

His dad turned and Eli saw a flicker of that old sadness on his face. He met Eli's gaze and smiled—and just as fast it was gone, leaving him to wonder if he'd imagined it.

He shook his head. "Poor Nina. I feel like the police have been convinced from the beginning that these juvenile delinquents out fooling around wrecked her on accident. One of the officers told me he's just waiting for the tip to come in, for one of the boys involved to get a case of the guilts and tell a friend or a girlfriend and someone makes an anonymous call."

Gale added a sigh. "And the holidays just complicate things even more. The DEA guys told me it's so quiet on Alex's property, it's like no one is even working there."

"They're not. His business is shut down until after the new year. He mentioned that earlier tonight. I'm still hoping we'll get lucky and someone will show up at his warehouse or his shop and lead us somewhere else."

"So what do we do? Do we ask him about the pickup? Tell the police?"

"Let's tell Yeats and see how he wants to handle it. This might be enough for a warrant."

CHAPTER NINETEEN

CHRISTMAS MORNING, AUBREY checked her phone as she let herself into her house. Plenty of time to run an errand at the base, go for a quick swim, come back home to shower and change and get over to her parents' for the afternoon. She'd spent a lovely morning with her sisters. Camile had fixed breakfast and they'd chatted about life as they lingered over coffee. And she'd tried to decide how she was going to handle Christmas dinner with Eli and his dad in attendance.

Talking with her sisters had made her think. Made her wonder if maybe she was being too hard on Eli. Sure, when she said it out loud, it did sound simple. His extremely protective nature, for lack of a better term, could be viewed as less controlling, more selfless, perhaps even romantic by some standards.

Except, she had worked so incredibly hard for her career success; harder, maybe even, than some of her peers, because she was a woman. Respect from within her profession, from her peers, meant everything to her. She couldn't have Eli, or anyone else, undermining that. Just the thought of her teammates finding out what he'd done made her go cold with terror.

But, on the other hand, when she thought about why he'd done it… As Camile had pointed out, the thought that he cared about her—loved her—that much and…

And why were there lights twinkling in the corner of her living room? A Christmas tree? A blast of happiness shot through her. Her first thought was Nina, but there was no way her sister could have pulled this off in her condition. Her mom? But as she stepped closer and took in the ornaments adorning the branches, she knew it could only have been Eli.

Colorful mermaids were interspersed with shiny silver knights; mermaids with flowing hair and sparkling tails. Knights, one with a coat of armor, another on horseback wielding a lance and shield. Where in the world had he found them? The mermaids she could understand. They lived in a beach town and were surrounded by beach towns. Every shop on Mission Street probably had a mermaid of some sort for sale. But the knights…?

Her eye was drawn to one knight on bended knee, his helmet in hand, a flower in the other. He seemed to be offering it to a smiling blond-haired mermaid lounging across the branch above. She reached out to touch it and that's when she realized the fastener had been glued on.

She removed a knight on horseback and examined it closely. Gobs of glue and fuzz were sticking here and there. She turned it over and realized he'd turned game pieces into Christmas ornaments. She placed a finger on the tip of the tiny lance he held and felt it pierce her heart.

Impulsively she slipped the ornament into her pocket. If only it was this easy to constrain Eli's protective nature, she thought. How nice it would be to simply put it in her pocket and take it out as needed.

THE BASE WAS quiet on Christmas, just like she knew it would be. Men and women were at their posts, of course, because people and boats didn't stay out of the water just because it was Christmas. But training missions were halted for the day and lighter than normal duties were assigned.

She let herself into the records room and headed for a group of file cabinets in the far corner. Personnel files were always locked, but she had a key. She knew she could probably get into trouble for what she was about to do, but she had to know.

A quick perusal and she found herself standing in front of the drawers where last names starting with *P* were housed. After unlocking the cabinet, she quickly located the file she was seeking: Pelletier, Timothy J. She pulled out the thick packet of papers, opened it up and began to read.

THREE HOURS LATER, her morning tasks accomplished, Aubrey walked through the door of her parents' house. Her mom met her in the entryway.

"Merry Christmas, Mom."

"Merry Christmas, sweetheart. Let me take those for you." She relieved her of the platter of sliced vegetables and yogurt dip she'd brought.

"I'm early, but I thought I'd give you a hand. I know the kitchen is usually Nina's domain, but since she's out of commission, I thought I could fill in. Where's Camile?"

"How thoughtful. Thank you. I would love some help. Camile is upstairs wrapping gifts. Nina will be here in an hour or so with Gale—bless that man's heart—he has been so good to your sister. He and Alex both. Your father is in the den watching football. And Eli and Tim aren't here yet."

Perfect, Aubrey thought. She had time to ask her mom some questions. She followed her into the kitchen. "What can I do?" She pointed at the sink full of potatoes. "Peel?"

"Yes, that would be wonderful."

They chatted while they worked. Aubrey tried to decide how to formulate her questions without giving too much away. "Mom, do you remember when Tim Pelletier got transferred?"

If she hadn't been watching from the corner of her eye, she would have missed the slight pause as her mom sprinkled salt over the now peeled-and-chopped potatoes resting in the large pot of water. "Yes?"

She lowered her voice. "He was the man you fell in love with, wasn't he?"

"Yes. But we never acted on it. I want you to know that."

Aubrey smiled at her mom. In an effort not to spread her black-and-white opinions around quite so freely, she said, "You mentioned that before and I believe you. And it wouldn't be my business if you had. I'm sorry to get so personal. There's a good reason I'm asking, I promise."

"Well, that's okay. I'm the one who opened this can of worms, aren't I?"

"I think it was time for the lid to come off anyway. Believe it or not, this all affects Eli and me, too."

Susannah nodded slowly and Aubrey could see she was trying to make sense of that. "You have to understand, honey, I was very unhappy there for a while. You girls were getting older and busy with friends and activities. As you should have been, but I was alone a lot. Your dad was…working all the time. He was never home and I was terribly lonely.

"I think if I hadn't fallen for Tim, it would have been someone else. He just happened to be around a lot. The feelings I had seem rather silly now. Tim was going through a tough time, too, and needed someone to talk to. I think he knew in his heart that what we felt wasn't real. I mean, he'd seen your father and I when we were happy. And those two were best friends."

She understood. Along with her and Eli, most military people felt that way; friendship was a bond, a brotherhood or sisterhood that could feel as strong as family. Like the way she felt about Alex. And Eli, too, for that matter. Right now, and in light of what she'd learned on base this morning, Aubrey was wondering just how tight it had been between her dad and Tim? Why *hadn't* her father been home?

"After Tim's transfer, things got better. Your dad seemed to come around. He started staying home more, paying more attention to me again. I realized that my marriage, my family, had to be what I made it. We fixed some things, worked others out, and now we're happier than we've ever been."

"I'm so glad, Mom." And she was. She almost had all the confirmation she needed. A quick trip up to the attic should do it. What to do with the information was another question altogether.

A bark announced the next guests as the front door opened. "Hey, we're here," Nina called out. An excited Marion pranced into the room ahead of a shuffling Nina, who had hold of Gale's arm. Camile came down the stairs, her arms weighed down with wrapped gifts.

Merry Christmases were exchanged all around. Gale helped Nina get settled in the cushy overstuffed chair by the fireplace. Marion curled up on the seat beside her.

Aubrey and Camile were arranging the gifts under the tree when a knock sounded on the door.

"Perfect timing," her mom said. "That would be the Pelletiers. The prime rib is done. Camile, will you go tell your father we need him to carve the roast?"

DINNER WASN'T NEARLY as bad as Aubrey expected. With lively conversation and enough food to feed an army, there were plenty of distractions.

Eli was his usual courteous and charming self, without being overly solicitous toward her. She appreciated his efforts and marveled at how light the atmosphere seemed. She knew simply from what was going on inside of her own head, and what she knew about each person seated around the table, that there were probably plenty of reasons to scrap the merry in Christmas in this year. But no one did.

Aubrey loved that.

After the meal, Dad offered to show Tim the latest geode he'd discovered while out rock hunting in Arizona. They meandered off toward the den.

"Enjoy your cigars," Susannah called after them.

Brian chuckled and waved as Gale and Marion helped Nina get settled in the living room. Her mom and Camile disappeared into the kitchen.

"Are you still mad at me?" Eli asked when they were alone at the table.

"I'm trying not to be," she answered without hesitation. "Thank you for the tree. It's beautiful and perfect. You have always been so good at knowing me and what I like. I can see how hard you worked on it, and I am overwhelmed that you would go to those lengths for me. I couldn't have asked for a better Christmas gift."

She hadn't realized he was nervous about it until she heard his relieved sigh. His shoulders relaxed as his big hands spread across his kneecaps.

At his next words she nearly caved.

"Does that mean you forgive me? You can forgive someone and still be mad at them, you know?"

"Have you been watching talk shows as well as HGTV?" She tried to keep things light because it was Christmas. She avoided answering the question because she couldn't. Not yet.

"I have another present for you. Well, it's just more good news, but I'm excited to tell you. You're back on duty."

"Really? Already?" Instantly her heart felt lighter.

"Yes, there wasn't much to it. I didn't go through the proper channels to suspend you like you assumed. I just asked Nivens not to put you on the schedule for a while."

"Thank you," she said, delighted by the fact that it wouldn't be on her record.

He reached out and took her hand, laying it gently on top of his open palm. He caressed it with his thumb.

His touch was so distracting, so mind-altering, she nearly gave in. She forced herself to focus on his face instead, which wasn't much better because his expression was this heart-tugging cross between nervous and sincere.

"I really am sorry, Aubrey. I know this will be hard for you to believe in light of the fact that I've repeatedly shown otherwise, but I understand now what you mean."

"I appreciate the apology, Eli. And I want to believe you. But those are just words. We've spoken words before and they didn't hold true. We can't... I can't do this until I know for sure that you won't do it again. You have to learn to let me be me, in spite of this scary and dangerous world."

He nodded. "I know. Believe it or not, Gale helped me to see that." He went on a little awkwardly. "If you had the power to keep me from flying, I wouldn't want you to use it, either. Even if you thought it would save my life, I would want the option to make that decision for myself. I should have given you that courtesy. Even as difficult as it is for me to do where your safety is concerned, I promise from now on to only protect you when you ask. I may not always get it right, but I will listen when you tell me you don't need my help. And I promise to always help you when you do ask."

Her mouth dropped open in surprise as optimism welled within her. *Did* he finally get it? "Wow. That's exactly what I've been trying to get you to see."

He grinned proudly, reminding Aubrey of the boy she'd fallen in love with. "I know it will take time and other trees and…stuff. But I will prove it to you."

She smiled and this time it was fueled by joy. "I will look forward to all of your trees, Eli." She leaned forward and pressed a kiss against his lips. "Thank you. And I take back what I said earlier. If you can really do that, then *this* is the best Christmas gift you could give me."

THAT EVENING, AFTER dessert and coffee, Eli and Tim left to visit the St. Johns. Eli had given her a lot to consider. She wanted to believe him. Her heart kept telling her it was worth it to try. But when it came to Eli, her heart didn't have the best track record.

Another issue kept turning over in her mind. Even though it was Christmas, Aubrey couldn't let it go. When her sisters and mom started a card game, she hurried up to the attic, found the box she was looking for, and silently thanked her dad for his unfailing organizational skills. It didn't take her long to find the tax records for the year she was looking for—the year leading up to Tim's transfer.

Then she went in search of her dad. The door to his den was open a crack. She pushed it enough to stick her head through and found him seated behind his antique Craftsman-style desk. He was smoking a cigar beside an open window.

She scratched her nails on the solid oak door and called softly, "Dad?"

He jumped. "Sheesh, Aubrey, you scared me. I thought you were your mom coming in to bust me. She *encourages* me to only smoke two of these a day and I'm over my limit."

She couldn't help but chuckle. "No worries, your stogie binge is safe with me. Can I talk to you for a minute?"

"Sure, hon." He waved her in. She'd always

loved this room with its nautical-themed collectibles and floor-to-ceiling bookshelves that took up one entire wall. They were crammed full of tomes on everything from Coast Guard and maritime history, the biology of coastal and marine life, to gardening and identifying rocks and gems. The latter of which he'd taken up when he and her mom had begun traveling south for the winters. She admired her dad's insatiable quest for knowledge as well as his seemingly endless supply of energy.

She came in, shutting the door softly behind her. After crossing the room, she pulled the cushy chair he kept in the corner closer to him. She sat and looked up to find him studying her intently.

"Are you okay?"

"I am. I want to talk to you about the past. About some things that happened twelve years ago."

He adjusted his chair so he was facing her more solidly, one elbow resting on the arm to allow the blue smoke of his cigar to curl out the open window. "Is this about your mom and me? And the, uh, trouble we had when you were in high school?"

"Mom warned you, huh? Only peripherally, Dad. And I wouldn't ask if it wasn't important."

He took a puff, studying her with assessing, narrowed eyes. In moments like this Aubrey supposed she could see why her sisters were intimidated by him. But they hadn't spent nearly the amount of time with him that she had. Her interest in the Coast Guard, her gift for swimming and her love of all matters water-related had bonded her to him from a very early age. She could see right through his rigid exterior.

"Important how?"

"Important for my relationship with Eli. And possibly for a, um, problem that Eli might have that is work related."

He tipped his head and she could see the questions, the curiosity, light in his eyes. "Promise to tell me when you can?"

She let out a relieved, "Of course. Thank you, Dad," even though she knew her smile revealed her feelings.

"I haven't helped yet."

"But you will. No matter how you answer my questions, the answers will get me closer."

"Shoot," he said.

"Twelve years ago, when Tim Pelletier was transferred, did you arrange the transfer at his request?"

"Yes. Well, I helped arrange it and I encouraged him to take it."

"Why? I mean, why did he want the transfer?"

Her dad's face contorted into a kind of half scowl, letting her know he was uncomfortable with the inquiry. "He was, uh… He was ready to get out of here. He wanted a fresh start."

"Why did he want to get out of here?"

"It's not my place to say."

Aubrey didn't think she could love her father more than she did in this moment. The sky-high level of respect she already held for him rose exponentially.

"Was it gambling, Dad? Was he in debt from gambling?"

In spite of his composed features, she knew her dad. She had her answer. She'd already had it from Tim's personnel file, but she'd wanted her dad's confirmation. And she wanted a bit more.

It was the conversation with her mom on the beach that had set this train of thought in motion. When Eli had mentioned that Brett West liked to gamble, she'd remembered that all those years ago Tim had liked to gamble, too. Back then, they'd just assumed it was something he did for fun. Unfortunately, and especially for someone with an addiction, the line between fun and financial disaster was far too easy to cross.

A look at Tim's personnel file had given her the confirmation she'd needed. He'd been in serious financial trouble and his habit had gotten him into trouble at work. The trip up to the attic had confirmed another part of her theory. Next to her mom's old cedar chest was a box full of her parents' past income tax returns. A quick perusal had confirmed that her father had worked an extra job during that year, a part-time evening shift at a nearby bottling plant.

"Did you pay off his debt?"

Exhaling a sigh, he stubbed out his cigar. "Aubrey, why are you—?"

"Because, for all these years, Eli believed that you forced his dad to take the transfer to punish him for something else…" She didn't add the part about her mom and Tim's almost-affair. "But since Eli has been back in town, he's been rethinking that assumption."

"Ah." Brian thrummed his fingers on the desktop. "Yes, I worked a second job to help Tim pay off his debt."

"Why didn't he ask the St. Johns for a loan?"

He seemed surprised by the question. "I don't think Carlisle knew. He was out of the

Guard by then. It was difficult enough for Tim when I found out what was going on. He didn't want my help, either. But I didn't ask. I just did it. I wasn't about to betray his trust and tell anyone—not even Carlisle. I didn't even tell your mother. These men were—are—my best friends."

Friendship. There it was again. There were few bonds that were tighter. In some ways they were tighter even than that of family, because with friendship you had a choice. You could choose where to put your loyalty.

She'd given her loyalty to Eli and Alex years ago. And even though things had gone south between her and Eli, she'd always had Alex. She'd do anything for him, and he for her. Truth be told, even when she and Eli were estranged, she would have done anything for him, too. How could Eli not believe this about Alex, too?

Friends, true friends, helped each other out, put the other first. Like her dad had done for Tim. They were willing to risk their lives for their friends, even their reputations, if warranted. But what happened when that friendship wasn't reciprocated? That would be the ultimate betrayal as far as she was concerned.

A one-sided friendship could also mean that you might be easily manipulated.

"Dad, I want you to know how much I admire you. How much I admire what you did for Tim."

"He would have done the same for me."

Aubrey couldn't help but wonder if this were really true. He'd allowed his son to believe that the man who was trying to help him was out to destroy him. Although, she reminded herself, Tim's pride had been on the line, his standing in the eyes of his son. So maybe that was, if not acceptable, then at least understandable?

She leaned her head against the high back of the chair. She couldn't tell Eli the truth about his dad. What purpose could it possibly serve other than to upset him? And embarrass Tim, and possibly drive a wedge between father and son? The irony of the situation seeped into her; of finding herself in the position of keeping information from Eli in order to protect him.

She thought about that and about this conundrum with Alex. Suddenly, everything seemed connected somehow and confusing.

Aubrey knew one thing. Her mom was right; the world wasn't nearly as black and white as she'd always believed.

CHAPTER TWENTY

TWO DAYS AFTER CHRISTMAS, Aubrey happened to be sitting behind the front desk at the pool. Her lessons were over and Tabitha, the regular receptionist, had a doctor's appointment. Aubrey had offered to fill in.

Aubrey heard the door open. She looked up from the lesson schedule she was working on to find a short, heavyset woman with bright blue eyes and the prettiest red hair she'd ever seen standing before her.

"Hello," she said with a friendly, dimpled smile. "I'm looking for an Aubrey Wynn. Do you know if she's here? Or where I might be able to find her?"

"I'm Aubrey."

"I thought it was you, but I wanted to be sure. Well, that was easy."

"I aim to please. What can I help you with? Are you inquiring about swim lessons?" She picked up a sheet of paper. "Or maybe our open swim schedule?"

"Oh goodness, no. I used to be a swimmer, though. Butterfly was my specialty."

"Fantastic. I love the butterfly, too. It makes me feel like a mermaid." Aubrey added a happy laugh. "That probably sounds weird, doesn't it?"

She let out a giggle. "Not at all. I always imagined myself as a dolphin." She reached out a hand. "Mary Justice. I work for DeBolt Realty."

"Coastal Christmas Contest DeBolt Realty?"

"That's the one."

"I owe you a big thank-you, then. I had so much fun with that contest. It pretty much consumed my life for six months. And I don't think Pacific Cove has ever had such a festive Christmas." *Even if mine didn't quite live up to what I helped create*, she added silently. But that didn't have anything to do with the contest.

"You don't know this, but I attended every event that Pacific Cove hosted."

"Really?"

"Yes, I was a judge. Your second event? The Visit with Santa?"

"Yes…" *Please don't let there be some kind of lawsuit or formal reprimand that would keep Pacific Cove from competing next year...*

"Quite frankly, I think you were robbed when corporate headquarters disqualified Pacific Cove. I believe it was a knee-jerk reaction."

"Thank you." Even though it didn't change anything, it was nice to hear. "It was unfortunate. We tried to appeal the decision."

"Appeal?" The bewildered expression on Mary's face was enough for suspicion to take root. "I'm not sure what you mean by that. I'm technically the contest coordinator. No one spoke to me about an appeal."

Aubrey tried to concentrate on her words. Mary described the call—the only call—that came in after the event was the one threatening a lawsuit if Pacific Cove wasn't disqualified from the contest.

Which meant... Alex. He'd assured her that he'd called the contest coordinator to argue their case for reinstatement. She'd asked him if he'd followed up on it. Twice.

"Anyway, I couldn't let it rest. I'd been at the Visit with Santa and it was the best I've ever seen. You could feel the excitement in the crowd. And when that little boy ran into the street and Santa scooped him up? I had tears. That's Christmas spirit in action right

there. I didn't think a thing of the street situation." She shrugged helplessly. "Kids are
kids, right?"

"Thank you so much. I can't tell you how
much your visit means to me. I was so upset
after that I—"

Mary interrupted, "You're welcome, dear,
but I'm not finished."

"Oh, I'm sorry."

"When you entered back in July, you had
to fill out a form about what you would do
with the money if you won. Do you remember that? How you talked about refurbishing
the pool you grew up in?"

Aubrey gestured around at her dilapidated
second home and said flatly, "Hard for me to
forget, Mary."

They exchanged smiles and Mary went on
to explain how she'd been so disappointed
after the phone call, and yet delighted about
A Visit with Santa that she'd gone ahead and
attended the treasure hunt hoping it could all
be resolved somehow.

"I saw you on the beach. With a tall man
and a little girl? Helping her find one of the
glass balls? I saw you slip it into a pool."

"Yes, that was me."

Mary smiled. "That sealed it for me. It just

exemplified the whole point of the contest—aside from the business aspect, of course."

Joy welled inside of her. Her efforts really had been worth it. They'd helped to make this Christmas special for a lot of people, even if her own hadn't quite worked out the way she would have liked.

Mary went on. "I found two of those hand-blown ornaments, by the way. So lovely. Anyway, I consulted our attorney and did some research. He said that while the safety *concern* was valid, the *violation* didn't break any laws. So a lawsuit probably wouldn't fly. But by this time it was too late—the grand prize had already been awarded to Remington.

"I went to the committee anyway. Long story short, we have made a special arrangement for funds to be awarded to Pacific Cove. We're calling it the Judges' Choice Award. For your pool specifically."

She handed Aubrey a check. Two checks actually. "I hope I made them out correctly."

She studied the numbers carefully, adding them together no less than six times, and coming up with the same outrageous total. Shock and joy mingled within her. "But this is way more than the original prize money amount."

"I know." Mary added a wink. "There's something else I need to share with you."

"I don't think I can take much more. I'm about to cry as it is. And let me tell you, Mary, I don't cry often."

Mary looked pretty happy herself. "I hope they are the good kind of tears. My father is Werner Patrick."

"Werner Patrick, the four-time Olympic Gold Medal swimmer?"

Mary awarded her with a satisfied nod. "I suspected you might know of him. That's the one. Well, he was also a very successful businessman. He had more money than he knew what to do with—more than my sister and I needed to inherit, that's for sure. And my sister and I agree that he would be delighted with us giving some of his money to a program like yours. That's why there are two checks…"

Aubrey listened to the amazing news that would make her dream come true. The pool was going to be saved, after all, along with funds to expand her program for kids who couldn't afford lessons. The phrase *too good to be true* flashed through her mind, but in this case she could rest easy. It wasn't too good because along with the good had come the realization of a horrible betrayal.

ELI AND GALE LISTENED with rapt attention to Aubrey's story, asking a few questions, but mostly absorbing the information.

"Why would he do this?" she finally asked. "Even though he wasn't crazy about Pacific Cove's participation initially, he really came through for me, helping out in so many ways. Just like this whole ordeal with Nina. He's gone above and beyond. Helping with Marion while she was in the hospital, bringing her firewood, taking her supplies, repairing the shelves in her canning shed..."

Gale was wearing a scowl, no doubt wondering if Alex had designs on Nina.

With wide, somber eyes, she added, "He knows how much saving the pool means to me, how much that contest meant. If he would do this—sabotage me like this—then I have to believe he's probably guilty of...more than I thought." She held up a hand, palm up and out, in Eli's direction. "Don't say it," she said. "Please don't 'I told you so' me about this."

"Aubrey, I won't. I wouldn't do that. I know how difficult this is for you, because in spite of what you've been thinking about me, I am not taking this lightly."

Dipping her chin, she placed one hand on her forehead. He knew she was trying to absorb it all. He was still hurting himself, trying to accept the fact that Alex was guilty, that Alex was not the friend he believed him to be. He couldn't imagine his life without Alex's friendship in it. It hit Eli hard, then, knowing how it must have hurt her when he'd left. Ending their romance had been one thing, but withholding his friendship had been truly grievous.

"Drug running or smuggling or dealing or whatever he's doing is horrible, of course, but this is unforgivable. To me." She pointed at herself. "This is personal. Why would he do this?"

"It's the promo, the commercial," Gale, who had been mostly silent, finally spoke up. "He didn't want Aubrey and the mayor to win because he didn't want that commercial shoot here in Pacific Cove. He's afraid of the town being in the spotlight. Afraid the attention and the publicity would put his operation at risk."

Eli felt another piece of the puzzle fall into place. He agreed. "You're right. That would explain why he's been so against the recent development, as well. I thought that seemed odd for Alex with his business presence here."

"Which means," Gale said, "that he's probably in even deeper than we think."

Eli looked at Aubrey. "I know your inclination is to confront him. But please stay away from him—you and Nina and Camile. We believe that Nina was run off the road because they thought Alex was driving that pickup. If they're willing to harm Alex, these people are not going to care who else gets in the way." Eli didn't say that Alex might be just as dangerous. He didn't have to.

The shock and resignation on Aubrey's face tore at him. She was tough, yes—tougher than any woman he'd ever known, and most men, too. But she'd been through an awful lot in the last few weeks. This emotional stuff was its own special kind of exhausting. It was mentally taxing.

He walked toward her and enfolded her hand in his. Her skin was so cold it seemed to seep right into him. He leaned over and kissed her softly.

"Why don't you go home and take a hot bath? Get some rest. I'll come over later when I can. And we'll talk about some stuff?"

ELI WALKED HER OUT. He gave her another kiss and she climbed into her SUV.

She started the engine, pulled away from the curb and headed in the direction of her house. She couldn't abide the idea of being alone. There was only one person she wanted to see right now, aside from Eli. And she knew he needed to do his job.

He was going to have their best friend arrested. Their third musketeer.

Alex…

She swallowed a sob. She couldn't go home. She needed to move, to do…something. At the end of the street, she turned right instead of left.

She drove out to Nina's farm, hoping for some solace. Instead that's where the heartbreak really began.

ELI WAS STILL pondering Alex's choices when he picked up his phone an hour later.

His dad answered on the second ring. "Hey, Dad."

"Hey, son."

"Are you still coming over for dinner? Gale is cooking."

"Um, actually, I'm not feeling well. Can we reschedule?"

"Sure. But what's wrong?"

"Just a headache. I'm going to turn in early tonight."

"Okay. Get some rest and I'll see you tomorrow."

"Sounds good. Hey, did I by any chance leave my jacket over there?"

"I don't know. Let me check." Eli walked and talked and finally spotted it on the floor behind a dining room chair. He picked it up. "Yeah, looks like you did."

"Good. I couldn't find it."

They talked for another moment. Eli clicked off. He went to hang the jacket on a hook by the door when something slipped out of the pocket. He picked up the paper and went to stuff it back inside. His eye was drawn to his dad's neatly printed note. His flight itinerary: AA 1254 EYW to PDX, 5:30 pm, 2A. Below that he'd written "SB" and underlined it. SB? Did his dad have a girlfriend? Eli hoped so. Maybe that would explain his good mood of late.

He'd told Eli he'd flown from Key West to Portland standby, so why did he have his flight information written down? And since when had his dad started flying first class?

So, he'd heard him wrong. Good for him on all counts, he thought, replacing the paper and hanging up the jacket.

He slid onto the stool behind the bar between the kitchen and dining area. Gale, bless him, was cracking eggs to scramble for dinner.

"Remember how the DEA guys said that it was almost like no one was at Alex's properties? And we figured it was because things were quiet for the holidays?"

"Mmm-hmm," Gale said as he added a splash of cream and whisked the eggs. "Do you know why free-range egg yolks are darker than eggs from caged hens? It's their diet," he explained without waiting for Eli to answer. "They eat more natural pigments."

"What does that even mean? 'Natural pigments'?"

"Like flowers and bugs and stuff. I read it online. Isn't that cool?"

"I think he knows. He knows we're on to him, and he's moved the drugs."

Gale paused the whisk he'd been using to mix the eggs. He stared down into the bowl and then tossed it all into the sink where it made a clanking sound.

"What are you doing?"

"Let's go," he said, already running for the door.

CHAPTER TWENTY-ONE

THE DOOR WAS unlocked so Aubrey knocked and opened it at the same time. Since Nina's ribs were still healing, she didn't want to make her move around unnecessarily. Marion greeted her with a happy dance and a wagging tail.

"Hello, gorgeous." She bent over and kissed the top of the dog's silky head. "If my sister didn't love you so much, I would dognap you. I would. I'm not saying it's right, but that's how much I adore you."

Marion nuzzled her hand in appreciation.

"Where's your mom?"

She let out one of those whine-yawns dogs do when they're anxious. Aubrey looked around, suddenly struck with a nervous bout of "been there, done that." She stood upright and called for her sister. "Nina?"

"Aubrey?" Her sister's voice instantly calmed her racing pulse.

"Where are you?"

"Kitchen."

She found her on top of a step ladder. The very top. She forced herself not to think about what would happen if she fell or had a seizure while she was up there. Instead she asked, "What are you doing?"

Nina pointed to the light fixture above her. "Changing a lightbulb."

"What about your ribs?"

"I'm not going to lie to you, Aubrey. They hurt. Bad. The pain you hear about broken ribs is not an exaggeration, FYI. I've been up here about ten minutes and I've barely taken a breath."

"Why are you doing it, then? That light fixture has, like, ten bulbs. It can wait. And you know there's a warning on that top step, right? You're not supposed to stand on it."

"You know," she said, slowly inching a foot down onto the rung below and then pausing, "for someone as brave and adventurous as you are, you are such a stickler for rules. There wouldn't be a step if you weren't supposed to step on it, right? And I'm up here because I'm really tired of not being able to do what I want to do. So I decided to do some stuff. Earlier today, I started taking down the Christmas decorations. Then Alex showed up and offered to help. This burned-out bulb has been bugging me."

"Alex?"

"Yeah, he brought some groceries out for me and offered to help haul the decorations out to the canning shed."

"What time was he here?" Aubrey asked, careful to keep her voice even.

"He got here about an hour ago."

"Got here? Where is he now? I didn't see any of his vehicles." Alex had several cars. She suddenly wondered if what she'd assumed were business vehicles had been purchased with drug money.

"He loaded the Christmas stuff in his pickup and drove it out to the shed to unload. Pretty clever, huh?"

"Nina, can you come down from there? There's something I need to talk to you about."

"Yes, I can. I'm done. This might take a while…" As she slowly moved one foot to the step below, Aubrey felt herself expel a relieved breath. When she reached the bottom she asked, "What do you need to talk to me about?"

"About Alex. There's something I need to tell you."

Marion let out a whimper and somehow Aubrey knew he was behind her before he said a word.

"Hey, Alex," Nina said.

"What about me?" His voice was the same jovial Alex, yet a frisson of fear tickled along her spine. She told herself not to panic. There was no reason to believe he was dangerous.

Forcing her mouth into a smile, she turned to face him. "Hey, there. You weren't supposed to hear that."

"Why not?"

Was she imagining the tightness in his tone? "Because it's a surprise."

"A surprise?"

"Uh, yep. I have a surprise for you. To thank you for everything you've done for Nina lately."

He leaned against the door frame, a enigmatic smirk on his face. "What a coincidence. I have a surprise for you, too."

And that's when Aubrey knew. The man staring her down was not Alex. Somewhere, at some point, while she was too busy with her own life to notice, that Alex had disappeared. Her mom was right; she could be oblivious. Because her friend had disappeared and she'd missed it.

"I love surprises," Nina said, shuffling closer. "Where is it?"

"In the canning shed," Alex said. "Come with me, ladies. I'll show you."

As ELI DROVE, Gale explained his theory while scrolling through his phone. "She told me about all the storage space she has out there. I saw it even, and it didn't occur to me."

Eli had seen it, too. He'd worked there for years. The farm would be the perfect place to stash drugs. Alex could have easily hidden anything out there while Nina was in the hospital. And she likely wouldn't have found it since then because she could barely move. It was a brilliant solution on his part. But then again, he knew very well how clever Alex could be.

"She's not answering."

"Call Aubrey."

"I am."

They waited. She didn't answer.

"Try Camile."

"Already on it… Camile? Hey, it's Gale… Uh, yeah, I am, thanks. Have you by any chance talked to Nina today?" They chatted for another minute before he hung up. He banged a fist on the dash. "Camile talked to her an hour ago. She was busy taking down her Christmas decorations. With Alex."

"I'm calling Les and Tom." They were the DEA agents who'd been handling the surveillance.

Eli tried to control his fear even as he pressed the accelerator to the floor.

THE FIRST THING Aubrey noticed as she stepped into the storage shed were the two wooden crates on the floor. The door to the cellar was open and she knew immediately what Alex had planned. Her only chance was to stall until she could figure out a way to incapacitate him. He probably outweighed her by close to a hundred pounds, but she knew he would be no match for her training and superior physical condition.

She pointed at the boxes. "Is that what I think it is?"

Alex shrugged. "Probably."

"What is it?" Nina asked, following her inside. "Is this our surprise?"

"Yes, Nina. Our surprise is that our friend Alex, who we love like a brother, is a drug dealer. Alex, please don't do this."

He answered with a harsh laugh. "You have no clue what you're saying, Aubrey. The problem, however, is that I don't know what clues you do have. But it's obvious that Eli has told you something, enough that I can't risk you trying to stop me from leaving. Please, get in the cellar."

"Really? You're going to lock us in the root cellar? How original."

"I have no choice here, Aubrey, and you know it. And before you get any ideas— Or maybe I should say before you decide to implement any of the ideas that I know are flying through that military-trained brain of yours, please take note of the fact that I have this." He opened his jacket and there was no mistaking the gun in the holster on his side.

Nina wore a look of total confusion. "Wait, is this a joke? What is going on?"

"I'm sorry, Nina." And he did look kind of sorry as he turned toward her. "I know you're in pain. So I'll give you plenty of time to get down the stairs. Lean against the wall for support, okay? Aubrey will be right down."

"What are you guys…?"

Aubrey reached out and squeezed her sister's forearm. She tried to convey the seriousness of the situation with her expression and her tone. "Nina, just do it, please. I'll explain later. Alex is in trouble."

"Not yet I'm not. Thanks to the use of Nina's farm. Thank you, Nina."

Nina stood frozen with shock as she stared at Alex. Her mouth opened as if she was going to say something. Aubrey willed her to cooperate with a look. Nina turned and shuffled toward the stairs. Anger and contempt welled in her as she watched her sister's snaillike descent. She knew every step must be agony.

"Alex, this is crazy. How could you do this?"

He shook his head. "I don't have time to explain my motivation to you. And I don't think I need to. Why does anyone enter into a business enterprise?"

"Money? You have all the money you could ever need."

He scoffed. "What does that mean? How do you know how much money I need? And it's not just money... You wouldn't understand."

Aubrey slipped her hands into her pockets, her fingers grazing the knight-shaped ornament Eli had crafted for her. She curled it into her fingers and held on tight, feeling the tiny lance bite into the flesh of her palm.

"Did you get Pacific Cove disqualified from the Christmas competition?"

He looked surprised by the question for a second. Then he rolled his eyes and said impatiently, "Yes, Aubrey, I did. I'm sorry about that. But it was clear to me you were going to win the stupid thing and I couldn't have TV cameras, reporters and people snooping around. Amazing what the threat of a lawsuit can accomplish."

Eli would come here. She knew he would. But how long would it take? If only she had told him where she was going. And how would he figure out where they were once he got to the farm? Once they were sealed inside that root cellar, it could be days before anyone found them. Slowly, she removed her hands from her pockets.

"You're my best friend, Alex. And I suddenly feel like I don't know you at all."

He scoffed. "This doesn't have anything to do with our friendship, Aubrey. As far as I'm concerned, you're still my friend. But I'm not like you and Eli. There are things that are important to me beyond honor and loyalty and love of country. Believe it or not, there are things that are more important than our friendship."

A noise sounded outside the door. As Alex glanced in that direction, Aubrey seized on the distraction, tossing the ornament to one side. She tried to cover the sound with a cough.

His gaze flew to her again. "We could talk about this all day, but it wouldn't change anything. You would never understand. Because you have everything you want. You're a hero in this town, a hero to your dad, to my dad, to Eli—" He stopped abruptly and pointed. "You need to get down those stairs now. We need to get going."

"'We'?" She repeated as she saw movement just outside the doorway. A figure came into view. "No," she said. No. No, no, no…

ELI TURNED ONTO the road that led to Nina's. As they neared the house, he felt some tension loosen his shoulders. Nina's and Aubrey's were the only vehicles parked outside.

"He's not here," Eli said aloud.

"Thanks, Les." Gale hung up. "He says they lost Alex earlier when they had to take a conference call. But the good news is that the call sealed the deal for the warrants. They've got them for his house and property. And the local police are bringing him in for questioning regarding Nina's accident."

They got out of the pickup and headed to the house only to find their relief was short-lived. Wild barking ensued as they knocked on the door. When no one answered, Eli pushed it open to discover a frantic Marion, barking and running in circles. A quick search revealed the house was empty.

Without saying a word, they headed out the door. An hour later, after thoroughly check-

ing the barn, the grounds and the other outbuildings, they stopped in front of the shed.

Gale looked down at Marion, who was
staring up at him anxiously. She let out a
bark. "Why didn't you get her a search and
rescue dog?"

"What?"

"I know Nina has epilepsy and this dog is
trained for that. But don't you think it's ironic
that since I've known her she hasn't had a seizure, but she's been lost twice?"

"Where's Nina?" Eli asked the dog.

Marion ran toward the shed, turned around
and sat in front of the door, eagerly looking
from him to Gale and back again. She let out
a whine as she trotted smartly in a circle.

Eli walked over and pushed the door open.
"I am going to call Grady and—"

That's when he saw something sparkle on
the floor. He'd know that knight anywhere.

He picked it up and showed it to Gale.

"Your ornament?"

"They've been here. Aubrey dropped this
for me to find. They're in trouble." Eli felt
his stomach drop. It must be bad. Aubrey had
asked for help.

INITIALLY, AUBREY WASN'T scared in the least.
Furious, yes. Scared, no. She wasn't afraid to

die. She faced death so often, she no longer feared it. She didn't know an RS who did. But she didn't want to go like this, at someone else's selfish hand. The fact that Alex would lock them in there was beyond cruel. Not only was Nina in constant pain from her ribs, she was terrified of exactly one thing in life. Spiders.

It was pitch dark, but Aubrey could hear her quick, frantic breathing. "Aubrey, I'm pretty sure there is one crawling on my back right now."

"That's impossible, Nina. There are no spiders down here. It's too dark. Nothing lives down here. What would they eat?" She had no idea if this was true, but she said it anyway. She'd say anything right now to calm her sister down.

"Me! I am dinner, Aubrey."

"Oh, sweetie, I'm so sorry." Aubrey lightly patted her back from her shoulders to her waist and back again. "There. See? Spider's gone."

"Thank you. I'm cold."

"I know. Me, too." Which wasn't really true. It had to be pretty cold before it got to her. Plus, she had anger on her side. Which made her think of Eli.

After she'd railed at him for not trusting

her, now she couldn't help but ask herself why she hadn't trusted him. When he'd told her Alex was guilty, she should have believed him. And when she'd learned about his dad, she should have told him. Maybe, if she'd told him immediately, they wouldn't be here right now. They were both guilty of wanting to protect the other. She'd given him so much grief about his actions when she'd been just as guilty...

When she saw him she would tell him all of this and more. If she saw him...and that's when she realized she was scared. But not for herself. She was terrified for Eli. And she was going to tell him that, too. How terrified she'd been for him and how she knew she would do anything to keep him out of danger, too. She finally understood why he'd done what he had for her. The thought of something happening to him filled her with so much panic she could barely think straight.

"You really think Eli and Gale will find us?"

"I know they will." *Eventually*, she added silently. She knew he would literally raze this place to find her if necessary. She could only hope it wouldn't be too late. And if they survived this ordeal, she hoped it wasn't too late for them. She should have told him about his dad. She hoped…

"I can't believe Alex is a drug dealer," Nina said. "He was like a different person when he made us climb down here. He seemed angry and…dangerous."

"Yes, he did," Aubrey agreed. Alex was guilty. That much was definitely clear.

So guilty.

But he wasn't the only one. And that was the part that had her scared.

"Aubrey? Nina?" Eli shouted as he continued farther into the canning shed. That's when he realized the shelving had been rearranged. Or, more to the point, a shelf had been moved. Right over the top of the root cellar door.

"Gale, help me move this." They slid the heavy wooden shelf unit out of the way. Eli grabbed the latch that opened the cellar door. Marion began barking wildly as if excited that her two human helpers had finally figured out the obvious.

As soon as the door began to give way, he heard his name. "Eli?"

At the sound of Aubrey's voice, Eli felt a wave of relief so strong it made him dizzy. He called out, "Yes, Aubrey, it's me and Gale."

"Nina and I are both here. We're fine."

He heard Nina let out a sob as he pulled the door all the way open. Gale had already moved around him and was running down the stairs.

He followed, grabbing Aubrey and holding her tightly in his arms. He held her for a moment, running his hands up and down her back, while he inhaled the absolutely irreplaceable scent of her.

"Get me out of here, Kohen," Nina said with a sob. "What took you so long? I told you I hate spiders." Her voice trailed off, lost in her tears.

Gale carefully lifted her in his arms and carried her up the stairs.

"I knew you would find me," Aubrey whispered, her face nuzzled against Eli's neck. "I knew you would help us."

His voice was hoarse and choked with emotion when he finally responded. "I'm so glad you asked me to."

Laughter mixed with her sob of relief. "I love you, too. Do you know that? I realized when I was down here that I haven't told you that. I love the way you love me. And I love that you'll do anything for me, even stuff I don't want you to do, because now I think I understand why you do it."

Eli pulled away and stared at her in wonder, hoping every bit of that love he felt was showing in his eyes. "I love you, too."

"I know," she said confidently. "We were stuck down here and I knew that, and it gave me so much comfort. But I was afraid that you didn't have that same comfort. I was afraid I wasn't going to get a chance to tell you back."

He grinned. "Yeah? Well, now that you know that, you should tell me every single day just in case someone decides to lock you inside a root cellar."

She laughed again.

"Did Alex say where he was going?" Eli asked, taking her hand and steering her toward the stairs.

"No, Eli, he didn't. But... There is something I need to tell you."

Sirens began to sound as they emerged into the daylight, signaling the arrival of the DEA and the police.

She stopped and tugged on his hand so he would face her. She stared into his beautiful eyes and saw his expression already full of pain and anxiety. She hated that she was about to make it so much worse. And in that moment she decided she would have done just about anything not to have to say the words.

"What is it? You can tell me anything, you know that."

"Eli, your dad. He was…with Alex."

His eyes closed on a look of sheer agony and her heart squeezed painfully with sympathy. She stepped closer and wrapped her arms around him.

"I'm so sorry." She whispered the words and was relieved when he hugged her tightly to him.

Gale called out to them from where he stood with two men she assumed were the DEA agents. A local police car had accompanied them and two officers stood nearby, as well.

Eli pulled away but kept her hand securely in his as they walked toward the house. They followed the agents inside where Aubrey and Nina gave their accounts of what had happened.

When they were finished, Les, one of the DEA agents, asked, "Did they say where they were going?"

Aubrey answered. "No, but I heard them talking about Savannah. Savannah," she repeated. "Wait! When I was on board the *Angela Sue* I heard the crew talking about the *Savannah B*. I didn't think anything of it at the time. But a boat would be—"

"Of course," Eli said, remembering the slip of paper in his dad's pocket. "It's a boat. The *Savannah Bound*. They're on Brett West's boat. The boat he purchased for Alex."

"Did you find them?" Aubrey asked as she let Eli into her house the following evening.

"Yes." He came in and collapsed on her sofa. "They've been arrested and detained in British Columbia. The DEA is already working on extradition with Canada. They have agents on the way up there to question them."

"Were they on the boat?"

"Yep. They left on the *Savannah Bound* just as we suspected. It was a lucky catch. Thankfully, the Canadian Coast Guard was on it. As soon as they got the information, they had their eyes on the water.

"Hard to believe, though, given there's so much water out there. They could have run up or down the coast, put in at any port and hopped on an airplane to anywhere in the world. They could have met another boat at sea…"

The same scenarios had been running through Aubrey's mind. Relief mingled with disappointment and a myriad other emotions she felt for her oldest friend and Eli's dad.

Eli had tipped his head back and was

now staring up toward the ceiling, long legs stretched out in front him. "My dad had a scrap of paper in his coat pocket that I'd found. He'd written his flight itinerary on it and the initials S.B. I was happy because I thought maybe he was seeing someone…

"I feel like I should have suspected or, at least, something should have occurred to me later…

"When we were bowling with Danny and Brendan, who have both been cleared, by the way, Brendan was talking about his dad's new boat, the *Savannah Bound*. It was the same boat my dad has in Florida, but a newer model. Expensive. Dad bought his about three years ago, right after Alex and I were down there fishing. I never thought to question how much he'd paid for it—or how he'd paid for it. He told me Alex helped him get a good deal. Which he likely did, but it wasn't for fishing. Obviously."

"Eli, don't be too hard on yourself here. Who could suspect their own father of something like this? It was hard enough to believe Alex was guilty."

"The DEA suspects that my dad's been in charge of Alex's distribution along Florida's coast. This was their getaway plan all along. When my dad flew up here, they knew the

DEA was on to them. Remember when I told you a tip came in that Coast Guard personnel were involved?"

She nodded.

"The DEA was able to identify the tipster. When they found him, he added the information that the suspect was working out of Florida but had connections on the West Coast. He was a former Coast Guard. My dad."

Aubrey hurt for him, for the disappointment—the complete devastation—she knew he must be feeling. "Eli, I'm so sorry."

"You know what's funny? I see now that he never really loved the Coast Guard. Not the way I do. He faked it for my sake." He raked a hand through his hair. "He faked a lot of things for my sake. Him and Alex both."

"I know," she said softly, her voice choked with sadness. "The part I don't get, though, is why? Why would Alex need to smuggle drugs? He has all the money he could want, right?"

"Nope. Apparently he's not such a great businessman, after all. The DEA interviewed Carlisle this morning. He cut him off about three years ago, around the same time my dad got the boat. Got tired of bailing him out financially.

"And the tough love seemed to work. Alex

appeared to get his act together. He was doing well. His business seemed to be thriving. Carlisle and Heather were finally proud of him. Thought he was really making something of himself. Poor Carlisle. He's devastated. I can honestly say I know how he feels."

"Me, too." Aubrey wiped at the tears on her cheeks.

"We're tied now, you know."

"What do you mean?" she whispered.

"Two out of the three people I loved the most have now broken my heart, too."

Aubrey felt like someone had driven a wedge into her heart. She steeled herself because she was pretty sure her next confession might cause it to split right in two. She stepped closer.

"I don't know if this is too soon. I know you have a lot on your mind. But I need to tell you something."

He stared up at her. "Okay."

"Your dad took that assignment twelve years ago because he was in debt. Deep debt. From gambling. He'd missed some shifts at work and was facing expulsion. I suspected there was more to his transfer than we knew… I found some information in his personnel file and asked Dad about it. My dad helped arrange the transfer to try and smooth things over for him. My dad also got a second job and helped pay down your dad's debt while they waited to learn his fate." She continued explaining the details she'd learned.

Finally, she added, "Eli, I'm so sorry. I'm sorry for not telling you. Maybe if I would have told you sooner you would have figured this out? I don't know. I wanted to but… I couldn't decide if you needed to know. I knew how much it would upset you, and I was afraid it would cause problems between you and your dad. Embarrass your dad…"

"You couldn't decide if I should know?" His blue eyes were piercing but unreadable. "You couldn't decide if I should be privy to this incredibly important, revealing and potentially damaging information about my own father?"

She whooshed out a breath. "I know how it sounds. It's exactly the same thing I got upset with you for doing. It's the same thing that broke us up."

He crooked a finger at her.

She eyed him warily.

"Aubrey, I'm absolutely both physically and mentally exhausted. I'm also heartsick and emotionally…defeated. Please come over here and sit next to me. I need you."

Her heart squeezed inside of her chest, letting her know it was still whole—hurting but whole. She could see the pain in his eyes and she hated having contributed to it.

But she could also see the love. She moved toward the sofa and sat next to him.

He looped an arm around her and pulled her tight against him. He held her there for a long moment.

Finally, he inhaled a deep breath and asked, "This has been bothering you? This failure of yours to disclose information?"

She nodded.

"Have you been afraid that this information—information that you kept from me because you love me and care about me and were worried about what it might do to me—would tear us apart? Again?"

"Yes."

He reached out and trailed a hand from her shoulder down to her fingers, which he entwined with his own.

Her soul seemed to take flight. She didn't deserve this man, yet she wanted to. And he did need her. She knew that now. And she needed him, too. More than she needed air. More, even, than she needed the water.

"That's impossible," he whispered. "Do you want to know why?"

"Because you're my knight and I'm your mermaid?" she croaked hopefully.

A mix of surprise and wonder flashed briefly across his face before settling into a familiar expression of love and desire that set her pulse racing dangerously. He reached out with his other hand and pulled her across his lap. He cupped her cheek and grinned.

"Yes," he whispered as his lips sought hers for a kiss. "That's exactly right. Because you're my mermaid and I'm your knight."

* * * * *

SPECIAL EXCERPT FROM

HARLEQUIN®

SPECIAL EDITION

*In the small Texas burg of Rambling Rose, real estate
investor Callum Fortune is making a big splash.
The last thing he needs is any personal complications
slowing his pace—least of all nurse Becky Averill,
a beautiful widow with twin baby girls!*

Read on for a sneak preview of
Fortune's Fresh Start
by Michelle Major, the first book in
The Fortunes of Texas: Rambling Rose *continuity.*

"I didn't mean to rush off the other day after the ribbon
cutting," he told her as they approached the door that led
to the childcare center. "I think I interrupted a potential
invitation for dinner, and I've been regretting it ever
since."

Becky blinked. In truth, she would have never had the
guts to invite Callum for dinner. She'd been planning to
offer to cook or bake for him and drop it off at his office
as a thank-you. The idea of having him over to her small
house did funny things to her insides.

"Oh," she said again.

"Maybe I misinterpreted," Callum said quickly,
looking as flummoxed as she felt. "Or imagined the
whole thing. You meant to thank me with a bottle of wine
or some cookies or—"

"Dinner." She grinned at him. Somehow his
discomposure gave her the confidence to say the word.

He appeared so perfect and out of her league, but at the moment he simply seemed like a normal, nervous guy not sure what to say next.

She decided to make it easy for him. For both of them. "Would you come for dinner tomorrow night? The girls go to bed early, so if you could be there around seven, we could have a more leisurely meal and a chance to talk."

His shoulders visibly relaxed. "I'd like that. Dinner with a friend. Can I bring anything?"

"Just yourself," she told him.

He pulled his cell phone from his pocket and handed it to her so she could enter her contact information. It took a few tries to get it right because her fingers trembled slightly.

He grinned at her as he took the phone again. "I'm looking forward to tomorrow, Becky."

"Me, too," she breathed, then gave a little wave as he said goodbye. She took a few steadying breaths before heading in to pick up the twins. *Don't turn it into something more than it is*, she cautioned herself.

It was a thank-you, not a date. Her babies would be asleep in the next room. Definitely not a date.

But her stammering heart didn't seem to get the message.

Don't miss
Fortune's Fresh Start *by Michelle Major,*
available January 2020 wherever
Harlequin® Special Edition books and ebooks are sold.

Harlequin.com

Looking for more satisfying love stories
with community and family at their core?

Check out **Harlequin® Special Edition**
and **Love Inspired®** books!

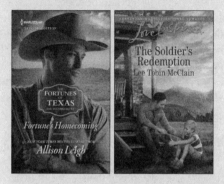

New books available every month!

"There's an open bottle of very expensive scotch on
the counter, just waiting for someone to enjoy it." She
laughed again, softly this time. "And I'd *really* like to
hear the story of how Danger Dan turned into a lawman."

Dan grimaced. He hated that stupid nickname Ryan had
made up, even if he *had* earned it back then. Especially
coming from Mack.

"Is your husband waiting upstairs?" Dan wasn't sure
where that question came from, but, to be fair, all Mack
had ever talked about was leaving Gallant Lake, having a
big wedding and a bigger house. The girl had goals, and
from what he'd heard, she'd reached every one of them.

"I don't have a husband anymore." She brushed past
him and headed toward the counter. "So are you joining
me or not?"

Dan glanced at his watch, not sure how to digest that
information. "I'm off duty in fifteen minutes."

Her long hair swung back and forth as she walked ahead of him. So did her hips. *Damn.*

"And you're all about following the rules now? You really have changed, haven't you? Pity. I guess I'm drinking my first glass alone. You'll just have to catch up."

He frowned. Mackenzie had been strong-willed, but never sassy. Never the type to sneak into her father's store alone for an after-hours drink. Not the type to taunt him. Not the type to break the rules.

Looked like he wasn't the only one who'd changed since high school.

Don't miss
Her Homecoming Wish *by Jo McNally,*
available February 2020 wherever
Harlequin® *Special Edition books and ebooks are sold.*

Harlequin.com

Love Harlequin romance?

DISCOVER.

Be the first to find out about promotions, news and exclusive content!

 Facebook.com/HarlequinBooks

Twitter.com/HarlequinBooks

 Instagram.com/HarlequinBooks

Pinterest.com/HarlequinBooks

ReaderService.com

EXPLORE.

Sign up for the Harlequin e-newsletter and download a free book from any series at
TryHarlequin.com

CONNECT.

Join our Harlequin community to share your thoughts and connect with other romance readers!
Facebook.com/groups/HarlequinConnection

HSOCIAL2020